~ ESCAPE WITH ~

JENNY COLGAN

By Jenny Colgan

Mure

The Summer Seaside Kitchen

A Very Distant Shore *(novella)*

The Endless Beach

An Island Christmas

Christmas at the Island Hotel

Kirrinfief

The Little Shop of Happy
Ever After

The Bookshop on the Shore

Five Hundred Miles from You

Little Beach Street Bakery

Little Beach Street Bakery

Summer at Little Beach
Street Bakery

Christmas at Little Beach
Street Bakery

Sunrise by the Sea

Sweetshop of Dreams

Welcome to Rosie Hopkins'
Sweetshop of Dreams

Christmas at Rosie
Hopkins' Sweetshop

The Christmas Surprise

Cupcake Café

Meet Me at the Cupcake Café

Christmas at the Cupcake Café

The Little School by the Sea

Class

Rules

Lessons

West End Girls

Operation Sunshine

Diamonds Are a Girl's
Best Friend

The Good, the Bad and
the Dumped

The Loveliest Chocolate
Shop in Paris

Amanda's Wedding

Talking to Addison

Looking for Andrew McCarthy

Working Wonders

Do You Remember the
First Time?

Where Have All the
Boys Gone?

The Christmas Bookshop

By Jenny T. Colgan

Resistance Is Futile

Spandex and the City

Jenny Colgan is the author of numerous bestselling novels, including *The Little Shop of Happy Ever After* and *Summer at the Little Beach Street Bakery*, which are also published by Sphere. *Meet Me at the Cupcake Café* won the 2012 Melissa Nathan Award for Comedy Romance and was a *Sunday Times* top ten bestseller, as was *Welcome to Rosie Hopkins' Sweetshop of Dreams*, which won the RNA Romantic Novel of the Year Award 2013. Jenny was born in Scotland and has lived in London, the Netherlands, the US and France. She eventually settled on the wettest of all of these places, and currently lives just north of Edinburgh with her husband Andrew, her dog Nevil Shute and her three children: Wallace, who is fourteen and likes pretending to be nineteen and not knowing what this embarrassing 'family' thing is that keeps following him about; Michael-Francis, who is twelve and likes making new friends on aeroplanes; and Delphine who is ten and is mostly raccoon as far as we can tell so far.

Things Jenny likes include: cakes; far too much *Doctor Who*; wearing Converse trainers every day so her feet are now just gigantic big flat pans; baths only slightly cooler than the surface of the sun, and very, very long books, the longer the better. For more about Jenny, visit her website and her Facebook page, or follow her on Twitter @jennycolgan.

JENNY COLGAN

Christmas
at the
Island Hotel

sphere

SPHERE

First published in Great Britain in 2020 by Sphere
This paperback edition published by Sphere in 2021

1 3 5 7 9 10 8 6 4 2

A CIP catalogue record for this book is available from the British Library.

ISBN 978-0-7515-8031-0

Typeset in Caslon by M Rules
Printed and bound in Great Britain by Clays Ltd, Elcograf, S.p.A.

Papers used by Sphere are from well-managed forests and other responsible sources.

Sphere
An imprint of
Little, Brown Book Group
Carmelite House
50 Victoria Embankment
London EC4Y 0DZ

An Hachette UK Company
www.hachette.co.uk

www.littlebrown.co.uk

*To the front line staff, all of you, who got up and
went to work every day while the rest
of us had to stay indoors.*

*You were, and are, the glue that holds
the world together. Thank you.*

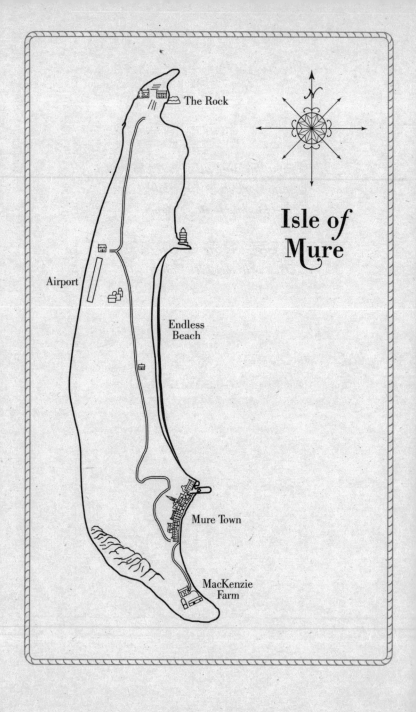

The Rock

Isle of
Mure

Airport

Endless
Beach

Mure Town

MacKenzie
Farm

Dramatis Personae

Eck MacKenzie —— Annie MacKenzie
(deceased)

Hamish MacKenzie

Innes MacKenzie —— Eilidh MacKenzie

Agot MacKenzie

Joel Binder —— Flora MacKenzie

Douglas Binder

Colton Rogers —— Fintan MacKenzie
(deceased)

Staff at the Rock

Gaspard – head chef
Konstantin – kitchen boy
Bjårk – Konstantin's dog
Gala – receptionist
Kerry – sous-chef
Isla Donnelly – scullery maid
Tam – general staff

Staff at the Seaside Kitchen

Iona
Malik

Residents of Mure

Lorna MacLeod – school headmistress
Mrs Cook – schoolteacher
Dr Saif Hassan – island doctor and Syrian refugee
Ibrahim Hassan – Saif's elder son
Ash Hassan – Saif's younger son
Jeannie – receptionist at Saif's surgery
Mrs Laird (also babysitter for Saif)
Vera Donnelly – Isla's mother
Malcolm (Malcy) Docherty – head of local council
Jan MacArthur née Docherty – Malcy's daughter and local philanthropist
Charlie MacArthur – Jan's husband
Christabel – Jan and Charlie's daughter
Wullie Stevenson – resident

Bertie Cooper – boatman
Hector McLinn – farmer
Cuthbert McSquib – farmer
Mrs MacGregor – resident
Elspeth Brodie – resident
Mrs MacPherson – resident
Anndra – builder
Billy and Effie – couple who run the airfield and the post office
Inge-Britt – proprietor of Harbour's Rest Hotel
Mrs McGlone – deputy head of local council
Colin – policeman
Fionn – fisherman

From the USA

Marsha Philippoussis – Joel's adopted mother
Mark Philippoussis – Joel's adopted father

From Norway

Konstantin Sundt-Knagenhjem Senior – Konstantin's father
Gunnar – artist

From London

Candice Blunt – journalist

Chapter One

Day and night, the great tankers plough the freezing water of the North Atlantic.

Vast up close – 200, 300 metres long, filled with cars and rocking horses and teddies and barometers and valves and bonnets and tea – they are nonetheless still dwarfed by the scale of the ocean.

Coming in from the west, they cross imaginary lines in the water that the comfortable and landbound hear about only as they fall asleep to the shipping forecast – Rockall, Hebrides and over the north of Fair Isle – when they loom into view of Mure, the tiny island between Shetland and the Faroes, home to fifteen hundred souls (in a good year).

The south-westernmost tip of Mure contains the village and the port, and the sailors of the tankers – often from the Philippines or Thailand, the great seafaring nations of the South Seas – are about as far away from home as they can ever get. They look out, often, on the little point of light marooned in the ocean, eyes starved of diversion from the endless dark waves.

You cannot be a seafaring man if prone to melancholy – you will live away from your family, in close quarters with other men, for nine or ten months of the year, so a positive attitude is best. But even the most sea-hardened occasionally get a little mournful for home, particularly when they pull up the binoculars and see the coloured houses of Mure crowded higgledy-piggledy on the wharf, all soft grey and pink and blue and yellow. The cottages and buildings cluster together, heading upwards from the waterside, in a cosy, haphazard fashion, as if leaning against each other for warmth on the bare island with its vast empty pale yellow beaches and low bending rushes.

There is no deep-water harbour on the island. None of the great container ships will ever land there. But more than a few like to mark her passing, as she is the last spot of land they will see before the Shetlands. Sometimes, through the binoculars, on a clear day in the summertime, you can see the children wave.

But now, in the pitch-black of an early winter's morning, it looks like a tiny pinprick of comfort in a world gone dark, as the huge ships chug past, making light work of the slapping waves, the motion so familiar that walking on land is a difficult adjustment for the men.

The island is so small that, at twenty knots, it doesn't take long for it to disappear behind you: for Apostil or Danilo or Jesús to go back to checking the radar and the fax machine, as they sail between Viking and on to North Utsire, and ultimately to the vast rich fjords of Norway, leaving the quiet island marooned once more under the cold stars – where, in the MacKenzie farmhouse, at the very southernmost tip of the island, the early morning fire is going and the coffee is heating on the stove, and Flora MacKenzie is currently in the middle of having a furious stand-up argument with her brother Fintan.

★ * ❆

'Colton's Bar,' she repeated. 'Absolutely not. I mean, I understand it, but also it sounds like a saloon where girls wear hot pants and fringing and cowboy boots and ask how y'all doing and we have a mechanical horse.'

'Nobody said anything about a mechanical horse,' grumbled Fintan, breathing in the scent of his coffee and the fresh rolls warming in the oven. Then he looked up.

'Hmm,' he said. 'Mechanical horse.'

'Do I have to take that coffee off you?'

Fintan rolled his eyes. 'Anything but that.'

It had only been a year since Fintan's husband Colton had died of cancer. Fintan had good days and bad days. This was not shaping up to be a good day. There weren't many good days.

Colton had left Fintan the Rock, the hotel he had always dreamed of opening on the island, and it was finally coming to fruition. But there were a million and one little details and he wasn't enjoying that side of things in the slightest. The hotel had been useful: it had kept Fintan phenomenally busy and helped keep the grief at bay – sheer exhaustion was his friend when it came to sleeping alone in a very big bed. Plus they had bookings for Christmas Day. They had to open, and quickly.

Flora technically had nothing to do with it.

But somehow, as she already had catering experience running the Seaside Kitchen down on the shore, she couldn't stop poking her nose in. Also, she was meant to be on maternity leave which,

3

as far as Fintan (and not just Fintan) was concerned, was leaving her with far too much time on her hands to interfere.

'Look,' she said. 'I think the Rogers Bar is fine. Just not so on the nose, you know?'

Fintan pouted.

There was a commotion at the entrance to the kitchen. Fintan was staying at the farmhouse, as was his brother Innes and his family. Innes's daughter Agot, five, was marching into the kitchen in her nightie, a serious look on her face, a thin wail rising behind her from the corridor.

'Bugliss Binder is awake,' she said with a sniff. 'I think he's a bad baby, Auntie Flora. He is very cross.'

'Douglas,' said Flora for the nine hundredth time. 'His name is Douglas.'

Agot and Fintan gave her a similarly dry look.

'What?' said Flora. 'She watches *Hey Duggee* all the time.'

'*Hey Duggee* is a very good dog,' said Agot loudly. Then: 'I'm not sure about Buglish.'

She marched over to the retired sheepdog Bramble and the two of them went outside to examine the vegetable garden. Agot had a very strong resistance to actually eating vegetables, but she liked watching them grow, even at this time of year.

'She's doing that on purpose,' said Flora, heading out. 'She can speak perfectly well.'

'She is,' said Fintan. 'And yet you somehow let it rile you.'

Flora headed towards the back room, even though the baby was barely crying, thinking Agot was ridiculous, and then she realised she was mentally having an argument with her five-year-old niece which was a waste of time if she'd ever known one, but it didn't matter, because by the time she got there, Joel was already with him, and Douglas had fallen silent.

4

He looked so like his father – black eyes and already, at five months, a shock of black curly hair – it was actually hilarious. Almost everyone who met him had felt the urge to put a pair of glasses on him.

She stood in the doorframe for a moment, watching them both. Douglas didn't smile much – he was not at all a smiley baby; his little face was grave and serious, as if he had been born knowing all the mysteries of a universe he would gradually forget as he grew older. He also shared his father's serious demeanour, being watchful and careful. For a long time, Flora had thought that Joel was like that because of his difficult upbringing – he had been in and out of foster homes since he was very little – but she was coming to think, that in fact Joel's demeanour was innate as, it had turned out, never was a baby boy smothered with so much love and affection as Douglas was, coming in to a home with many uncles at close quarters and his grandfather, Eck, who worshipped him and did many of the babysitting duties. Then there were his adopted American grandparents, Mark and Marsha, who sent vast care packages of ridiculously expensive baby clothes imported from France, via New York, which were frankly a little too good for the muddy farmyard and changeable climate of a small very northern Scottish island, but Flora made sure he was dutifully photographed in them all anyway.

Joel didn't fuss Douglas or sing to him. He just lay down on the bed next to him and the two of them eyeballed each other. It was the oddest thing, as if something intangible flowed between them through eye contact alone. Joel's large hand would reach out so Douglas could clasp a tiny finger, and then they would commune. Flora didn't know if this was normal, but it was sweet. Sometimes Douglas would flap at Joel's heavy gold watch and Joel would let him. Usually, after fifteen minutes of this, they would both be asleep, the long body gently cradling the tiny one.

Flora was supposedly on maternity leave with Isla and Iona running the café perfectly well, somewhat to Flora's annoyance. But it was Joel, her workaholic boyfriend, who appeared to have taken parental leave most to heart, and Flora couldn't help occasionally feeling just a little jealous. Which was, of course, completely ridiculous. Everything was great. Fine. Great. Sure, Douglas cried at her and was totally calm with Joel but she didn't mind. Not a bit.

Chapter Two

'Well, which is the best one?'

Isla Donnelly's mother Vera was looking at her over the old teapot with the flowers and the chip in the top.

Isla, staring at it, realised something she had never quite put into words before: she hated that teapot. It was the stupidest thing she could imagine, hating a teapot. It was possibly because her mother treated it like a precious heirloom she needed to be more careful with rather than just a dumb, crappy teapot.

She sipped her tea.

'I don't know, Mum,' she said again, trying not to get riled, which wouldn't help.

'So, the MacKenzies need someone up at the new posh hotel?'

Vera Donnelly sniffed loudly. She didn't think much of the new hotel. Not the kind of thing Mure needed, in her opinion, and Vera had a lot of opinions. Too fancy, too expensive, who wanted that kind of thing?

Regardless, it was set to open this Christmas, and Flora had offered to help Fintan by moving one of her café staff up there.

Isla sighed. She was in fact indeed quite terrified, but she would never tell her mother that. Not good to give her the ammunition.

'Well, one of us will stay and take over more of the running of the Seaside Kitchen and one of us will go up to the Rock.'

Isla and her best friend Iona had worked in the Summer Seaside Kitchen for years, and neither was looking forward to being separated. Isla in particular was very much the shyer of the two, especially when she wasn't with Iona, and was absolutely dreading being without her cheeky chum.

'Yes, but which one is the *best job*?'

'I don't know.'

Vera carefully picked up her treasured teapot and daintily poured herself another cup of tea.

'You know I just don't want them taking advantage of you,' she said. 'That Flora treats you like a scullery maid.'

'I've just been learning on the job,' said Isla, who adored Flora and didn't have quite her mother's expectations. It was difficult being Vera's only child. She hated constantly adding to her disappointment.

Isla's main goal was to stop herself being Vera's only area of attention.

'What are you doing today, Mum?'

'It's *Homes under the Hammer*!'

'You know there's a choir rehearsal tonight ... you should go to that.'

'Bunch of busybodying old gossips. No, thanks!'

Isla pulled on her coat and pulled her tam-o'-shanter down over her unruly dark chestnut curls, which pinged out every which way, unusual on the island where people had fair or red hair depending on whether they were descended from Celts or Vikings. There had once been a rumour of Spanish invaders making it as far north as Mure, which would have made more sense of her green eyes, although the pale skin, lightly freckled in the summertime, was purest Scotland to Isla's eternal chagrin.

A nor'wester was blowing down from the Arctic Circle straight into Mure, and it made walking in a straight line quite difficult, but it wasn't far to the Seaside Kitchen, down two cobbled streets and on to the seafront.

The little café was always warm: the baking ovens through the back never really quite cooled down and on the freezing winter mornings it was cosy even before Isla lit the golden lamps that, together with the cheery spotted tablecloths and the pretty pictures on the wall, made the café so inviting. Iona would already be brewing up coffee and together they could make a start on the scones, pies, tarts and cakes for the day, while Mrs Laird popped off the freshly baked bread, the coffee machine hissed and ground in a comforting fashion and the day could begin. And it wouldn't be long before the first chilled worker arrived, fresh from milking or a fishing boat or waiting on the earliest ferry of the morning.

'Bye, Mum,' she said.

'Aye well. Good luck then,' said her mother grudgingly as she left, and Isla reminded herself it was only because her mother loved her and wanted the best for her. Even when it felt unpleasant.

Chapter Three

Two hundred miles to the east, expensive sheets on a bed were ruffled and crumpled. A pale figure was lying on them, unconcerned and snoring heavily. A heavy scent of stale booze was in the air.

A short man with an exceedingly tidy haircut entered the vast room, paused in front of the bed and coughed loudly. Nothing happened.

'AHEM,' said the man.

There was an unpleasant hacking cough from the bed, followed by a snorting and some grunting. A large arm grabbed the shiny coverlet and pulled it over the incumbent's head.

'Go away, Johann,' came a very croaky voice, muffled beneath the covers.

'Johann has been sent away,' came the voice. There was a pause in the room.

'Huh?'

The young man who emerged from the covers had fair hair sticking up in every conceivable direction, a very tiny amount of stubble and a confused look in his round blue eyes, which became markedly rounder as he registered who he was talking to.

'Papa,' he said, and there was a notable tremor in his voice. He clutched the covers round him. The man staring at him looked disappointed. Again.

'Um,' said the figure in the bed. 'I mean, hello. Good to see you. You don't normally ...'

He glanced round at the large, lavish suite. There were pillars in the corners, gilt on the cornicing and vast, ancient mirrors lining one wall.

Unfortunately there were also underpants and socks on the floor, empty bottles, books scattered everywhere, a snorting, pig-like dog called Bjårk, who hadn't woken up yet but had left muddy pawprints all over the wildly expensive rug and black and white tiled floor, and at least four towels.

'I don't normally come here, no,' said the boy's father, whose name was Konstantin. The boy's name was also Konstantin. There had been Konstantins, in fact, all the way back to the early seventeenth century, when they had first become dukes of Hordaland, and the grand castle had been built on the beautiful Folgefonna peninsula. Titles in Norway had been theoretically abolished. Of course, every-one still knew about them though. An unbroken line. Which, the older Konstantin reflected sadly, was about to be broken when he kicked his dissolute only son down the one hundred and eighteen marble curved steps of the grand entrance hall. 'Because it's a revolt-ing pigsty.'

'That's Bjårk's fault.'

The hairy creature didn't stir.

'Do you recall what happened last night at the state banquet?'

Konstantin screwed up his face.

'The snowball fight,' he said finally. 'Yes, wasn't it brilliant?'

He remembered the palace windows blazing light as they ran about outside, exhausted, freezing and soaking, but laughing their heads off.

'It was *not* brilliant,' said his father. 'You hit the archbishop on the ear.'

'Well, he should have joined in.'

'You put snow down the neck of my financial advisor.'

Konstantin shrugged.

'He's an old stick.'

His father shook his head.

'No. You behaved like a thug.'

'We were having fun!'

'And, worse than that, you behaved like a bully to people older and weaker than yourself.'

'With a *snowball*.'

But he wasn't stopping now.

'This is after the ice races.'

'I accidentally tripped up . . .'

'The entire professional team . . .'

'They were in the way!'

The boy pushed out his lower lip and suddenly looked a lot younger than twenty-four. His father shook his head.

'You know, if your mother was still with us, she wouldn't have stood for this.'

The boy pouted more.

'That's not fair,' he said, but now his voice was quiet and sad.

'We were too soft on you . . . afterwards,' went on the man. 'I didn't want to upset things . . . didn't want to make you study too much or get a job or work hard. And look at you now. Twenty-four years old and in bed in the middle of a Tuesday.' He shook his head sadly. 'I got it wrong. I got it so wrong.'

He turned round, his younger years at Sandhurst still apparent in his gait. Konstantin stared after him, stricken.

At the door, his father turned back one more time.

'I'm tempted to disinherit you.'

'You wouldn't! For a snowball! Don't be silly, Papa; you can't mean that.'

'This is a big job. And you do nothing, you learn nothing, you work at nothing except drinking champagne and playing with that fat idle hound of yours.'

Konstantin frowned and covered Bjårk's ears.

'Be as mean as you like to me, but don't upset Bjårky.'

'It's all a joke to you, isn't it?' said the older man. 'All a joke. And I am going to fix that.'

And he opened the heavy white door with its gilt handle, and let it slam behind him.

* ❄

The younger Konstantin sat up in bed, Bjårk snuffling underneath his hands. It would blow over, wouldn't it? Surely. His father was always getting these ideas into his head, insisting he should go to college, or into the military, or get a job, and nothing ever came of it in the end. The much-loved only child, who'd come along late in life, whose mother had died when he was fourteen . . .

Mind you, there was no still Johann. That was odd. He looked at the grandfather clock in the corner. No breakfast either.

Normally he needed four strong cups of coffee, some excellent rye bread thickly spread with *smør* before he could even think about a steaming hot bath and a read of the sports pages. His paper wasn't even here. He frowned to himself and reached over to ring the bell. But nobody came.

Chapter Four

Flora caught up with Fintan and they walked through the lobby of the Rock. It had felt like it would take for ever to get finished, but it was done: sound and warm and dry and very beautiful. And Christmassy, even though it was only November. The trees were arriving shortly, but the staff had already hung the great scalloped green boughs tied up with tartan ribbon, their scent filling the air. There were bowls full of oranges studded with cinnamon cloves, the great log fire at the entrance was lit and gentle music was playing in the background.

Originally a tumbledown old croft on the very northern tip of the island, the Rock had been converted by the brash American developer Colton Rogers, with absolutely no expense spared. There was also no taste spared in terms of what an American thought a Scottish hotel was supposed to look like, which meant tartan carpets, lots of open fires, muskets on the walls, vast stags' heads everywhere and a library full of old hardback books that had been bought from an aristocratic book dealer down Kirrinfief way, without Colton reading a single word of any of them.

It was a little kitsch, maybe, but Flora couldn't help admitting to herself that she rather loved it. It was just so warm and cosy all the time, which in the winter at Mure meant a lot. And being done up for Christmas put it in its absolute prime.

There was underfloor heating in the bathrooms, and heated towel rails filled with fluffy towels, and great deep baths for which the hot water never seemed to run out. The kitchens were pristine and full of the latest equipment, Flora noticed enviably, ready to churn out bread and pastries, high teas and fresh lobster, buttery scones, creamy Cullen skink and sharp cranachan. And, behind the bar, forty-five different types of whisky waited tantalisingly, together with a menu of delicious local cocktails.

Flora and Fintan looked at each other. Flora was excited by all the possibilities; Fintan's shoulders were slumped, his entire countenance a mask of misery and defeatism.

'It's never going to pay its way in a billion years,' said Fintan bitterly. 'We should just get rid of it. Colton didn't leave me a fortune,' he went on anxiously. 'He just left me this place. We'll tear through the money in five minutes.'

Colton had donated the vast bulk of his considerable fortune to medical research. He'd left the hotel and his home to Fintan, but Fintan couldn't bear to live in the vast echoing house by himself, so Joel and Flora were renting it while Fintan stayed back at the farmhouse.

'And I don't know how to run a hotel! I don't even know what VAT is!'

'It's like a very complicated puzzle the government sets you for fun, but if you get it wrong you go to jail,' said Flora, but Fintan wasn't listening.

'I already can't get staff! And how am I going to tell them what to do? What if the people here want to leave because they hate me? What if nobody comes? How much would we have to charge? I should sell it. I should sell this whole place.'

Flora stood warming her hands in front of the fire. There was a skeleton staff, all of whom seemed great. They just needed a chef and a bit of help in the kitchen. Fintan was panicking.

'But it's all Colton's,' she said softly. 'It was his dream. It's exactly how he wanted it.'

Flora eyed the huge antlered stag's head above the fireplace and reflected that, for better or worse, it certainly was that. Fintan sighed.

'It's all that's left of him. How could I sell that?'

His voice was anguished. Flora didn't know what to say.

'Well, how would you feel if you did sell it?' she tried gently.

'We met ...' said Fintan abruptly. He now appeared to have completely changed his mind about selling it, and was somehow blaming Flora for implying it. 'We met for the first time on the lawn. We got married out there, or did you forget?'

Flora stayed silent. She understood Fintan's bitterness and grief. She had just slightly hoped that he might get a bit more excited about moving forward, find energy in working on the new project to make it as wonderful as Colton always hoped it would be.

Fintan, however, was still fuming at the world, specifically the Rock section of it, the amazing boutique property that was now technically his to do as he liked with. To most people, Flora reflected a little glumly, it would have been a wonderful legacy. Fintan seemed determined to be having none of it.

She tried to help.

'We'll just need to charge a lot of money,' she said. 'Get the right people in.'

'Rich nobbers.'

Flora shrugged. 'There are plenty of nice rich nobbers.'

'Are there though?' said Fintan, looking cross.

'Well, you married one for starters.'

'Yes, but he . . . he was a one-off.'

Flora smiled sympathetically as they walked on to the dining room, which had cosy soft leather banquettes at the windows, and comfortable tweed chairs, and wide, dark oak flooring. There was panelling along one wall, with expensive and terrible oil paintings of stags and Bonnie Prince Charlie. It was completely empty and still.

Flora looked around. 'So many tables,' she said, half to herself. The Seaside Kitchen had twelve tables, at least two of which were permanently occupied by knitters who worked with the Fair Isle companies.

Then there was the mums and babies group who spent copiously on the organic purees she put together each morning with whatever she had to hand, plus a long line of extremely hungry fisherman, farmers, hikers, birdwatchers and holidaymakers, who wanted sausage rolls and haggis pies and hot soup. She knew her clientele back to front and was fond of all of them. That she could manage. But this . . . even though it was technically a 'boutique' hotel, it was still an awful lot of doing. Was Fintan up to it?

As if hearing her thoughts, Fintan let out a great sigh.

'All I ever wanted to do was make cheese.'

Flora looked at him. His handsome face was so tired; he'd lost too much weight and was still in the throes of such a strong grief.

It made her vow to appreciate her own situation more.

Especially when she remembered how much she'd worried

about Douglas before he'd arrived. She had been told subsequently by the other mums she met around the place that this wasn't uncommon at all. People who desperately wanted to be parents, who had fantasies about how perfect it was all going to be, had a very difficult time of it when their baby wouldn't sleep or eat or wasn't the perfect heavenly dream they'd expected, or read about in magazines or looked at in advertisements, and they didn't lose their baby weight by 'running about after the baby' like celebrities said they did. Was it just possible, she'd heard one mother muse, that those celebrities might in fact be talking out of the cracks of their arses?

Flora had by no means lost her baby weight, but was filing it very far down on her list of Current Things to Worry About. He wouldn't have mentioned it in a million years, not being an idiot, but Joel thought it suited her; it made her so pretty and rounded and soft.

From the second Dougie had arrived, Joel had behaved like a man poleaxed by love. Sometimes with reluctant parents – the accidental pregnancies, the slightly (or in Joel's case, extremely) ambivalent fathers – the force of the extraordinary rush of love that the babies brought with them could knock them over, take them completely by surprise, and Joel was the worst of the lot. Flora complained that he had never once appeared so gaga about her, but she didn't really mind, she supposed. He had been so worried about whether he would take to parenthood – as a foster child, he'd been moved around from house to house, never once finding a home – that he had been mute and difficult and anxious all the way up to the birth itself (an unusually speedy process which Flora found increasingly difficult to remember anything about but as soon as the gawky squawking tiny blood-, shit- and goo-covered alien – or, counterpoint, the most beautiful miracle ever in the history of human existence – was placed on Flora's stomach by the midwife, Joel had been hit by a lightning bolt.

And any ups and downs Flora felt after the birth – and there were absolutely loads of them, notably how it feels to become a mother when your own mother is no longer around to share it with you – were somehow balanced out by Joel's extraordinary, all-encompassing love for the baby and for her. Finally, her doubts about whether he was, with his difficult past, capable of loving at all were set aside. She knew she was lucky. She didn't even know where the resentment came from. So she ignored it, hoping it would go away. She was so lucky.

* ❊

'I'm just so miserable,' said Fintan. Flora looked at him. Time was running short. She'd hoped and hoped and hoped that he would perk up, come back to himself for long enough to consider taking the job on. But he was listless and sad and nothing could motivate him. If it was ever going to happen, she knew, there was only one person who could do it.

'Okay,' she said finally. 'Well, I suppose I could help out a bit.'

'We've been through this! It's called *interfering*.'

Flora gave him a Big Sister look.

' . . . and I thought you were on your fancy maternity leave.'

Flora chose to ignore him.

'Look. You love doing all the food and stuff, right?' she said. 'That's your area. Best of everything. We have a little money. And even if we lose it all – well, we never had any to start with, right?'

Fintan shrugged.

'But this is Colton's dream . . .'

'And his dream was to have the absolute best of everything, right?'

Fintan nodded.

'Well. You go do your part. Find the best chef, get the best local ingredients, make sure the food is amazing. Let me handle the rest.'

Fintan stared at her. His entire demeanour changed. Flora could tell he really didn't want to accept. But also that he really, really needed to.

'Yeah, I'm not going to do *much*,' she said. 'But I've got experience of hygiene regs, fire checks, all of that now. I can help you out when Joel has got Dougie.'

She didn't dare even hint that she might quite like having a project while Joel and Dougie were carrying on their massive love affair.

They both looked around. The dining room still seemed huge. But Fintan's face showed something she hadn't seen for a long time. A tiny bit of hope.

Chapter Five

So it was that Flora came to be interviewing her own staff at the Seaside Kitchen. They were doing a brilliant job during her maternity leave and the place was as bustling and jolly as ever, she observed, not without a touch of envy, and young Malik who'd been drafted in to help seemed competent and popular too.

Flora sat the girls down.

'I feel like Paul Hollywood,' she grumbled. 'Not necessarily in a good way.'

The girls looked at her expectantly, Iona cheerful, Isla terrified. Flora smiled encouragingly.

'The Rock needs kitchen staff, and the Seaside Kitchen needs looking after just as normal till I get back.'

Iona frowned, then grinned rather wickedly.

'By "looking after", do you mean making too many giant

custard creams and then secretly eating them by yourself by the cold store?'

'Um, no,' said Flora, blushing.

'Do you mean going behind the larder to snog your boyfriend?'

'I . . . I do not mean that,' said Flora, biting her lip a bit. 'And this is insubordination.'

'Well, not if I'm going to be management. Is Isla going to be management too?'

'I think I'm going to regret this,' said Flora. They were just young girls, after all. Maybe this wasn't a good idea.

'You were right about the big custard creams though,' mused Iona. 'We should do more. Bourbons and jam sandwiches – people loved them, and they're easy to do; you just need the moulds. Mark-up's good. Oh! And pumpkin spice.'

'What?' said Flora, carefully pretending she knew what Iona meant.

'We need to get pumpkin spice.'

'Um, what is that?'

Iona looked unsure for a moment.

'I don't know *exactly*. But it's what you have to have on your coffee this time of year. Instagram says so.'

Flora blinked.

'Instagram?'

'Yeah. You have your pumpkin spice latte and post it on Instagram.'

'And it makes your coffee taste of pumpkin?'

'I don't know.'

Iona started scrolling through her phone.

'It's just what everyone's doing, that's all. And people take pictures of the biscuits.'

'Do they?'

Flora had noticed, in the last year or so, people taking pictures of themselves more and more outside the pretty frontage of the little harbour café, but hadn't thought much of it; customers were customers, and tourists did tourist stuff and even if these days it meant all of them lining up at the exact same angle to take exactly the same photograph, well, she didn't really think about that very much.

'We need an Instagram page.'

Iona was quite pink in the face now and Flora realised she was entirely serious, and also that she'd thought about this a lot, and hadn't just been cutting sandwiches the whole time.

'We need to show off how lovely it is here and have people come in and link and make sure that tourists come even if it's just to see us. And ...'

Flora frowned.

'Hang on ... have you been having these brilliant ideas all this time?'

Iona looked perturbed and didn't say anything.

'Am I a terrible boss who never listens to anything?'

'You never asked,' said Iona.

This wasn't at all the way Flora had predicted the morning turning out.

' ... also I think we should do more organic baby food for the mothers' group. The mark-up is ...'

'Okay, okay, you've got the Seaside Kitchen,' said Flora, smiling. 'Just turn us into millionaires by Christmas please.'

She looked at Isla, who was standing there quietly.

'Are you happy to come up to the big house?' she said. 'I know it's not as glamorous a job, but there's lots of opportunity to learn in a bigger kitchen, try out different skills, cooking as well as baking ...'

'Does she have to wash pots?' said Iona.

'Everyone has to wash pots,' said Flora. 'That's how small businesses work.'

Isla looked at Iona a bit sadly.

'It'll be hard to be separated,' she said quietly. In fact, she was gutted to be leaving her best friend. She didn't like things changing. She wasn't very good at it.

'You'll be great,' said Flora.

'I don't know if I have good ideas like Iona.'

'That's not really how you should approach a job interview!' said Flora. Then, when she saw Isla's face fall: 'I'm kidding! I'm kidding. I've seen you work your socks off here for three years. I know how good you are. I'm lucky to have you both and you're both getting raises.'

'And a marketing budget,' said Iona.

'*Iona!*' said Flora crossly. 'I am intensely cross with you for not telling me all this before.'

'Take it up with management,' said cheeky Iona. 'Oh no, that appears to be me!'

Flora shook her head. 'Okay, Isla,' she said. 'You come with me. I'll talk you through it up at the hotel. And the call's already gone out for other staff. It's going to be fun!'

Isla was already working out what to tell her mum.

Chapter Six

Konstantin was perturbed. There was no breakfast at all. Not delivered, and not in the great dining room. He ended up heading down to the kitchen where normally Else would pet him and find a titbit for him to eat. After his mother had died, he had been so spoiled and coddled by the kitchen staff (even if they'd been allowed to refuse him, which they certainly were not) that he had been a lonely, podgy boy. When his father sent him off to boarding school at fifteen, hoping this would straighten him out, it had got better and worse all at once. Worse because he was initially unbelievably miserable. Better because the enforced sport and meagre rations had got rid of the flab immediately. And then worse again as, to try and make himself popular, he had done his best to get in with the worst gang in the school. Since his father was extremely busy trying to keep up with ceremonial duties, as well as manage his own grieving, he hadn't always been able to keep on top of his absent son's behaviour too.

* ❄

Having an unusually large stipend, even for a boarding school boy, allowed the younger Konstantin to become accepted into an unruly gang of reprobates who liked to take weekends in Montenegro, Gstaad, Monaco and Biarritz. They would stay in the flashiest hotels and see just how much they could get away with, which – as a group of northern white aristocrats – turned out to be an awful lot. School hadn't been so bad in the end. He'd stuffed up his exams, of course, but these things happened. There wasn't much incentive to take exams when you already drove a nicer car than the head teacher ever would.

And being an excellent shot, a good and brave horseman and a tremendous skier took work, didn't it? And effort. His father never recognised *that*. Even when he'd been tipped to join the national ski team, the discipline and expected hours were, quite simply, unbearably dull – not to mention the nutritional requirements – and he hadn't attended any practices at all.

Now Anders, his father's personal secretary, had taken him aside and was talking to him, but every word of it was going in one ear and out the other.

So Anders was doing his best to explain, yet again.

'We've found a job for you, and you're going to be beginning in a week.'

Konstantin screwed his face up in a charming appeal that had always worked like gangbusters with most of the palace staff.

'Yeah . . . noooo.'

'I'm afraid it's your father's orders,' said Anders.

'He's not the boss of me!'

'I've been asked—' Anders was not a cowardly man, but he hadn't been looking forward to this in the slightest. 'I've been asked to inform you that all of your credit cards have been stopped as of this morning. Your phone contract has been cancelled, and you'll be leaving in five days. Your tickets are in this envelope.'

Konstantin gawped in astonishment.

'WHAT?!'

'Your horses have been restabled and ...'

Konstantin immediately looked around for Bjårk, who lumbered over (he really was frightfully overweight).

'You're not taking Bjårk Bjårkensson!' His face grew grave. Now he was listening. 'He stays with me.'

'I'm not sure whether that will be possible.'

'You can't banish me and not him! He behaves worse than I do!'

As if to prove this, Bjårk slunk over to the breakfast table and, disappointed to find it empty, let out an almighty fart and disappeared under it, snuffling for crumbs. His large hind end started shaking the exquisite rococo legs of the gilt table and Anders rushed over to steady it before it crashed onto the parquet. He rolled his eyes.

'Well, I'm not going anywhere,' said Konstantin.

'You aren't today,' said Anders. 'Your father has impounded your cars. But next week, I'm very much afraid that you are.'

Konstantin blinked. This couldn't be happening. It just couldn't.

Gradually, the meaning began to sink in. If his cars were gone, then ...

'You took my PHONE?!'

Chapter Seven

On the rare occasions Fintan had had the funds and free time to go to Glasgow, he had absolutely loved it. He adored the wet, majestic city with its vast sandstone tenements; the glittering straight roads he imagined they had in New York; the expensive Merchant City with its designer clothes shops and mysterious-looking restaurants.

He loved the people. Marching down from Buchanan Street, every shape and size, from every corner of the world. Students, tourists, businessmen. It felt like the centre of the universe. He loved the Glasgow girls, with their tans and long eyelashes and brightly coloured clothes, often inappropriate for the weather, and who cared a jot for that? They yelled, they laughed, they looked like stunning tropical birds compared to the duller colours of home.

But most of all he loved the men. Or rather, a certain type

of dangerous, slender, short-haired man, who might give you a glance here or there, or walk boldly up Sauchiehall Street hand in hand with his boyfriend. The city smelled of opportunity and excitement and sex, and Fintan had loved it ever since his mother had first brought him there, a wide-eyed and extremely confused fifteen-year-old, to do the Christmas shopping, ladling everything onto the little prop plane that would take them home again. It had been quite the adventure. They had eaten oysters in Rogano's and looked at the beautiful art school. Fintan had never seen anything like the variety of shops and things to buy and he'd been paralysed by choice. His mum had bought him a discounted Tommy Hilfiger sweatshirt and he had worn nothing else for a year. And he had sworn he would go back there, be a student there, make his life in the city.

But he hadn't. His mother had got sick and he'd had to look after her, and then the farm had really needed all hands on deck, and that dream had got away from him. Of course, he had discovered a new love of food and cooking when Flora had come back from London. And then he'd met Colton and fallen in love, and everything had changed in the very best way, and for a short time he'd been the happiest man in the universe, and firmly believed that everything had turned out for the best.

That had not lasted long.

And now here he was, trudging the damp, shining pavements of the old place again, the leaves wilting beneath his feet, umbrellas overhead, pipers trying to make money on the corners of the huge stone buildings. He didn't raise his eyes to look in the extravagant shop windows. He didn't glance at men walking into coffee shops that might glance back at him. He just thought over his life, of the ways he had and hadn't taken, the other roads and other doors.

He arrived at the employment agency in a very low mood indeed. Flora had suggested, at the beginning of the year when things were very bleak, that he take a little of Colton's money and go lie on a beach somewhere, and he'd gone to Cancun by himself and drunk cocktails under a palm tree and cried himself sick. It had not been entirely successful.

People did keep telling him not to worry, it took a long time. The problem was, they'd say that, with their heads tilted and a sad face on, and he knew they meant it and he knew they were concerned. But then they went on, and bought one of Flora's sausage rolls, or patted the next dog they saw, or went to the library and exchanged the latest novels. But he was still here, stuck in his misery. They did two minutes a day and thought they were being helpful when it was all he could do not to snarl at them, to not feel enraged at the way they carried on their totally normal lives, now made even more perfect by being able to mentally pat themselves on the back for doing a good deed to poor wee Fintan.

Grieving set his teeth on edge. And more than this, it was dull. So dull. To be missing Colton every second of every day; to wake up every morning and remember the whole sodding thing again; to know, because he'd been told, that it would never go away, not entirely, that this was just it now and oh, by the way, loads of people lived like this so he might as well get used to it.

He didn't want to get used to it, he thought, kicking a pile of leaves with such savagery that a passing taxi driver eyed him warily. He didn't want any of this. He didn't want to be going to some lousy chef agency. He wanted to be lying in their vast bed in the Manse – before it turned into a hospital bed, before that bed was donated to a hospice on the mainland. Way, way back, even though it was only a year or so. He wanted them to be lying there, going through CVs, laughing at things together, making French toast and those hideous vitamin things that Colton would wince and gulp down with a shudder. Fintan had assumed it was because he was being Californian about things.

It wasn't.

But no. He was out, on his own, doing a job he didn't even know if he was suited for. It was all right for Flora, he thought. Her life had worked out absolutely fine. She had her boyfriend, had a baby, had the house even. Fintan couldn't bear to live in Fintan's mansion, so he'd made Flora rent it. But he still resented them being there. He wanted it bricked up like a shrine, kept exactly how it had been when they had been in love, with nobody else walking through it, no babies laughing or fires crackling. Every time Flora changed something, he winced. Flora, aware of this, tried to tiptoe around the place, so as a result nobody was particularly happy with the arrangement.

He arrived at the large red sandstone building. Happy Hospitality was the name of the company. He snorted to himself. Whatever.

Chapter Eight

The young recruiting agent was pretty and enthusiastic.

'Well!' she said. 'You are quite the conundrum! Lots of our chefs want to work with their own kitchen.'

Fintan stared ahead stonily, ignoring the cup of coffee the receptionist had brought him.

'. . . but the location is quite . . .'

'It's far away, aye,' he said shortly. 'It comes with accommodation.'

'Yes, but often people aren't sure whether they want to uproot their entire lives . . .'

'Is that so?'

'But we do have a *few* people for you to meet!'

The woman smiled brightly and buzzed in the first person, a morose bearded man with a bright red nose and trembling hands. Fintan internally sighed. He had thought that recruiting a chef to a state-of-the-art kitchen, with a mandate to build a creative menu using whatever local ingredients they wanted to source, would be enticement enough. Mure had an embarrassment of riches in that regard: local shellfish, oysters, lobsters and crayfish, all pulled from the ice-cold water each morning; rich green vegetables that kept their flavour in the soil; samphire glistening like emeralds along the wide beaches; careful crops of wild mushrooms; venison from the mainland, rich and dark as chocolate; elderberry and juniper gin brewed on the island; rhubarb to beat the band.

As well as luxury accommodation on a beautiful island ... he'd thought it would be a dream come true. But now, in the city, burn-out followed burn-out: old chefs who'd seen it all; tourist hoteliers, whose limit was scampi and chips or chicken in a basket. Time-servers and bedraggled kitchen casualties who he wasn't entirely sure weren't just after the free room and board. Cheffing was a punishingly difficult career, with high rates of drink and drug-taking. Not everyone got out of it unscathed. And the people that Happy Hospitality had lined up for him were hardly the cream of the crop.

He'd hoped he might find someone with as much passion as he had, who could see the amazing potential of their little island at the top of the world. But he sat through interview after interview with little light. The idea was that he would talk to everyone, then the ones whom he liked would cook something in the kitchen set up in the offices. But so far he wouldn't let anyone he'd met make him so much as a sandwich.

'I'm not sure this is going to work out,' he said as he and the recruitment consultant took a break. He tried the coffee this time. It really wasn't bad.

She nodded.

'I do realise ... it's just the location ...'

'Yeah, you said,' said Fintan. 'The location is amazing, actually.'

'We do have a couple more people for you to see,' said the woman. Fintan glanced at his watch. The plane didn't leave till the evening and he didn't have anything else to do; there was nowhere he wanted to go, nothing he wanted to see. The bright lights of the shops and gay clubs and restaurants had no appeal for him any more. It was, he reflected once again, so dull being so joyless.

'Okay, bring it on,' he said.

The woman glanced at her phone worriedly. The next interviewee was late. Rather late. Bordering on very late.

'I'm sorry,' she said awkwardly. One just pulled out … Apparently one of their friends was in earlier …'

Fintan's brow furrowed.

'What does that mean?'

The recruitment agent's lips twitched.

'Oh, nothing,' she said.

'What?' said Fintan, then he gradually realised.

'What, because they'd met *me*?'

'I couldn't possibly say,' said the agent, whose name was Marian and who thought it was a fiendish disappointment that Fintan was gay because she had a terrible soft spot for handsome angry men. Although, she reflected, that had brought her nothing but grief in her life, so this was something of a lucky escape. Regardless, word had already got around and nobody wanted to work for a misery guts in a place where if you were lucky the thermometer might hit twelve degrees in July.

Fintan folded his arms.

'For fuck's sake,' he was saying crossly, just as the door burst open.

'I AM LATE!' announced the tall, very skinny man standing in the doorframe. He was wearing a rather grubby T-shirt and

35

jeans. His arms were completely covered in spiky tattoos and he was unshaven and looked none too clean. His accent was heavy. Fintan internally sighed. So the whole day would be completely wasted. No decent chefs would ever want to come with him. Flora had tried to cut down on everything he had to do and still he hadn't managed to properly handle the one thing – the kitchen – that he was meant to love, that he was meant to be looking after.

'Yes, thank you, Gaspard,' said Marian primly. Her lips thinned. She liked sullen men, not ridiculous ones.

Gaspard came in and threw himself insolently onto a chair.

'So. A keetchen. In the ocean.'

His accent was so French as to be absurdly comic. Fintan wouldn't have been at all surprised to learn he came from Basingstoke and was putting it on.

'I thought you were back in Marseille,' said Marian, flicking through the CVs.

Gaspard gave a shrug.

'Eet ees feelthy like wild dogs on street. Also. There ees wild dogs on street.'

'I've heard Marseille is nice.'

'Not my Marseille.'

He had two days' stubble on his cheeks and really did look in profound need of a bath. He also sat sullenly, his arms folded, as if furious at being in a job interview situation – which indeed he was – as Fintan attempted to explain what was going on up at the Rock. He looked around even as Fintan was still talking.

'You want me to cook, *ou quoi?*'

Fintan was caught mid-spiel.

'Well, I'm just trying to explain what—'

'*Oui, oui*, but eef you hate what I cook, then this is a waste of everyone's time, *non*? Eet ees pointless talk talk talk bleh bleh bleh.'

Without waiting for an answer, he stood up and stalked into the small kitchen.

'Maree-ong!' he shouted. 'You have NUZZING! NUZZING ees here.'

'You know this guy?' said Fintan.

Marian nodded.

'Is he a dick?'

'Um.'

Marian truly didn't want to be unprofessional.

Fintan, reading her face, groaned.

'But,' said Marian to the sound of a gas burner being turned up high and popping loudly. 'He can cook.'

Chapter Nine

Fintan went in to watch what Gaspard was doing. What Gaspard was doing was having a cigarette out the window in blatant defiance of the fire regulations and the many signs posted around the walls.

'What are you doing?' said Marian.

'Sweating the onion,' said Gaspard. 'Nobody does eet properly. They do not leave eet long enough. They rush rush rush. And *so. Dégueulasse*.'

He shook his head sadly and leaned back, so far out of the window Fintan thought he might fall out.

Fintan couldn't help himself. His lips twitched, ever so slightly. Gaspard tossed his cigarette out of the window and went back to the pan without washing his hands. Hearing Marian's anguished sigh, he theatrically returned to the sink and did so. Then he added some finely chopped bacon, reduced some white wine he had already sampled straight from the bottle and gave Marian a big telling-off on *terroir*, explaining that if you bought wine for cooking that was worse than your normal wine you were an idiot, and if you bought that wine for both cooking and drinking you were also an idiot and so what was she? Finally, he added a topping of a cream sauce and some quickly seared scallops in another pan with fennel on top and served them all the lightest most delicious meal Fintan had had in some time, particularly after ferreting around in the back of the cupboard and finding a slightly more acceptable bottle of wine.

'*Tenez*,' he grumbled, throwing his food down him like a lanky bear.

He disappeared after Marian insisted on his leaving the building for another cigarette.

'I'll take him,' said Fintan.

'Are you sure?' said Marian. 'He's a pig. And he doesn't last long in jobs.'

'So why did you show him to me then?'

'Because we were . . . a little short on CVs.'

'Well,' said Fintan as Gaspard rolled back in, shouting at the top of his lungs what were patently obscenities in French down his phone. 'You've got him off your hands.'

'For now,' said Marian, glumly collecting the plates. 'See you in a week, Gaspard.'

Chapter Ten

The following week, Isla walked up the steps of the hotel somewhat tentatively.

She'd been to the Rock before, normally to help waitress at parties. But that was different: then she was just in and out of the back door in a black skirt and a white shirt, handing round haggis canapés and refilling people's glasses, except for Wullie Stevenson, who wanted his filled a tad too often, even by Colton's generous standards.

She'd never really thought of it as anything other than the big house, the hotel. She'd never considered that one day it might be a place where she worked every day.

Nervously, she fiddled with the zip of her padded jacket. Would she be able to handle such a big job? Flora seemed to have confidence in her but wasn't it just that Flora was so distracted with the baby and that grumpy boyfriend and Fintan being so miserable that she didn't really care?

Isla hadn't always lacked confidence. Not when her dad . . .

Well. There was no point thinking like that now.

The huge oak doors were propped open and a bright fire was burning in the grate. The receptionist, Gala, was a beautiful American girl, a niece of a colleague of Colton's who was supposedly on work experience and had got rather more than she bargained for, but she was friendly enough.

'Isla! Yeah! Sure! Got your name right here!' she chirruped.

Isla glanced around. Beyond the welcoming hallway, with the flickering fire, the kitchens were cold and bare and the restaurant was sitting unused and empty. There were so many chairs to fill, so many mouths to feed. Flora kept saying it was just a bigger version of what she was already doing and that there'd be a boss in place, but she wasn't sure. Not at all.

She passed on through the heavy oak doors at the back of the restaurant into the kitchens. They were huge! Vast state-of-the-art burners and grills, walk-in freezers, a wood-burning oven for bread – wow! Colton had stinted at nothing. Lines of empty shelving for butter, eggs, flour, everything she could conceivably need, tidy and neat and brand-new.

Well, maybe, she thought. Maybe she could make this work. Her dad, she thought, would have been pleased. Roddy had adored his only child. Lost in a fishing accident, the industry as dangerous as ever it was, his death had broken everyone's hearts. Especially his daughter's. It had also turned her mother's heart hard as flint, everyone said.

* ❈

The very top row of the house with its servants' quarters had been repurposed to be as comfortable as possible for seasonal staff: Gala had already taken the best room on the corner.

Fintan had gone down to the dock to meet Gaspard off the ferry and Isla had gone with him. She looked up at him shyly, slightly terrified of him.

'Hello? I'm Isla? In the kitchen . . .'

'Oh yes, hello.' He sank into his habitual sullen silence in case she started to talk about Colton or ask him how he was doing, something he was tired of and normally discouraged.

'I am a bit worried,' said Isla in that quiet way of hers, 'that he might not be very keen when he arrives.'

'They,' said Fintan. 'There's a kitchen assistant coming too.'

Sure enough, it was an absolute pig of a day. Hail was blowing into their faces; Isla was barely visible inside the zipped-up hood of her Puffa; Fintan had an expensive overcoat and a cashmere scarf but the tips of his ears were bright pink.

He smiled ruefully.

'It's not Antigua.'

Isla pulled open her bag.

'I brought hot chocolate,' she said. 'To kind of welcome him . . . them if they'd had terrible journeys. Would you like some?'

Fintan was about to say no – he ate rarely these days and never really felt hungry or thirsty – when he felt how cold his fingers were, even inside the leather gloves he was wearing.

'Okay,' he said.

She poured him out the cup of the most delicious frothy hot chocolate he'd ever tasted, sliding in a couple of marshmallows for good measure. He warmed his hands, then took a sip of the rich, not-too-sweet goodness. It tasted like Christmas and home and warmth all at once.

'Oh my,' he said. 'That's fantastic.'

Isla smiled.

'We've been perfecting it in the café for years. Have you not tried it?'

'It's not very good for you.'

Isla didn't say anything as she disagreed with him thoroughly and thought a delicious satisfying milk-based beverage on a cold day probably didn't do anyone any harm. She caught sight of the incoming ferry bouncing on the grey sea.

Fintan stared out at the pounding waves against the dock that had been the background noise to almost everything he'd done for so long that, like most people on Mure, he couldn't even hear them any more. He took another sip. It really was good.

'We need to serve that in the bar,' he said.

Isla nodded.

'You could put a shot of whisky in it and have it like Irish coffee,' she said. 'Only better.'

Fintan nodded too.

'It would be better,' he said. 'I should write that down.'

Isla pulled out her phone.

'Hot chocolate with booze,' she said into it. Fintan looked at her.

'You talk to your phone?'

Isla flushed instantly. She hated anyone singling her out for anything.

'Uh, yeah,' she said quietly. 'When I have to remember some-thing but I don't want to take my gloves off.'

'That makes a lot of sense,' said Fintan. The ferry started to churn backwards as it docked, and they fell into a watchful silence.

43

Gaspard had spotted the lean, confused-looking boy in the corner of the bar in the nearly empty ferry. November was not what you'd call peak season for island-hopping in the far north of Scotland, and there was barely anyone on board: a few farmers with Land Rovers stowed downstairs, who had come back from market enjoying a wee dram at the bar; a clutch of ladies who'd been shopping and to a show in Glasgow, giggling and cheerful and dressed up, albeit with their fleeces pulled back on over the top now they were heading back to the real world again; and an athletic, blond-haired boy looking sulky and completely out of place.

'Hey,' Gaspard had said. 'You live in theese end of world? Huh? You can tell me about it?'

Konstantin shook his head miserably.

'I've been banished,' he said in neatly clipped English with just the trace of an accent. 'I'm being punished.'

'Me also,' said Gaspard. 'Except I have done notheeng wrong. NOTHEENG!'

He marched up to the tiny brass bar and rang its heavy ship's bell, which was really only for decoration as the barman's face made perfectly clear when he'd straightened up from the shelf where he'd been putting glasses away. Gaspard had made several questions about the wine, none of which the young rating could understand or answer, then pointed at one bottle and took the whole thing. After seeing Konstantin looking increasingly miserable, he grabbed another glass and bade him sit down and tell him the whole sorry story, fuelled with more of the terrible wine which didn't taste quite so bad by the time they got halfway through it.

The long and short of it was that by the time the boat churned into Mure, as the light was failing over the horizon and the gleam of bigger ships the only light to be seen, both of them were a) great friends and b) completely roaring drunk.

$$* \text{ } *$$

Fintan was rather taken aback.

'*VOILA!*' yelled Gaspard, turning his face into the wind, where hail had started and spiked into his face like daggers. 'Welcome to hell, *non*?'

Konstantin lurched off, the difference in the motion between the two states of land and sea and the frankly rough wine having a predictable effect. As Isla watched him, horrified, he wobbled across the gangplank and threw up heavily over the side.

'Oh Christ,' said Fintan.

Chapter Eleven

Gaspard kept up a constant slew of loud questions as Fintan grimly drove everyone up to the Rock, Isla silent by his side. Konstantin had come via some kind of client of Joel's, and Fintan was utterly dismayed. What kind of young lad got drunk on their way to their first job?

And Gaspard looked like he was hell-bent on proving why he couldn't get a job anywhere except at the tail-end of nowhere – nobody wanted to work in the islands, and nobody wanted to work for him. Fintan felt bitterer than the acidic wine sloshing in the men's stomachs. This whole enterprise – Colton's pride and joy, the dream of his life – was going to fail. Fintan was going to fall flat on his face.

'So you 'ave cellar?'

'You can't stay here if you drink,' Fintan said steadily.

'I 'ave not 'ad one seengle drink on this soil!' protested Gaspard noisily. 'Not one! It was my final celebration of life as a free man.'

'This isn't prison,' said Fintan gruffly.

'Oh, yes, yes, it is actually,' said the young man, who up until now had been very green and quiet. Suddenly he stood up in the back and shouted, out of nowhere:

'STOP THE CAR!'

Assuming he was going to be sick again, Fintan did so. Konstantin got out of the car immediately and started bombing towards the boat, which was filling up ready for the return crossing.

'Well, he didn't last long,' observed Isla. They all watched him, waving his arms and shouting, charging down the hill to the men putting away the gangway.

'WAAAAIIIITTT!' he yelled, as the small party watched him in consternation.

'I hate this job,' said Fintan despondently.

'Me also,' said Gaspard, pulling out a cigarette and lighting it – somewhat miraculously – in the full force of the oncoming wind.

* ❋

'I forgot my dog!' Konstantin panted to the tall, kindly captain of the ferry, who had been very unimpressed with both of the men coming to work on Mure: he took as keen an interest as everyone else in the success or failure of the Rock.

'Did you now?' said the captain. Grudgingly, he opened the rope that blocked off the gangway and Konstantin, slightly fuzzily, ran into the hold where Bjårk was filling his travelling box a little snugly.

'BJÅRK! I am so sorry. I am a terrible, terrible person,' he said.

'Well, so everyone else says. I was probably just having a bad day,' he added, kneeling down.

Bjårk, as it happened, was happily in the process of forgiving him as he wanted out and ideally a snack too, and then perhaps another snack. Indeed, Konstantin felt in his pocket and found a packet of crisps that he'd bought at the bar and he'd completely forgotten were in there. He opened them up, sniffed them – they were a flavour he was not familiar with – and passed them all on to Bjårk, who didn't care either way.

The captain was still staring at him.

'You give crisps to your dug?' he said incredulously. 'The dog you didn't even remember you had?'

He shook his head and felt sorry for Fintan. Konstantin returned a haughty stare. He was used to everyone being nice to him and fussing over him. Being cross with him wasn't really done, unless of course it was his father.

Instead of responding, he hauled Bjårk – who didn't want to leave the huge raft of fascinating smells coming from all over the boat – up the gangplank with every ounce of dignity he could muster which, given he was half-drunk, splashed with water and was heaving a vast hairy beast whose muzzle was covered in crisp crumbs, wasn't much.

* *

Fintan and Isla stood outside the car, watching them approach. Gaspard was delighted and waved cheerfully from the back seat.

'Hey! *Monsieur Chien!*' he shouted cheerfully. Bjårk wagged his tail in return.

'Okay. Now we can go,' said Konstantin stiffly, arriving back.

'But . . . but . . .' Fintan started to stutter. As he did so, the dog walked up to him and licked his palm. He smelled inexplicably of prawn cocktail. His tongue dangled cheerfully.

'We don't have room for a dog!'

Isla gave him side-eye. Colton's two dogs, ridiculously expensive huskiess, lived around the Rock perfectly happily, and everyone quite liked having them around even though they were trained to tear you limb from limb on hearing a key word that Colton appeared to have taken with him to the grave and Fintan was terrified of saying by accident one day.

'We absolutely didn't say dogs were allowed.'

'Okay, fine,' said Konstantin. Bored now, he made to turn round and catch the ferry back. Isla gave Fintan a hard stare.

'Okay,' said Fintan finally. 'Okay. Get in. We'll sort it out later.'

And the very strange party continued on their way in silence in the Land Rover.

Chapter Twelve

It didn't help that Flora liked almost anyone who came with a dog attached. Back at the hotel, she had found the whole thing patently hilarious, to Fintan's fury. She looked Konstantin up and down. It was very unlike Joel to make this kind of request for anyone and it had been very hush-hush, so she knew absolutely nothing about the younger man except that he was Norwegian and, by the look of things, a bit of a drip. He stood tall in the doorway, his blond hair flopping over one eye, gazing at the Rock as if it was the worst place he'd ever seen.

'Okay, Isla, can you show Konstantin where he's going to be sleeping and take him round the kitchen? And is it Gaspard . . . ?'

But Gaspard had already disappeared. From the back of the long corridor, Flora could already hear the *whoosh* of a burner being turned on. She frowned. Fintan had mentioned he was 'temperamental'. It appeared to be rather worse than that. Crazy, drunk and covered in tattoos seemed about the size of it. Fintan himself looked absolutely disconsolate and desperate to get away even though he should be settling everyone in and leading his new team. Oh lord. This was like herding cats. She felt a sudden wish to be at home, snuggled up with Dougie and Joel, ideally in front of some really, really terrible television. She had a bad feeling about—

'OH, HELLO! COOEEE!'

Flora turned round slowly. There was Jan, who led the Outward Adventures group.

Flora would never like to say she had a nemesis. But if she had a nemesis, it would have been Jan, who had never quite forgiven her for getting off with her boyfriend years ago. For like two seconds. Actually, Flora suspected (correctly) that Jan found it slightly more annoying that Flora had never given it a second thought afterwards, not once she and Joel had found one another.

Jan's baby, Christabel, was strapped to Jan in a woven home-made baby wrapper that looked oddly confrontational. She was red of face, with Charlie's heavy eyebrows and a permanent frown.

'Hello,' said Flora, smiling at Christabel at least.

Jan blinked, and her voice took on an instant pitying tone.

'Oh, Flora. Where's little Douglas?'

'He's at home with my dad,' said Flora. 'Ten minutes down the road. I'm just going there now.'

Jan smiled pityingly. 'It's so hard to be apart, isn't it? Such a shame you can't have him with you. What a shame you don't get any maternity leave.'

'I'm on maternity leave now, actually. Just popped in.'

There came the sound of loud swearing in French from the kitchen and Fintan immediately headed off in the opposite direction, shouting, 'Flora, can you see what that is?'

'You know,' said Jan, 'I never put Christabel down. Never! It's called attachment parenting. It's how our ancestors would have done it in the old days.'

Before catching scrofula and dying at thirty-two, thought Flora, just managing not to say it out loud.

'We're always together, she and I. Mummy and baby! How it's meant to be.'

Christabel screwed her face up crossly.

'Of course, it's different with girls.'

'Is it?' said Flora, genuinely curious, then annoyed with herself that she'd fallen for it. She knew she should always keep her distance. The problem was, Jan was the only person she knew with a baby and she would have loved to have asked her lots of things – like, was it normal to want to get away from your baby sometimes, or was it all right to be a bit resentful of being knackered all the time? But Jan was obviously having an absolute ball.

'Oh yes. Girls and their mums. It's a special thing.'

Flora thought about her own mum, who had died far too young and smiled ruefully.

Jan was now talking to the baby.

'Poor little Douglas doesn't get to spend time with *his* mummy, does he?' said Jan in a baby voice, bouncing Christabel's fingers up and down. 'Poor ickle baby Douglas.'

'Is there something you want, Jan?' said Flora, realising too late she'd betrayed her frustration, which in Jan's world would totally be chalked up as a win.

'Oh. Yes! Christmas lunch for the Outward Adventures sponsors. But, Flora, these are . . . these are important people. Sponsors and people coming from the mainland. You know, the Seaside Kitchen is all very adorable and so on but these people . . . they'll be expecting something quite good.'

Flora tried to breathe in through her nose and out through her mouth. The most annoying thing about this was that they needed a soft launch; a chance for the kitchen to run through its paces before they opened properly at Christmas.

'Well, we have a new chef, so we'll have a new menu for you to take a look at.'

'Oh *good*,' said Jan, clapping Christabel's little fingers together, 'Not that you're not, you know, wonderful at what you do. But a real chef . . .'

There was a bang from the back of the kitchen. Gaspard marched through into the main hallway. Despite the fact that there were brand-new whites ordered in for him with his name on them, he was wearing a pair of filthy old checked trousers with a packet of cigarettes hanging out the back of them.

'Your fridge – no good. Your oven – no good. Your cupboards no good. You need to change – *pouf!* – everything.'

Jan blinked.

'Yes, I'm sure that's true.'

Gaspard stopped.

''Ello, tiny baby,' he muttered in a soft voice much different to anything Flora had heard so far. 'Ah, she is very *sage*.'

'She isn't,' said Jan crossly. 'She's pink, thank you very much.'

Christabel, however, was cooing loudly in Gaspard's face. She had her father's pale colouring and round cheeks.

Jan was waving her hand in front of Christobel's face.

'I'm sorry, I don't like smokers near the baby!'

Gaspard gave her a long look, then glanced at his hands as if he had a lit cigarette there he hadn't known about (it was, to be fair, always possible). As he backed away, Christabel started to bawl.

'So,' said Jan fussily. 'Send over the menus please. We'll be thirty.'

Gaspard blinked.

"Ow can I send over menus?"

'Just – tell – us – what – you're – making,' said Jan, talking very loudly and clearly as she liked to do when speaking to foreigners. 'We'd like one full turkey and all the trimmings, one vegetarian option and one gluten-free.'

Gaspard gave her another long look, then glanced at Flora as if to clearly say *what in the hell do you expect me to do with this woman*. Flora felt caught between a hard place and, well, the Rock, she supposed.

'We'll get you something as soon as possible,' she said to Jan, who looked sceptical as she turned to leave.

'Of course, obviously we'll be expecting a big discount,' she said. 'Seeing as it's for charity and you're just basically having a test run. You should probably do it for free,' she added pointedly.

'I think for everything to be great for your charity event you should buy good produce,' said Flora smoothly. Jan's family was one of the richest on the island. 'Which costs money, I'm afraid.'

'Produce which all mysteriously comes from your farm,' said Jan. Flora put her best smile on again and hustled her out of the door.

'I am not doing turkey,' Gaspard was already threatening within earshot.

'It's Christmas!' said Flora. 'Please! We'll never hear the end of it. Please do turkey at Christmas.'

'Turkey is 'orrible! Is huge dry chicken! Huge dry unhappy chicken!'

'I'm sure they're not . . .'

'Do not eat unhappy animals! Is unhappy! That is why . . .' He paused for emphasis. ' . . . so many fights at Christmas.'

Flora looked at him.

'What are you talking about?'

'People, they are so sad, they fight at Christmas, boo hoo. Everyone sad. Is all *EastEnders*.'

'That's a fictional television show.'

'Christmas Christmas Christmas, fight fight fight.'

'You're saying people fight at Christmas because turkeys are unhappy?'

'*Exactly*, yes.'

There was a pause.

'So what would you ... ?'

'*L'oie*. Goose. You have goose at Christmas. Delicious goose.'

'And geese are happy?'

'You know geese?'

'I do,' said Flora, who had been terrified of geese since she'd been taken to a wildlife park on the mainland as a child and one had nearly broken her arm.

'Geese, they are fierce! They are strong! They hate everyone. CACAR!'

'That's not the sound a goose makes! They honk!'

'A goose, he has an 'appy life. I 'ate you, he say. CACAR! Everybody move. Happy goose.'

'Not foie gras.'

'Oui, foie gras! 'Appy, 'appy goose, something to eat, yes please.'

'No,' said Flora. 'No foie gras: it's cruel.'

'Okay,' said Gaspard, not in the least bit perturbed. 'Free-range goose.'

'Thank you.'

'CACARRRRR!'

'ONNNNKKKK!'

I like him, thought Flora.

Chapter Thirteen

It had happened the previous month. Entirely, Joel knew, with him in mind, Colton had left a large bequest to a fostering charity on his behalf. This was embarrassing enough in itself, but they'd also asked him to speak, which he did, about his own childhood and his new life in Scotland with a baby, and Colton's hotel.

Afterwards, Joel had found himself next to a portly, short Norwegian man.

'You have a new baby?' the man had asked him.

Joel nodded.

'How's it been?'

Joel half-smiled, which was more or less as demonstrative as he ever got in company. He had been up with Douglas at four, giving him a bottle as Flora slept, happy as Larry. He'd reminded himself to get started on Colton's Christmas lights – there had been a hefty bequest in there to make the island more Christmassy, and looking round at the smart room he was in in London, with a huge silvery-sharp tree, and cutting-edge modern baubles, he made a mental note to remind himself again. Unfortunately, someone had just offered the possibility for him to show off pictures of Douglas, which made it immediately fall out of his mind again.

'Oh, he's ... he's amazing,' he said. He whipped out his phone to show pictures of the dark-eyed little baby boy. The other man smiled sadly.

'Ah,' he sighed miserably. 'Then they grow up.'

'You have children?' said Joel, who was of the unshiftable view of new parents that their children would of course be different.

'A son,' said the man. 'Layabout, more like.'

He blinked.

'He needs a job, in fact.'

There was a pause.

'What kind of job?' said Joel carefully. He wasn't especially happy about bringing on board people's privileged children: they tended to take up more time than was strictly necessary and be frankly horrified that they were expected to work every single day, and that people might occasionally tell them that what they had done wasn't wonderful and perfect, and that they couldn't just get immediately promoted.

'Oh, anything,' said the man. 'He should really start at the bottom. He's never held a proper job. Have you got anything an idiot can do?'

Joel smiled.

'Probably but I'm sure you wouldn't want to ...'

But the man was warming to his theme and took another swig of his wine.

'No, do it,' he said. 'Get him cleaning floors. Washing pots. I insist! I'll sponsor the charity too if you do it. Yes. This is it.'

And so Joel could hardly refuse. And so it was arranged.

Now, Isla stood in the kitchen, looking at her watch. It was time for the new kid's – Konstantin – shift to start. Everyone else was there but he hadn't shown up yet. Which was not ideal considering he only lived upstairs. Gaspard was late too but she had kind of been expecting that. Still, it was frustrating.

The double swing-doors that led to the dining room suddenly burst open and two people came through: Gaspard and a plain, doughy-faced woman.

'Thees is Kerry. She is my sous-chef.'

Isla frowned.

'Does Fintan know?'

Gaspard shrugged.

'I don' care. I need more help. Ees beeg job.'

Kerry was already tying on a cap round her head. Isla tried to smile hello, quite excited about the possibility of a female friend in the kitchen to take Iona's place, but Kerry returned only a stony look.

Gaspard looked around.

'Where is my boy who cleans pots?'

'I don't think he's up yet,' ventured Tam, a stolid redhead from one of the most northerly farmsteads who absolutely didn't care what job he had to do in this hotel as long as it didn't involve walking up and down the side of a hill in the pouring rain all day for the next forty years like his father, three uncles, three brothers and nine cousins were all doing. He would scrape the floor with a toothbrush if it meant not wearing nine jackets and getting sewn into his underwear.

'Well, go get him!'

Tam frowned. 'Where is he?'

Gaspard shrugged. Isla sighed.

'You know?' demanded Gaspard. Isla flushed bright red. She didn't like being picked out to do anything.

'Same place as you, on the roof ...'

'Go! Get him!'

'But—'

'Feerst thing in my kitchen!' Gaspard flexed his arm, and all his tattoos stood out. His face suddenly looked rather menacing. 'We say "*Oui, chef*". Okay? You are in a real kitchen now, leetle girl! Ees real job, not pretend! Okay? You understand? Not pretend?'

Isla froze.

'*Oui, chef!*' he repeated.

She had absolutely no idea what he was talking about as everyone stared at her.

'Come on!' he snarled.

And then he paused, leaving an excruciating silence until he drew out of the utterly humiliated Isla a rather half-hearted ' ... wee chef!'

He nodded curtly and Isla scampered off up the stairs, feeling wretched. It had been all right being shy in Flora's kitchen. Iona could pick up the slack for noisiness and Flora was kind enough that she never seemed to notice. And actually Isla even spoke up from time to time. It wasn't impossible, when she felt comfortable.

But when it came to foreign men yelling at her or, like now, asking her to do something utterly preposterous like go up to a strange man's bedroom ... her face was absolutely flaming and she wanted to burst into tears, and the thought of how it would be to burst into tears on your very first day in a new job was so awful she couldn't face thinking about that either, so she bit her lip incredibly hard and went past the corridors leading to the Rock's twelve beautiful boutique rooms, and up a hidden staircase to the old attic rooms. All were open except for one at the very end of the hallway. She pulled herself together and knocked loudly.

There was no answer. She tried again, harder.

'Hello?' she said. Then, louder: 'HELLO?'

She touched the door which, to her horror – she had been hoping to turn back and say that she hadn't found him – started to creak open. It was too late now: she was stuck there and would have to hope for the best.

'Um . . . Chef sent me upstairs to . . .'

There was still no sound of movement from inside the room. Curious, she pushed the door open further and glanced inside. The bed was completely unmade; possessions were strewn everywhere. But the room was empty of people. And the window was wide open.

She frowned. Surely he wouldn't have made his escape: they were three storeys off the ground. And it was only a job, not prison, whatever he thought. She blinked. Had he gone?

It was freezing in the room: the wind blew right in off the sea and there were little flecks of rain bouncing off and around in the maelstrom. The curtains were dancing; papers were jumping off the desk.

Isla found herself going to the open window, her heart beating quickly. She was suddenly struck by the most horrifying thought: what if he'd fallen? Tried to climb out and slipped on the wet pipes?

Slowly, she advanced.

'Um . . . Konstantin?' she said, the odd consonants taking shape in her mouth. No answer.

As she moved towards the window, there was a sudden flurrying noise and a *wouf!* as a massive hairy something exploded in her face. She screamed and dropped her phone.

'What?' came a voice. Shocked, she'd fallen back a few paces into the room and tripped backwards, sitting down heavily on the unmade bed. There was little space in the room for anything else. A bemused-looking figure with rumpled hair appeared at the window, standing as if in mid-air, half his body visible in the frame. Isla was so shocked she could barely speak. In his white shirt and pale skin, she thought for one terrifying moment she was looking at a ghost.

'Oh,' he said, eyes wide. 'Santa got my letter!'

He had a slightly flat, barely traceable Scandinavian accent. Isla jumped up as if the covers were hot.

'Where . . . ?' she stuttered. Konstantin showed her that the window of his room led out onto a flat gravelled area, the top of the window below – dangerous, unfenced, but wide enough for his big dog to stand and, she could now see, have a gigantic pee.

'I don't think you can let your dog pee on the roof.'

His face puckered.

'Well, he cannot fly so you see I have no choice.'

Isla blinked. Konstantin shivered and jumped back in through the window, encouraging his clearly overweight dog to do the same behind him, even as he scrabbled and whined for help and he ended up hoofing him over ungraciously.

'So what are you, the welcoming committee?' he said, still smiling. He was used to having a certain effect on young women.

'You're needed downstairs,' stuttered Isla, pink to the tips of her ears. 'It's time to work.'

'Really?' said Konstantin, pouting. 'Are you sure you wouldn't rather stay and have a quick ... ?'

He had been about to say 'cup of coffee' in the hopes of staving off work a little longer, but Isla had been brought up to be very wary of strange men, though there weren't many on Mure, which was why they were all so terrified when one appeared.

'GET BACK!' she shouted. 'GET AWAY FROM ME!'

'No coffee then?' protested Konstantin as she stared at him menacingly, reversing back out into the corridor.

He added impishily: 'You know, it was *you* who turned up in *my* bedroom.'

Finally, Isla found more words.

'Piss off, you disgusting sex case!' she screamed. Then she turned and bolted back down the hall.

'*Woof!*' said Bjårk.

Konstantin frowned, thoroughly awake now. He'd been called a few things in his life but that seemed rather harsh.

'Sorry!' he hollered down the corridor, but it was too late.

Chapter Fourteen

'Listen to me,' commanded Gaspard. Konstantin had made it down ten minutes later, but, being unused to a uniform, he was wearing his trousers back to front. Isla moved as far away from where he was standing as she possibly could.

'The next time this 'appens, you will be doing all the potato peeling, you understand? For one week, two week, four week . . .'

'Yes all right,' said Konstantin, who was confused. Surely they'd been friends yesterday in the bar?

'You do what *I* say in theese keetchen. Then all will be 'appy. Or you do not do as I say and boo hoo there is absolute *tristesse*, you understand?'

Nobody did understand but they could make a stab from his scary tone of voice.

Gaspard had been through a lot of restaurants and found that his manner tended to make people afraid of him and leave, unless they were good, committed or – and this was very much what he was counting on at the moment – if they had absolutely nowhere else to go. He didn't care which.

Modern-day restaurants, with their cost centres and portion control and budgets, didn't suit him. But here ... he'd sneered at the kitchen at first, but it wasn't bad, not really; done by someone with money to spend. Here, there was a chance for him. And nobody was going to stand in his way this time, certainly not some posh teenage drunk and a clutch of locals who probably shared one eyebrow between them.

Konstantin had assumed Gaspard was kidding about the potatoes. He emphatically was not. The third time he took the skin off his knuckles – he'd never peeled one in his life – he muttered strangled epithets while he ransacked the first aid box. His hands were a riot of blue plasters. Everyone ignored him. After the potatoes, he started washing pots as everybody else got to try out cooking stuff. This was absolutely rubbish, incredibly boring and took hours. He tried to catch the eye of the girl who'd been upstairs but she was resolutely not looking at him. Gaspard just shouted. The blank-faced girl, Kerry, worked like a robot and ignored everybody. Not only were his hands cut, but they also became red and chafed from the hot water. He smelled absolutely terrible; the aromas of food got everywhere. How could it be so hard and boring at the same time? He hated his stupid father with an absolute vengeance. He hadn't even been able to tell his friends where he was going. Not only had they stopped his phone contract, they'd also stopped his data use. He was completely alone in the universe because of his stupid father, having to grovel and make himself filthy with a bunch of random dicks. It was a joke that had gone far too far.

Konstantin had never felt so sorry for himself in his entire life.

Chapter Fifteen

They were doing a test run for Jan's charity dinner. Joel had made a stupid joke about how he would come so he could get a chance to see Flora, which had not gone down well and which he'd regretted almost immediately. Flora had sat with Douglas all afternoon, glowering, showing him seagulls on the shore until his little fingers were pink – he hated his mittens and tried to bite them – as he pointed at the waves and she grew increasingly freezing. By the time they got into the Seaside Kitchen for a coffee, Douglas was cross and tired and screamed the entire place down, to the point where even the fondest regulars were finding their smiles growing a little fixed. Why was this so easy for everyone else?

So Flora was looking forward to going up to the Rock and testing the kitchen's wings, even with Fintan drumming his fingers anxiously on the white tablecloths.

Iona was coming too to take pictures for the hotel's Instagram account (who knew there was one?), and Innes and Eilidh, his once-upon-a-time ex-wife, newly reunited and making a great show of being disgustingly lovey-dovey all the time, had shown up for moral support.

They'd tried to leave Agot behind with Eck, who didn't hold with fancy new food, but she was having none of it and had turned up at the front door of the farmhouse in her ballet skirt, her *Frozen* slippers, some alarmingly applied lip gloss and one of her mother's handbags, looking at them with an expression which would have been cute in a five-year-old if it wasn't quite so uncompromising.

'I'll be coming to dinner,' she enunciated clearly. 'I have thought and thought and now I have decided. YES.'

'Well, I'm not sure that's—'

'Yes, I think so, Daddy. THAT BABY is coming.'

Innes was a helpless pushover where Agot was concerned, and Eilidh was just so pleased they were back together again – and the frankly thrilling idea that boring old Mure island was going to get a fancy hotel, thus not being quite the dead arse-end of the world she'd left in a snit two years before – that she wasn't going to halt Agot either, as a result of which she marched straight to the Land Rover fully confident.

'Well, it'll be worth it to test how the restaurant deals with really difficult customers,' whispered Flora to Fintan, who nodded emphatically in agreement.

There are two ways of getting to the Rock from the south where the village is. Driving up the island was always an option but on sunny days, Bertie Cooper will run you round in the boat to the headland – it's not far, only five minutes or so, and it's delightful on a dusky pink evening to be out on the water. You might see a dolphin and you'll certainly hear the seals barking at you as you land at the jetty with the torches shining up ahead towards the building itself. Fintan had always thought it was one of the most beautiful landings in the world.

This was not one of those times. The wind that had nearly blown Konstantin and Bjårk Bjårkensson off the roof the previous week was bucking harder. The ferry that day had taken a few runs to get to where it wanted to be, and even then the passengers disembarked a trifle greener than they had hoped to be. Gusts were also flapping smaller cars out of the way – the farm's and the Rock's battered old Land Rovers could be trusted to take them the few miles up the narrow bumping track that served as the inland road, but you wouldn't want to be in a little tin can, however much Flora might have hankered after a chic pastel Fiat 500.

Grey clouds dropped out of the sky as night was now falling at four p.m. Sheep huddled close to the mountainside, trying to keep themselves warm, and Flora inhaled the sleepy baby beneath her in the car, snug in his best woolly hat with ears (all hats came with ears these days, Joel had observed, puzzled; he didn't know why) and lightly twirled one of his fine black curls.

'THAT BABY is very hairy,' observed Agot from the opposite seat. She was cross because she was in a baby chair, 'EVEN THOUGH,' she complained the entire way, 'I AM NOT A BABY.'

'He is,' smiled Flora. 'Hairy babies are lucky.'

'Yes,' said Agot. 'He is lucky he doesn't have to sit in a STUPID BABY'S CHAIR or eat STUPID DEAD UNCLE COLTON'S FOOD.'

'Agot,' remonstrated Innes. She had started calling him 'Dead Uncle Colton' after the funeral and although everyone had furiously tried to get her to stop, Fintan told them he didn't mind it. In fact, it was comforting because she brought him into every conversation, every game she played. She didn't lay a tea table for her dollies (who were usually to be heard getting strict tellings-off – who knew where she had even learned how to do that given that Innes was useless at it and the primary school specialised in encouraging play not discipline) without including Dead Uncle Colton in the family line-up, and was absolutely convinced that he watched every single thing she did. Fintan found it an unending comfort. Sometimes Flora, watching the little sprite with her white-blonde hair and tiny dancing figure, wasn't entirely sure she didn't see ghosts.

'That's enough.'

Agot lifted her stubborn little chin and stared out of the window crossly, pausing briefly en route to shoot Douglas an utterly filthy look. Flora sighed inside. They were meeting Jan and Charlie there too, so they could 'discuss menus'. Please, please let it go well.

Chapter Sixteen

Meanwhile, in the kitchen, all was chaos. Gaspard was shouting and everyone felt like crying. The last week had been an absolute trial for everyone; like *Big Brother* without the calm cooperative atmosphere. The Norwegian guy was absolutely hopeless, so there was never a pot or pan when you needed it. Kerry wouldn't do anything without checking with Gaspard first, which meant Isla being in charge of cakes and puddings was useless when the sous-chef was standing around doing nothing except eating crisps while Isla was going nuts. Tam was fine, but his job was bringing in supplies; he wasn't around for long enough to help with anything really useful.

Also, slightly worse, Isla's initial coldness with Konstantin after the way he'd behaved had hardened into an awkward stiffness. He hadn't done anything really awful since, just ignored her, but she didn't know how to talk to him except to tell him how to peel potatoes without skinning himself when he was helping with food prep, or how garlic actually worked, something Gaspard had found so astonishing he'd actually stopped cooking to watch. There was a bad attitude in the kitchen, and they all knew it.

'Okay. Tonight. Try not to be idiots, *non*?' Gaspard was saying, just as Konstantin dropped the most enormous pan on the stone floor. The noise sounded like a bomb going off and Isla even let out a tiny shriek. There were patent French expletives and Konstantin, white as a sheet, looked like he was going to walk out of the kitchen, even as a pot boiled over just behind him. Everyone froze as Gaspard marched towards Konstantin.

'You want work in thees kitchen or not?' he snarled.

'*Not*,' snarled back Konstantin.

'Well, you can leave.'

'Well, I *can't*,' said Konstantin.

It was unbelievable, but true. His phone, debit and credit cards had all been stopped and he'd called the bank to absolutely no avail because he didn't know any of the passwords. His friends and relations had been warned by his father not to sneak him any dough, and given that most of them were also completely funded by their parents, and were absolutely terrified by the amount of attention their mums and dads were paying towards the older Konstantin's experiment, meant they were very much toeing the line as well.

He couldn't quite believe it, but he was somehow meant to survive – and feed Bjårk – on the tiny pittance they got, which wouldn't quite cover a single restaurant meal back home but here was supposed to last him a week. It was a joke. A stupid, ridiculous joke, and he was near constantly tempted to storm off and tell them all where to stick it.

Except he couldn't. He had literally no way of paying his way off the island, and even if he got off, by the time he'd saved up for a plane ticket, what would he do: sit at his father's feet and beg for forgiveness? His pride wouldn't let him do that. Well, okay. It wasn't so much that because in fact he'd already tried it. And his father had graciously said, thanks for the apology, now get on with your work and I'll see you in six months.

He was stuck, and mutinous, and he stared at the pot on the floor. The room went silent.

'Pick that up or you go now,' said Gaspard unwaveringly. They all glanced at the windows. Hail was hurling itself against the glass. A lovely night to be cosy in front of a roaring fire with a good book and a glass of whisky. A frankly ludicrous night to storm off in a snit. The atmosphere in the room grew as icy as the windows.

Meanwhile, the dining room looked as beautiful as ever, the big log fire crackling merrily away, gleaming off the tinsel. 'Scots Nativity' was playing gently, and the scented air gave everyone a thrill. It didn't matter how old you were: Christmas was coming! And that was always the most exciting feeling. Agot stomped over, irritated that the tree hadn't come yet, but when she realised the highly polished wood was very slippery, she took off her shoes and was soon skidding round the room in her stripey tights. Flora noted mentally 'health and safety' and filed it away till later to mention to Fintan.

Colton had bought a vast amount of old vats from a distillery closing down, and the wood on the fire had the deep aroma of peat and whisky. With that and the soft chairs, it was, Flora always thought, the most comfortable place you could be, with the anticipation of a good meal ahead. Gala had greeted them happily and brought them drinks, and everyone was stretching out good-naturedly. Agot stopped skating and got happily buried in her sketch pad with her felt-tip pens, as usual drawing everyone in her life including Dead Uncle Colton but missing out Douglas which was, Flora supposed, something of an improvement from when she'd presented them with a mass family portrait with everyone in it *including* Douglas, but with a huge black scribble across Douglas's face.

Jan, Charlie and, irritatingly, Malcy, Jan's large father who'd done very well for himself and liked everyone to know it – and hadn't been scheduled to come – had arrived bang on time, which made Flora anxious. She glanced at Fintan, who patently didn't care. The problem was, the Mathiesons were big spenders on this island. Golf club dinners, big parties and weddings. They needed to impress these people. She wished he'd at least try.

There was no menu first off, which Flora looked worried about and Innes frowned at. Fintan was drinking and not paying attention which was almost as worrying to Flora as the lack of menu. Well, perhaps this was the modern way and it would be something unexpected and magnificent. She ordered some wine from Gala, and they tried to chat even though there wasn't even a piece of bread on the table.

'I'M HUNGRY,' came a warning voice from underneath the table, but you couldn't say it wasn't a shared emotion.

Inside the kitchen, Gaspard was holding up a knife as if it was a weapon.

For the first time in his life, Konstantin was on his hands and knees, picking something up. He didn't know what to do with the pan and was grateful when Tam came and took it from him to put away in a cupboard.

'CHOP!' said Gaspard.

And finally, the cold wind still blowing outside, Konstantin decided that for once discretion was the better part of valour, so he picked up an onion and a knife without the slightest enthusiasm, and stared at them.

Gaspard had already moved on and was shouting about stock. Kerry and Tam were keeping their heads down, waiting for it to pass. Konstantin tried stabbing the onion and let out a heavy sigh. Isla was just next to him.

'Just chop it,' she hissed. She couldn't believe they hadn't got more prep done this afternoon but apparently Gaspard had been out and become distracted by a field full of wild garlic he hadn't been expecting, as a result of which she was now chopping up head after head of them for later. She smelt pungent, she knew, and it would be seeping through her pores for days.

She snuck a look at Konstantin. He was doing a truly horrible job, hacking at the defenceless onion like it had insulted him in some way. Isla edged away from him a little.

Konstantin noticed, and hacked again even more viciously. Great. Here he was, locked in a dungeon in a howling storm, and even the kitchen girl didn't want to talk to him. He wanted to tell her that where he came from, the girls who worked in the kitchen *loved* him . . . then he started thinking of what was going on at home right now. The run-up to Christmas in Norway was incredibly beautiful. The Christmas markets went up early and the delicious scent of *gløgg* filled the air, as the warm gingery mulled wine was poured over crushed almonds and raisins in the bottom of the glass, and topped with a little aquavit so that you lifted the entire warming scent of Christmas in your own two hands, steam curling off the top.

This year, they had had early snow. You could see it on the hills, such as at the high airport in Oslo, which was thick with it, around which the dark fir trees seemed to go on for miles. They'd take the horses out and go steeplechasing even as the snow fell thickly and the night came on early, finishing for drinks by a roaring fire at the lodge his father kept up near Lillehammer. After Christmas, as the weather hardened, there was skating and of course skiing, the toughest courses, the fastest mountains, to build up your appetite for long hearty lunches, filled with laughter and bonhomie at the best time of year.

Here the snow was pathetic, wet and bitty, he imagined fiercely. It would barely lie at all, totally useless with all this wind.

Up until now he'd only felt cross and annoyed at being, according to him, kidnapped and forced into servitude. Now it felt worse than that. He felt exiled from everything he loved. He thought of the pretty houses of Trondheim, or of heading out into the woods to catch a glimpse of the northern lights, later sitting in the hot tub at his friend's cabin. He was almost unbearably homesick. *And* he'd had to hide Bjårk in his room to keep him out of the kitchen, which wasn't going to work well for very long, judging by the impassioned moaning that had started up as soon as he'd left the room.

He heaved a great heavy sigh and looked down at his work again, just in time to watch the incredibly sharp knife Gaspard had bought him slice deeply into his thumb.

Once again, the kitchen froze. The blood didn't trickle out: it arced straight up in the air, right over all the already chopped vegetables, spraying across the brand-new factory-fresh whites.

'*Faen!*' yelled Konstantin, even though the pain hadn't kicked in yet, just the shock.

'*Merde!*' said Gaspard in disbelief, running his hands – themselves scarred and pitted, like all chefs' – through his thick dark hair.

'Uh-oh,' muttered Isla, mostly to herself. Then, seeing to her amazement that nobody was doing anything, least of all Konstantin herself, she got up and went to him.

'Come here,' she said.

The boy was white; his already pale skin had all the colour drained out of it. 'It's just a cut,' she said, glancing at it. He looked at her, still shaky, as she led him to the sink and started running the tap.

'It looks worse than it is.'

Konstantin was still staring at his thumb in disbelief.

'I didn't realise we were serving finger food,' Isla surprised herself by saying, even as he blinked and put his finger under the running water, wincing as the cold touched the cut.

'That knife was really sharp,' he grumbled.

'Yeah,' said Isla, looking closely to see if he needed a stitch. 'Like some kind of kitchen knife or something.'

Everything with blood on it was bundled into the bin just as Gala came in to see if they were ready to start taking food into the dining room. A single glower from Gaspard made it very clear to her that they were not, and she scurried out again, going to find some crisps behind the bar.

Isla examined the wound again. Konstantin had very long fingers on a large strong hand that didn't look like it had done a day's work in its life, as indeed it had not. She frowned. 'I think you'll be okay. I can get Saif to put a stitch in it if you like.'

Saif was the local GP, who was just sitting down to dinner with his two sons Ib and Ash, and wouldn't have been best pleased to hear he was being called out in a howling gale to fix a ridiculous kid. Gaspard came up to them and frowned.

'*Non*,' he said. Then he clicked his fingers for the word. '*Colle, colle* … GLUE. That is it: glue.'

Gala immediately brought some superglue from behind her reception desk.

'*Oui!*' said Gaspard brandishing it. Konstantin and Isla looked at one another anxiously.

'Let me just google that,' said Isla, getting Konstantin to hold his finger up in the air while she retrieved her phone. 'Well, the internet says it's fine.'

'The internet says the royal family are lizards,' grimaced Konstantin.

Nonetheless, he held out his finger and let Gaspard stick the two edges of skin back together. Isla then wrapped it in a blue bandage she'd got out of the first aid kit. They were, she noted, running low.

'Do you need to sit down for a bit?' she said, feeling some sympathy for this ridiculous person, so far out of his depth.

'*Non*, there is no time,' said Gaspard. 'Start again! With the onions! This time, keep all of your fingers please!'

Chapter Seventeen

Back in the dining room, they were on their third bottle of champagne – Fintan didn't mind depleting the cellars Colton had built up for the two of them. At least it was staying in the family. Flora had a glass. She was barely drinking because, although she'd expressed, she was still feeding Douglas, even though he was sleeping beautifully in his car seat under the table.

Jan of course wasn't drinking a drop, as she'd told everyone who came into earshot at any second of the day, going on to speculate how she'd probably never drink again she felt so much better than she'd ever felt and goodness, didn't Flora's eyes look bloodshot, was she sure she was all right? Christabel was still strapped to Jan. She was getting very big – it couldn't possibly be comfortable – but it did mean Jan could pull the conversation round to the genius of her child every five seconds. Charlie was sitting looking anxious.

By contrast, the boys were getting stuck in, particularly as they appeared to have slightly mistaken the concept 'champagne' for 'beer' and were more or less drinking it by the pint. Innes kept looking at the other MacKenzie brother Hamish as if they might get up and start wrestling in a minute like they used to when they were children. Agot was banging her knife and fork on the table and singing a song about being hungry and how cruel the world was to five-year-olds. Eilidh was getting a little loose around the eyes, which Flora knew from experience meant she was probably going to start telling the story about how she had reignited her marriage, then getting up and starting to snog Innes at the table which Innes didn't mind in the slightest but the rest of the MacKenzie siblings found a little unnecessary. And if Fintan had more than a certain amount, it was odds to sods he was going to collapse into tears are some point which was fine but not ideal in front of the staff he was supposedly managing in the business he was supposedly running. They desperately needed some food to mop it up.

Flora excused herself and crept into the kitchens. What she saw took her rather by surprise.

* ❋

'I can't even smell cooking,' she said, outraged. She looked at Gaspard.

'Where is the bread?'

He scowled.

'I am not happy with the bread.'

He pointed to the fresh loaves that had been made in the bakery that morning.

'Why not?' said Flora.

'Ees local flour?'

'There is no local flour, you dimbulb,' said Flora. 'It doesn't grow here. This stuff is perfectly good.'

Gaspard screwed up his face.

'And the butter is perfectly good – I know that because it comes from *my farm*.'

Isla had never rarely seen Flora so cross. She scuttled to the fridge and got out the butter.

'It's fridged,' said Gaspard, pouting.

'That's *your* fault,' said Flora. Konstantin quickly looked away. Someone had told him to defridge the butter but he hadn't known what they meant and had therefore completely ignored it.

'Isla, take this out,' said Flora, 'before Innes falls off something and Hamish starts making aeroplane noises.'

Isla vanished into the dining room. Through the door came a noise which sounded like Douglas revving up. Jan was enjoying every second of this, Flora could tell.

'What are you making?'

'I 'ave no good stock.'

'Well, you're not making it now! What are you making?'

'I am going to make coq au vin.'

'That takes *hours*.'

'Is new kitchen! Ees expected!'

'Absolutely bloody not,' said Flora, almost trembling. 'No way. You can't. Make something – anything, I don't care. But just make it now.'

She marched to the big fridge and hauled it open.

'Here,' she said. 'There's steak.'

Gaspard looked at it.

'So boring,' he said.

Flora was already in the freezer cupboard. She looked up and down all the shelves, shivering in the low temperature. She was sure she'd seen it in here somewhere ... somewhere ... behind the fresh food and the cooking materials ... *Aha!*

She returned from the cold store victoriously, holding her bag high.

Gaspard looked at what she was holding.

'Ees *impossible.*'

'Um,' said Isla, coming back into the kitchen. 'Um, Fintan says if we don't get some food out, he's going to sack everyone.'

This was a complete lie. Konstantin raised his head from where he was trying to make his six-foot frame seem completely inconspicuous. He saw a look of complicity shoot between Flora and Isla and was impressed. He didn't think the girl had it in her.

Triumphantly, Flora handed over her freezer find – a large packet of oven chips. Gaspard took it from her as if she was handing him a dead snake to cook.

'*Allez,*' he said, coldly furious, and struck a match as Iona turned on the burners.

*   *

Back in the dining room, Jan seemed to have forgotten her pledge to drink absolutely nothing as she had been sipping small amounts from a glass and getting rather giggly, a situation in which Flora would have dearly loved to have found herself instead of pretending everything was fine when she was in fact incredibly worried.

Everyone dived into the bread in starvation; it disappeared in minutes. Thankfully, the butter didn't disappoint: it was a smoked garlic flavour Fintan had developed to seed through, and was so delicious Flora could have licked the bowl just as she noticed, with a sinking heart, that Agot was actually licking the bowl.

Fintan was calling for more wine which almost certainly wasn't going to end well. His eyes had taken on a slightly glassy look, which tended to warn of the arrival of tears. Sure enough, he was mournfully looking round the room, which was filled with ridiculous, expensive tartan tchotchkes that Colton had insisted on. His presence was still so strong: his loud, cocksure American accent ringing out; his easy laugh; his quick anger and even more surprising kindness. Yes. It was hard.

'Well,' Jan was saying, looking pointedly at her watch and getting slightly unsteadily to her feet. 'It's nice to know that at least you *tried*, Flora.'

'Oh no, I'm sure it won't be long,' said Flora in a panic.

'I mean, I thought I'd give you a chance. But this ... I mean. It's difficult to run a business. My darling Charlie and I have been doing it for years, of course. We know what we're doing, don't we, darling?' Charlie stared at the floor. Malcy laughed. 'But you can't just walk in out of nowhere and start from scratch. It's just not possible!'

'I don't come from nowhere,' said Flora through slightly clenched teeth. 'I come from down the road.'

'Yes, but all the gadding about? Marrying foreigners and whatnot? You don't really understand what the local community needs now, do you? I mean ...' She gave a little laugh. 'A bit of dinner at least, don't you think? And how are you going to cope with travellers from further afield? I mean, people do have standards, you know. They'll want a little more than a cheese scone! Which I notice we don't even have.'

Irritatingly, she was right about this. Flora cursed herself for not even having thought to bring up some baking. Mind you, she had felt it would be insulting to Fintan and demoralising to the kitchen if she'd arrived with back-up. Meanwhile, short of being able to Instagram the food, Iona had taken to putting sunglasses on the stag's head and photographing that instead.

'Okay, Jan,' she said finally as Jan smiled graciously in triumph. 'It's all very new—'

Suddenly there was a clatter at the swinging doors and Gala appeared, all flustered but smiling, and balancing the first three plates of food.

Chapter Eighteen

It was extraordinary. Wizardry.

It was a simple steak and chips – but what a steak and chips! The meat was soft and bloody, with a dark caramel crispy outside and a melting inside. There were crispy fried onions (courtesy of Konstantin) on the side, perfectly salted, like the best seaside treats. The chips were triple-fried in goose fat and satisfyingly crunchy. The salad was tart and green, and next to it all was the most wobbly, mustardy, perfectly set hollandaise sauce Flora had ever tasted.

It was an absolute rave, completely and utterly delicious.

Without saying another word, Jan simply sat back down. Flora half-smiled. Obviously, there was wanting to walk out – and then there was how insanely hungry you got as a feeding mother.

Gala poured the wine, a particularly beautiful private bottle of Colton's, and brought cola for Agot which she wasn't actually allowed, but nobody could stop eating for long enough to explain this. The room fell into a reverent silence, punctuated occasionally by people saying 'Oh my God' and 'Bloody hell' and Iona trying to photograph plates before they got emptied. Even as she was eating it, Flora felt sure and slightly sad that every single steak and chips she had in her life after this would be a completely pale imitation of this meal; a true disappointment. She felt like Edward in Narnia, looking at the empty box of Turkish Delight when she'd finished, staring regretfully at the empty plate.

There was a little scraping of knives and forks and then everyone sat back, Innes letting out a contented sigh.

'Well,' said Jan eventually. 'Well. I suppose that might just ... I mean, it's a little plain.'

'It was magnificent,' said Fintan crossly. 'Gala, could you get the chef out?'

Gaspard came out, looking mutinous. 'And what?' he said.

'That was amazing,' said Flora, meaning it, and everyone else added a round of applause. Gaspard tried to look like he was still cross with them but couldn't quite manage it. A tiny twitch appeared on his thin lips.

'I have no time! No food! And my team are *vrai* cretins.'

'But it was still magnificent,' said Flora.

Gaspard sniffed.

'Bah *oui*.'

Chapter Nineteen

Konstantin, exhausted from all the new experiences, was absolutely ready to retire to bed. Working past nine o'clock was, he mused, hardly a practice for gentlemen. He wondered too that he had never once given a thought in his life to all the serving staff, the waiters, the barkeeps, the servants at the palace, who stayed up as long as he wanted them to stay up. His feet hurt and his back was sore from bending over to chop, and his hand was throbbing from the cut, even though the bleeding had stopped. How did people do this every day? And how long was he going to have to do it before he either collapsed or got to go home? His father could not be serious about six months.

He heaved a sigh and turned towards the door. A small cough met him as he left, and then a slightly louder one. He turned back. The little scullery maid Isla was standing there, blushing as usual, and looking apologetic. Tiresome. He wanted to go to bed.

'What is it?'

She gestured to the kitchen, which was covered in grease and spattered remains of chip fat and onions.

'What?' he said again, but with a steady sinking feeling in his stomach. They couldn't be serious.

'Um, we kind of need to clean up,' she said, so quietly he could barely hear her, and that accent was totally ridiculous.

He held up his bandaged finger.

'Uh, I know, but I'm in terrible agony.'

'LAZY BOY!' came the voice from the other side of the kitchen. 'WORK! I make deener for you. You clean.'

Konstantin noticed that Gaspard had fired up the grill again and appeared to be about to make them all the rest of the steaks. He then also noticed that he himself was completely and utterly starving; he had been too worked up to realise just how hungry he was. He hadn't eaten all day and the steaks smelled absolutely unbelievable. Gaspard was smearing them with garlic butter and the pan was sizzling with lightly popping fat.

'But do eet properly!'

'I do it properly!'

There was massed laughter from everyone in the kitchen. 'No, you don't!'

Konstantin was annoyed. He'd been slogging his guts out, for God's sake.

'Okay,' he said crossly to Isla. 'Show me. How to do precious washing up your proper way.'

She looked at him.

'It's like you've never done the washing up before!' she said incredulously. He didn't like that one bit; she sounded like she was looking down on him. And also, it was true.

Isla took the hose tap and the scourer in disbelief and showed him how to wash out the pots before putting them in the dish-washer that ran fast and hot, and left him to it.

It took him ages, particularly with Gaspard jeering that he had no idea what it was going to be like when they got a *real* kitchen going and how he was going to have to get ten times faster than that and his finger really was hurting now and he was having, in fact, a very, very bad night indeed, which got even worse when they handed him a mop and bucket.

He could only imagine the laughter of his friends if they could see him now. They certainly wouldn't believe it. Well done, Papa, he thought sullenly. You wanted to bring me down a peg or two and you've certainly done it now.

At last, having done a frankly terrible job of mopping, he sat down at the staff table and Gaspard *finally* handed him a plateful of food. The combination of tiredness, his finger, his predicament and the amazing scent and taste of the food was so overwhelming that for the tiniest split-second, Konstantin thought he might cry.

Isla, sitting opposite him, noticed this in some surprise. It made absolutely no sense to take a job and then hate it so much. He was such an odd person.

'Go to bed,' she said when they'd finished and there was just the staff meal to clean up. 'I've got this.'

Konstantin was instantly taken aback by the kindness and, annoyingly, how obvious it was that he was completely shattered. But he couldn't think about that now; despite his hunger, he had half a steak wrapped in a napkin to have when he got upstairs, so he simply nodded and scuttled away without a backwards glance, fed Bjårk, took him out on the roof again and fell into bed, absolutely out for the count.

Chapter Twenty

Stupid Buglish was in the way again. If there was one thing Agot really hated it was how distracted her beloved Uncle Joel had become ever since the baby had arrived. Even when Joel had been on the outs with various other members of her family, Agot had adored him from the get-go, which Joel found slightly alarming. He didn't really know how to talk to children. This was a hundred per cent what Agot liked about him. He treated her entirely like the small adult she fully believed herself to be.

This was one of the long number of things Douglas had completely ruined in Agot's eyes. Uncle Joel was always staring at the stupid baby or picking up the stupid baby or asking her if she'd seen what the stupid baby could do now. The number of things the baby couldn't do – dance, play shinty, sit up for a tea party, look at pictures of ice skating, watch ice skating on television, talk about ice skating and pester her father to watch old Torvill and Dean videos and skate about the kitchen floor on clean dishcloths pretending to be an ice skater, much to the annoyance of anyone else trying to get anything done or anyone who didn't want 'Bolero' in their heads for the next six months – were huge. Agot was trying to shout louder to get them to pay her some attention, but it didn't seem to be working.

Seeing Joel coo over the stupid baby the next day in the kitchen gave her an idea. She went through to where Flora was squinting at her phone. Everyone looked all day at their phones, then if she wanted to do it they said 'No, no phones for you, Agot' even though if it was bad why did they do it all day and then they would say 'Agot, you are being too noisy' and she would absolutely not be noisy if she had a phone. Why was everyone so STUPID? And why was Christmas SO FAR AWAY? When you are five, four weeks is for ever.

'Auntie Flora,' she said conversationally.

'Darling,' said Flora, who had been looking at flour sourcing and wondering why the hell Fintan wasn't.

'I think,' said Agot seriously. 'I think Uncle Joel does not love us any more.'

'Do you?' said Flora.

She glanced above Agot's head and saw Joel dancing with the baby in the kitchen, Douglas giggling and reaching up his little fingers. It was a pretty sight.

'What makes you think that?'

'Because it is true,' sighed Agot in a world-weary fashion. 'He loves THAT BABY now.'

'I think it's possible to love more than one person at once,' said Flora. Agot frowned.

'One time,' she said, 'I dropped Big Fox and Daisy Duck and Jamford into a puddle at the SAME TIME because it was a wet, wet, WET day.'

Jamford was a small stuffed cow she dragged along with her, the origin of whose name was lost in the mists of time.

'And,' she said darkly, 'I picked up Jamford first.'

Flora thought about that.

'Well, yes, I can see that,' she said. 'But you picked up Big Fox and Daisy Duck next, right?'

Agot shook her head solemnly.

'No,' she said. 'Jamford was very muddy so I had to fix him.'

'And you left Big Fox and Daisy Duck in the mud?'

She shrugged.

'Oh, maybe Daddy got them.'

Flora looked at her.

'I don't think Uncle Joel would leave you in the mud,' she said.

'Not ME, silly,' said Agot. 'You!'

Then she clambered up in Flora's lap.

'Hmm hmm hmm, oh look, a phone,' she said, repeating it herself and getting gradually louder until Flora handed it over. Agot sat back with a contented sigh while Flora glanced over at Joel, who had to go to London that night and was patently unhappy about it.

*⁎ ❄

Back at the Seaside Kitchen, Iona had filled the official Instagram feed with beautiful shots of the previous night to go with all the lovely pictures she already had of the café. She wasn't getting much traction, and everyone else was getting annoyed with her as she insisted on lining up every single thing perfectly, buying so many fairy lights that their electricity bill was going up, and using a ruler to straighten the edges of her

Battenberg cake to make sure it looked absolutely flawless in the photographs.

She lobbied Flora to buy new artistic-looking cake stands, which Flora was dead set against – it was hard enough to have the funds to keep the lights on through the winter as it was. And now she was stuck with old Mrs McClocherty, who was waiting to get served at the till, and Mrs Barr behind her, who was having to deal with the wait for cake by listening to an exhaustive list of Mrs McClocherty's latest medical symptoms.

Iona reflected that she needed something better than this.

Chapter Twenty-one

The success of the dinner somehow softened the atmosphere in the kitchen. And Gaspard was also softening to what was available on the island. He pulled in a huge side of locally smoked salmon one afternoon to experiment with canapés, and insisted they all tried a bit.

'You 'ave to learn,' he said, 'only have what is good.'

'Won't that make it very expensive?' asked Isla shyly.

He glanced at her.

'Yes,' he said. 'You pay sheet, you get sheet, okay? We must get out and see the *terroir*.'

'I don't know what that is,' said Isla. 'But the Seaside Kitchen has millionaire shortbread.'

Gaspard snorted loudly and led them on.

They strode down the long road to the village. It was snowing, the sky grey and low and the fresh flakes bouncing into their faces. Konstantin had brought Bjårk, who was happily stamping his massive paws in and out of frozen puddles that cracked every time and surprised him anew every time. Isla was snuggled in a teddy bear coat Iona had made her borrow, now she was commuting. Konstantin had frowned when he'd run into her at the kitchen door.

'You look like a bear,' he'd said.

'So?' said Isla, who was nervous and not paying attention and not really in the mood to go out in the freezing cold with a temperamental chef and a spoilt man-boy. Kerry and Tam were getting to stay back and do prep in the nice warm kitchen, and she'd much rather be with them, however many dirty looks Kerry shot her.

'So you are buyer for the Rock,' said Gaspard.

'I don't need to be the buyer,' said Isla. 'I know exactly where to get everything from: bread from Mrs Laird, dairy from Fintan and Innes, smoked fish from Andrew Linhorn and fresh fish from right outside my front door.'

'Well, then you must show me, and we can make sure together. It is important for a kitchen to understand provenance.'

'Can I come?' Konstantin had asked earlier.

'You are pot boy. Is not necessary for you. Scrub pot cupboard please.'

But Konstantin had looked so pained and sad that Gaspard had relented and the boy had practically bounded upstairs to grab an extremely expensive-looking coat and scarf and his ridiculous dog. He was like a teenager, his long legs stretching out during the journey as the snow finally fell away and the breeze dropped and a watery winter sunlight appeared. He cracked as many puddles as Bjårk did, covering a lot of ground as though he was just delighted to be out in the open air, which indeed he was.

Near the entrance to the farm, they were stopped in their tracks by a loud voice.

'YOU ARE A BAD DOG!'

'*Hei*,' said Konstantin. 'I don't think he is a bad dog.'

He looked down. Agot came up to his knees.

'He broke my skating rink!'

Everyone looked at the muddy, icy puddle in which Bjårk was standing.

'I am going to the 'Limpicks and now I cannot practise.'

'You're going to the Olympics to ice skate?'

'YES!'

'This is Fintan's niece, Agot,' said Isla. 'Agot, this is Konstantin. He works at Colton's hotel and this is his dog Bjårk.'

Agot turned to Bjårk with undisguised dislike.

'I don't like his dog.'

Konstantin looked at her, insulted.

'That's a puddle, not an ice rink.'

There was a pause. Then Agot turned tail and rushed back to the farmhouse, bawling her eyes out.

'Well done,' said Isla crossly. 'She's five. And your boss's niece.'

'Well, she should have better manners,' said Konstantin, going slightly pink.

'So should you! She's a *child*!'

'I am now concerned we will be banned from their dairy,' said Gaspard. 'You – keep your mouth shut.'

Flora came down towards them, holding hands with a howling Agot. Konstantin immediately went forward to meet them.

'I am very sorry,' he said, crouching down in front of the child, although he still sounded sullen. 'My dog should not have broken your ice rink.'

'That's because he's a very bad dog,' said Agot, and Konstantin bit his lip to stop himself saying any more before he straightened up again.

'Okay,' said Flora. 'Is that it?'

'I am not sure,' said Isla to Flora quietly as they headed up towards the dairy, 'which one of them is more spoilt.' And Flora would normally have leaped to defend her family. But today, with Douglas being fretful because his dad was away, she just laughed. It had been a challenging day. The baby had grizzled and growled and she had found herself jealous of Joel sitting on a plane, both hands free, drinking a cup of coffee, reading the paper, even though she knew he didn't want to go and sit in meetings; didn't want to leave them. But the day stretched ahead, and she'd been up three times in the night and her brain was a fog and there was so much laundry to be done but she couldn't put the baby down. Sharing a laugh with Isla was definitely an improvement.

Chapter Twenty-two

Flora brought everyone into the kitchen where she had made Fintan lay out a selection of everything so Gaspard could choose what he wanted and how much they were going to use. The idea of using another supplier was not on the table, but Fintan hadn't wanted to do it at all so Flora had talked him round by stressing how important it was, and how the more of their produce they could use, the better it would be for everyone.

So there were plates laid out with butter: salted, unsalted, garlic-smoked, olive, plus an exquisite fleur de sel, which had full large salt crystals in it and, when spread cold on fresh warm bread with a cracked exterior and a yeasty crumb, could make grown men weep.

It was warm in the farmhouse. Bramble got up from his normal spot – practically lying in the fire – to say hello to Bjårk, who returned the bum sniff then, both of them satisfied neither was interested in fighting or shagging the other, casually followed him back to the fire and lay down with him back-to-back. Bjårk had been walking for approximately twenty minutes: the lazy creature now required approximately forty-eight hours of recovery rest. Agot, performing skating moves to herself in the corner, gave him the occasional dirty look.

'So what ees this?' said Gaspard, indicating the first butter, and Fintan took him through their processes, the difficulties of getting certified organic, how their cows were smaller given the grass was not lush this far north but hardy and sweet, and how Highland coos were some of the best out there. Gaspard mentioned something about how Brittany cows could almost certainly beat his in a fight, but Fintan didn't really notice and after the first bite, neither did anyone else.

Konstantin had originally been slightly taken aback by the shabbiness of the vast old farmhouse kitchen, with its range, piles of papers, back copies of *Farmers Weekly*, old horse brasses on the walls, a clutch of Agot's plastic toys in the corner and old boots lined up by the fire to dry. It wasn't shabby-chic; it was just actually shabby. The plates were mismatched, half from Eck's old wedding service, with delicate tulips painted on them and scalloped edges, and half modern pastels Flora had ordered from the mainland for the Seaside Kitchen to supplement the ones she's sourced locally, with the farmhouse benefiting from the overspill and the chipped. There weren't quite enough chairs and even the few available were also mismatched and a little wobbly on the flagstones, with the rugs here and there.

But it was filled with the scent of the coffee brewing in the little pot on the stove top as well as the fragrance of warm bread rising in the air, the crackle of the fireplace, the comforting *swish swish swish* of the dogs' tails, the tick-tock of the ancient grandfather clock in the corner, the gentle twitter of BBC Radio nan Gàidheal in the corner, the pouring of tea into cups and the clatter and chatter of old conversations steeped into the walls – the daily chat about the weather forecast; the grain price; the good health of sheep.

Sitting down on the least comfortable chair – he had somehow been last to choose, having been used to being offered the best of everything; it was very confusing – Konstantin found his eyes heavy, practically drifting off, as people ate and talked and the clock ticked in his ear. It had been a very stressful time.

'Konstantin? Konstantin . . . ?'

There was a voice that sounded like it was coming from far away. He was sure, suddenly, that he was once again in trouble for something – knocking off the bursar's hat or spilling champagne down the exiled princess of Romania again. When he opened his eyes though, instead he saw a group of people smiling at him. He blinked.

'What do you think of the cheese?'

'I haven't had any cheese.'

'Your plate is empty.'

Everyone looked at Bjårk, who was licking the inside of his mouth reflectively.

'He likes it,' said Konstantin, blinking.

Gaspard's face was grave.

'You know,' he said. 'Of course, the only cheese I would really wish to serve is French.'

'We do know,' said Flora brightly. 'But you're not going to!'

'But if I have to – if I absolutely have to serve something else . . .'

'Which you do.'

'Then this is . . . *pas mal*.'

And Flora beamed at Fintan.

Chapter Twenty-three

The snow had swept away by the time Jan's grand charity dinner came round in early December. Joel was back home, having mentioned the new hotel to everyone he'd met on his travels, of course. Flora wasn't crazy about this: would there be lots of his gorgeous, skinny blonde exes showing up? Joel was not remotely worried about this; instead he was pondering on what to do about these extra Christmas lights Colton had stipulated. He had contacted a few firms in London, all of whom had given him the traditional London shrug-off, laughing at him, saying 'You wot, mate?' and suggesting that only an absolute idiot wouldn't have started planning this eleven months ago. Whatever Flora thought, Joel didn't actually miss London in the slightest.

He looked good in his suit. Flora was having trouble zipping up her old black velvet dress, which was extremely annoying. Unbelievably annoying, in fact. Jan kept wanging on about how she'd accidentally lost all her baby weight so quickly after Christabel, it was amazing really, baby weight was a myth held on to by lazy people. This was obviously nonsense but still, thought Flora, knowing she had a healthy and beautiful baby wasn't really helping with the fact that she also had a horrible and unrelenting zip.

'Let me breathe in really hard and you zip it,' she said to Joel, who made a face.

'Just wear something else,' he said, kissing her shoulder. 'You'll feel bad all night if you're uncomfortable.'

'Are you calling me fat?'

'No! You look amazing!'

'Well, if I'm not fat, I'll still fit this dress,' said Flora crossly, sucking herself in as Joel tried not to stab her with the zip by mistake.

'Right,' she said. 'Let's go. If Gaspard can pull this out the bag again and Iona gets enough photos for Instagram, I think this might be a bit of a success.'

She desperately hoped so. Fintan had done basically nothing, and she didn't really have the marketing skills to open a hotel. If they had some lovely pictures, they could get some brochures done and hopefully all would go well for the real launch.

But anyway, this was Fintan's problem, obviously. She should, Joel kept pointing out, just relax and enjoy it.

It seemed like the entire island was there, mostly because it was. Jan and Charlie were from two very old Mure families, and there were few people who weren't connected with them somehow. Everyone supported their work: they brought impoverished young people from built-up cities on the mainland, taught them how to camp and look after themselves, gave them outdoor experiences, but really it was more than that as they got fresh air, learnt self-reliance and could take a break from whatever might be going on at home. Jan and Charlie were undeniably a force for good. Most of the money to fund this endeavour came from the lawyers and office johnnies they charged vast amounts to sit in a freezing tent and eat beans and tell each other it was a bonding experience (it was: they all tended to bond very tightly indeed as to how much they hated Charlie and Jan for putting them through such a miserable experience).

The building looked ravishing as usual, and Flora had booked the lovestruck ferryman Bertie Cooper who had never got over his teenage crush on Flora, even though she now had an actual baby of her own. He was an optimistic sort.

'Quite the night,' he observed, rowing her and Joel round in choppy waters. Joel was looking at the island behind him, frowning.

'Wouldn't want anyone to accidentally tip over the edge, leaving babby without a daddy,' said Bertie quietly.

'Well, no,' said Flora, puzzled, then went over to Joel.

'What are you thinking?'

'I was thinking,' said Joel, who had barely celebrated Christmas as a child and had felt the lack very keenly, 'that when you look at it from out here, there's hardly any lights on the island at all.'

'Yes, well,' said Flora. 'That's because we're out at sea on a boat and people very rarely decorate for people passing by for two minutes on a boat. The next nearest people who could see it are in Norway.'

'Hmm,' said Joel. 'Only I was thinking ... it is Douglas's first Christmas ... I really need to get on it.'

'I'm aware of that, thank you,' said Flora, smiling to herself at the sheer amount of extraordinary woollen garments that had already come her way from her older customers. With more to come, she knew. That poor child would get eczema before he was two.

'I haven't managed to allocate Colton's lights provision yet.'

They looked at the dull island. There was a council ruling every year that the money which other places set aside to use for their Christmas decorations actually went on extra street lighting.

School finished in the dark in the winter months, and the school itself was at the very top of the hill above the village. Extra lighting and handrails on the hill down meant more children could walk to and fro on their own without parents having to drive up and get them, increasing danger to the other, still-walking children. It was a sensible arrangement. But it left the island rather devoid of decorations elsewhere. Joel hadn't noticed it last year. This year, of course, everything was completely different.

'Cool,' said Flora, whose mind was on other things as they completed the short journey and Bertie held out his hand to lift her off.

'You're looking lovely,' he said, lightly depositing her on the quayside.

'Thank you!' said Flora, genuinely grateful as it helped cheer her up quite a lot about the zip situation. Bertie was happy. He'd made her beam. There was always hope.

Chapter Twenty-four

One night, thought Lorna MacLeod, getting dressed for the dinner in her flat near the tiny school where she was headmistress, and thinking about Saif, the island's doctor who had come as a refugee from Syria and with whom she was passionately in love – even though he had no idea if his wife were still alive. Oh, and she taught his children.

It was frankly an incredible mess, and now the end of the year was nearly upon them, she was doing a mental tally and not liking in the slightest what it showed.

One night at the beginning of the year, snuck under the cover of darkness.

One night in the springtime, when the boys went camping with the Scouts.

Three nights: they had managed a long weekend in Edinburgh,

when Jan and Charlie had taken the boys on an Outward Adventures course they had had free places for.

Saif had been bowled over by the city's dark, extravagant beauty, its glorious, brimming-over atmosphere, the tiny closes and cobbled steps, the hidden-away bars and vast vistas.

They had stayed in a turret of a hotel they could barely afford, climbed Calton Hill in the rain, eaten every type of food they couldn't find on Mure which was frankly pretty much all of them – they even found, on the corner of an ancient square, a Middle Eastern restaurant which Saif pronounced 'not bad' as Lorna laughed her head off at the sight of him absolutely stuffing his face with baba ganoush.

She had a couple of photos of the two of them – the sun had shone down sporadically and they had grabbed a spread of an extraordinary amount of unlikely food from Valvona & Crolla, and sauntered to Princes Street Gardens and sat out and had an actual picnic in the shadow of the castle, and she had taken a selfie of them both, his head next to hers, laughing and slightly embarrassed at the same time, always feeling guilty.

But she took the photo anyway, even though she knew a million times over that she couldn't post it anywhere, couldn't put it on her social media. She sent it to Flora, who was half-dead from breast-feeding and couldn't do much more than send a weak thumbs up. But Lorna looked at it all the time. They could be any couple in that photo. They could be normal. If they weren't in secret. If she wasn't his children's teacher. If his wife wasn't missing. If they could go public . . .

Well, there was no point in thinking about that. They couldn't go public, they just couldn't. Little stolen moments – occasionally when he was on call. She hated them being furtive, they both did: it felt grubby and tawdry.

It also felt wonderful, which was very much a part of the problem.

Oh, and Hallowe'en. Which really oughtn't to have happened at all. She blushed slightly. Well, it had been very dark. There had been a lot of parties and a lot of people in and out of houses and the boys had been away with all their schoolfriends for hours – children could always roam freely on Mure; it was safe as houses.

Six, she counted on. Six nights in a year. This couldn't go on. She brushed out her lovely thick red hair crossly.

* * ❄

The little jetty, in contrast to the rest of the island, was absolutely festooned with lights, twinkling in large jars, leading the way to a red carpet which was laid up the steps to the Rock's front door, where a piper greeted them with a lamenting air.

It was beautiful, and the people disgorging behind Joel and Flora oohed and aahed their way appreciatively up the steps, even though the cold wind was blowing straight off the sea. At either side of the door were two gas braziers jetting fire into the night, which looked incredibly impressive too, and all the windows glowed the cosiest yellow and orange, temptingly warm and cosy. The scents of champagne, ladies' perfume and crackling wood drifted out on the air along with, of course, that of the great heavy Christmassy wreaths everywhere.

Flora felt a flush of pride. It was going to be okay. The Rock was going to be fine. Several of the guests from the mainland were staying over tonight, some in the main house, others in the guest cottages that also came with underfloor heating and all the mod cons dotted around the grounds. It's where Joel had lived when they'd first been working on Mure. Even thinking about the guest cottages now gave her a little frisson. She looked at Joel to see if he was thinking the same thing, but he appeared to be texting Eck, who was babysitting, and who didn't pay any attention to his phone or know how to text, so she wasn't sure how useful that was going to be.

Inside, Gala was standing with flutes of champagne and sparkling juice for the guests, and waiting staff recruited from the village were already circulating with canapés. The fires were burning high and everywhere were groups of well-dressed, happy-looking people; many local but utterly unrecognisable out of their tweeds and fleeces. Mrs Doherty sparkled in a glittering diamanté shirt and bright fuchsia lipstick that Flora would wager (correctly) was the only lipstick she had ever owned; the farmers scrubbed up well in ancient handed-down kilts, patched and mended. Jan was wearing a bright purple satin dress with puffed sleeves. Flora thought she looked like a Quality Street but kept that to herself as Jan swept in to see Joel.

'Come on, darling, I have to rush you away,' she said. 'You don't mind, do you, Flora? He has to meet the sponsors.'

Flora did mind, very much. This was the first night they'd had out, just the two of them, since Douglas had been born. She was hoping to say a quick hello to everyone then grab a bottle of champagne and retire to one of the as-yet-uninhabited suites. She had been hoping for that very much. Perhaps a bit of dancing first (Joel did *not* dance, but he liked watching her at it), followed by an amazing dinner, then ... well, she had quite a lot of plans for Joel Binder that evening, as it happened.

But here he was, allowing himself to be impounded by Jan. Charlie came up, smiled at her apologetically and kissed her on both cheeks. Jan turned round and gave him a stony stare which meant that the nice little chit-chat about baby sick Charlie had been very much looking forward to with Flora – he couldn't discuss anything tough about child rearing with Jan as she insisted it was all brilliant and everything was perfect at all times – was not going to be on the cards at all. So he smiled apologetically again and backed out of the entry hall. Flora eyed the big stag's head over the door.

'Just you and me, kid,' she muttered, handing in her coat.

*　＊　❋

In the kitchen, Konstantin was once again despairing. He'd been supposed to have been practising chopping vegetables all weekend, as they got closer and closer to Christmas. Instead, he'd spent the time hiding in the airing cupboard, the warmest place in the building when it wasn't open for guests, reading *Ivanhoe* and composing desperate missives in his head to his friends back home to launch a rescue mission. He needed to buy a phone, and actually considered stealing one.

'Can I borrow your phone?' he asked Isla brusquely.

'Please?' she suggested mildly. He grimaced.

'Please,' he said, feeling like an idiot. She handed it over and he took it, then stared at it, frowning.

'I can't remember anyone's number,' he said.

'I know,' said Isla. 'Where's your phone?'

He shrugged.

'It doesn't work any more.'

'You can get credit at the shop,' said Isla. 'When we get paid.'

'Credit?'

'Phone credit.'

108

'Will that make my phone work?'

Isla wondered if Konstantin was in fact educationally sub-normal.

'Uh, duh?'

Konstantin looked so upset she nearly laughed.

'You can log in to Facebook if you like,' said Isla finally when he showed no sign of handing the device back.

'I'm not on Facebook,' he scoffed.

'Fine,' said Isla. 'Give it back then.'

'No, no, hang on. I can sign in to Snapchat and DM.'

He fiddled with some buttons.

'Sure, use my data, you're welcome,' said Isla, but it fell on deaf ears. Konstantin had never paid a phone bill in his life. He tapped a few buttons. Then a few more. Then he really did swear.

'What now?' said Isla.

'I can't remember the password.'

'Well, ask them for a new one.'

'I have,' said Konstantin. 'They've texted it. To my phone.'

Isla couldn't suppress a grin, which he noticed.

'It's not funny,' he said, roughly handing back the phone.

'No,' said Isla. 'But can I ask ... why are you here? Without a phone or any money?'

Konstantin sighed. He was too embarrassed to say he'd been banished. So he shrugged.

'I'm meant to be learning things.'

'Well, you can start back at those potatoes.'

So Konstantin was in a filthy mood because he was falling behind, and Gaspard was in a filthy mood with him because, as he – Gaspard – never ceased to tell him, when he was seventeen years old he had learned to chop for six hours a day in order to save up for his very first set of knives, the knives he still carried today, because if you wanted to excel at something you had to practise it. Which was exactly what Konstantin had heard from his music teachers, sailing teachers, maths teachers, English teachers, science teachers and art teachers his entire life. He felt about three feet tall.

'Faster! Faster!'

The menu was simple – pâté, followed by red wine-braised venison with hasselback potatoes, roasted carrot and turnip and a beautiful vegetarian haggis dish for the non-meat-eaters, but the timing was crucial. There were sixty people out there, all of whom needed feeding at the same time, and if half the room had nothing and half the room had rapidly cooling plates, you could be assured that absolutely nobody would be happy.

But, Isla was starting to notice, things were coming good. The ovens worked brilliantly and fired the potatoes in record time, and the whisky sauce was smelling absolutely delicious. The selection of local pâtés had been made in advance and stored in the huge fridges; the mushroom, white pepper and brandy one was so very delicious Isla simply couldn't imagine it was made from things you could find on the island, but Gaspard assured her both that this was the case and that he absolutely, one hundred per cent wasn't going to poison anyone and Isla had stared at him for a long time and he had said, 'Ees joke,' but she wasn't completely convinced.

Outside, she could hear the happy din of pleased punters as the champagne kept coming, and people readied themselves to open their cheque books. It was nice to have something like this on Mure, when everyone could get together and complain about the people who visited the island. And because it was getting into Christmas party season, there was a nice feeling of kicking everything off in style. She wished her mother would have come. She'd brought her an invitation to get her out the house for a while.

Her mother had harrumphed and told her it was a completely stupid waste of time and the MacKenzies were going to ruin themselves up at that big house, and everybody knew it, and Isla would be out of a job, and they'd hardly want her back at the café, it was running much better since she left.

Iona slipped into the kitchen.

'You're not supposed to be back here.'

'I know!' said Iona. 'Hee hee! I came to laugh at you because I don't have to work nights. Oh, and take reportage photographs.'

Isla didn't know what those were but decided it was best to keep quiet.

'Hey, who's that?' said Iona in, as usual, a voice that wasn't nearly quiet enough. She meant Konstantin, who was dolefully chopping the slices in the hasselback, wearing an oven glove because Gaspard didn't trust him enough not to cut off a finger or two again. It didn't matter that Iona was being loud though because Gaspard had the food mixer blaring away, drowning out all sound.

'Ugh, he's a drip,' said Isla. 'Some dropout. He's absolutely useless.'

Which would have more or less been fine, had Gaspard not chosen that exact instant to mute the food processor.

Silence fell in the kitchen, apart from the radio burbling away in the background. Konstantin's pale skin suddenly flushed bright pink, right to the tips of his ears. He concentrated on chopping, the knife sounding clumsy and unruly on the board, and very loud in the suddenly hushed kitchen. Isla went bright red too, not helped by Iona bursting out laughing.

There was no time to dwell on any of this, however, as Gaspard batted his hands at Iona to get her to leave his kitchen, then rallied his staff to go faster and faster. The potatoes were beautifully crispy, like tiny toast racks, roasted in local duck fat, sprinkled with rosemary and crystals of sea salt – he used, Isla noticed, quite an alarming amount of salt in almost everything. Perhaps that was a cheffing secret she was previously unaware of.

'Okay,' shouted Gaspard. 'Are we ready to go? Thees is our first big night of service so we are ready. Table one, you go, table eight!'

Everyone nodded, looking serious. Isla and Konstantin were plating up together. She sidled up, face flaming.

'Uh, sorry about . . .'

He gave her an extremely imperious look.

'What would I care what you think?' he said, blinking.

Stung, Isla went bright red once more, hating him, and back to plating up. The waiters moved at lightning speed as Gaspard looked at the big clock on the kitchen wall and shouted, 'Three, two, one: LET'S GO!'

Chapter Twenty-five

In the dining room, there was a pleasant hum of conversation. The pâté had been cleared away, and people were re-spreading napkins and refilling glasses ready for the new course. There was a pleasant clink of conversation, dominated by Jan who was also going to be starting the speeches afterwards, she kept telling everyone, about how this was for the children really, which Flora knew already, and how amazing it was that Christabel was sleeping through the night already so they could easily leave her with a sitter. Flora narrowed her eyes at this last bit. It couldn't be true, could it? Well, maybe it was true, she thought, but Jan was following one of those evil, regimented baby care techniques that involved them being left to cry themselves exhausted for hours on end. Flora decided this absolutely had to be it.

'Yes, they're just so much happier in a lovely structure,' said Jan.

'I thought you never put the baby down,' said Flora in a voice that came out much more accusatory than she'd intended. Jan blinked at her.

'Well, yes,' she said. 'For the first few months. It made her happy and secure enough to be left whenever and however.'

She smiled beatifically as Flora ignored her phone, which was bleeping, almost certainly a message from Innes, saying that Eck was complaining that Douglas was yelling blue murder and Agot was joining in.

Flora headed over to speak to her friend Lorna who was looking beautiful in a new green dress, earrings sparkling.

'Wow, look at you!' she said.

'I know,' said Lorna. 'Too much?'

'Mrs Mathieson is wearing a diamanté fascinator *and* a jewelled comb.'

'Okay, compare me to somebody else.'

Flora gave her a hug. Lorna didn't even pretend to hide what she was feeling: Flora was her only confidante.

'So he's not coming?'

'I'm not sure he's really a posh dinner kind of a person.'

'You don't know what kind of a person he is,' said Lorna too quickly, then bit her tongue.

'Sorry.'

'Don't be,' said Flora. 'Don't think I'm not sympathetic, because I am. Do you want me to fake a medical emergency so we can call him? Nothing disgusting, just a fainting fit or something?'

'No, don't,' said Lorna, pointing at Mrs Laird, Saif's usual babysitter for his sons, who was wearing a gold dress with batwing sleeves from the 1980s and cackling wholeheartedly with her mates over a gin. 'If we ruin Mrs Laird's night, she'll start spitting in the flour.'

114

'I'm sure she wouldn't,' said Flora, watching Mrs Laird cackle once again. 'But yeah, let's not take the risk.'

'I wish,' said Lorna. 'I wish I could give him up.'

'There are men here,' said Flora.

'There are men everywhere,' said Lorna. 'Have you seen the Highlands Tinder?'

Flora allowed that she had not.

'Loggers. Fishermen. Farmers. Renewable power analysts. Rig workers. Ferrymen. The Highlands has about ninety per cent of Britain's available men *and* a lot of them are fit.'

'But?' said Flora softly

'But none of them are him.'

'You do look beautiful,' said Flora again.

'Thanks,' said Lorna, reminding herself not to drink too much. The temptation to go over to his house would be huge, and the repercussions potentially disastrous. The concept of waking the boys was so unutterably traumatic and disgusting she couldn't bear it.

'More fizz?' said Flora eagerly.

'No,' said Lorna regretfully, covering the top of her glass with her freshly manicured hand. 'No, thank you.'

The doors to the kitchen were suddenly flung open and Flora turned her head interestedly to watch the food come out. Instead, she was greeted with absolute mayhem.

☆ * ❀

In Bjårk's defence, he had been cooped up in Konstantin's bedroom a lot, and even when he was taken out, it was for gloomy walks around the small headland at the north of the hotel, as

Konstantin looked out at the wind farms across the water and felt terribly sorry for himself. It wasn't entirely his fault that he needed some exercise, plus he was desperate for company. Back at the palace, it was considered perfectly normal for Bjårk to wander the hallways, almost always ending up in the kitchens where the staff spoiled Bjårk as much as they spoiled Konstantin – there was always a titbit or two for them, while the dog obligingly accepted treats, hugs and confidences.

'Let's go', shouted loudly, sounded very much like what they called out '*La oss gå!*', which was what they called out in Norway when they were chasing stags through the woods, or racing their horses across a crisp snowy field just for the fun of it, as the low winter sun made everything sparkle like diamonds. It was a call to arms, a call to run.

And Bjårk, lonely, bored, on his way to the kitchen to see what smelled so absolutely wonderful, couldn't help but respond to it.

Like a big furry bullet, he shot straight through the kitchen and through the door, *bang!*, straight into one of the waitresses, who shrieked and toppled the artful collection of plates on the vast tin tray. The noise it made was unbelievable. Someone in the room screamed as well, so surprised by the sudden cacophony. This startled Bjårk so badly he ploughed headlong into the nearest table, knocking it straight over, drenching several white shirts with bright red wine. Someone else had started yelling. Now there was a rampage.

Gaspard appeared at the door.

'*Mon Dieu!* The dog! The dog! Breeng 'eem to me! I shall keel him and serve him as delicious next course!'

Konstantin appeared next, white-faced.

'Bjårk! Bjårk! Heel! Come here! *Heel!*'

But Bjårk was cavorting now, having discovered some cracker

bits he'd upturned on the floor, and he was eating and dashing about, unable to see beyond the tables, badly confused. He was so big and hairy – and an unknown dog – that people were unwilling to lay a hand on him in case he bit it off. Some old farmers did make a grab for him, but he was still bucking about, tail waving madly now, having a fabulous time as he caused absolute havoc. It didn't help that at that point the piper thought it was his cue to come in from the outside (where his fingers were freezing off) and immediately start up a noise incredibly loud even in the big room, startling the most hardened bagpipe listeners, never mind poor old Bjårk, who leapt even harder and started barking trying to join in.

'BJÅRK! KOM HIT!'

'I WILL KEEL YOUR DOG AND THEN YOU! IT SHALL BE A BOUILLABAISSE AND YOU MAY BOTH FLOAT!' said Gaspard, waving a meat mallet – the closest object he had to hand – in the air, and going after Konstantin, who ducked straight under him to get out of his way. The entire room was in chaos between people genuinely upset at losing their dinner in this way, and everyone else, who was doubled up in helpless laughter as the entire kitchen staff chased a bouncing dog round and round the tables.

'Och, everyone, be quiet!' shouted Flora finally, and she grabbed a piece of the venison from the nearest broken plate. This was all so awful, but she couldn't let herself think like that right now. Instead, she knelt down and opened her hand to the dog.

'Come here, sweetie.' She spoke in the soft voice that worked incredibly well with Bramble, Douglas and, as it happened, Joel.

She held her hand out steadily as Bjårk paused in his bounding for a second.

'There we are, come and try this,' she said softly and soothingly. The dog paused and she didn't move, so he stealthily made his way towards her.

Just as he opened his mouth to take the meat, Konstantin pounced on him from behind with a makeshift lead made from two tea towels hastily tied together, and managed to restrain him for long enough to pick him up, whereupon Bjårk immediately tried to wrestle his way out of Konstantin's arms and knocked over another table. As if for the final word, the table hit the wall hard, and the huge stag's head that was hanging on there collapsed and fell off, hitting the ground with a clang. Bjårk, confronted with what he thought was a live stag, instantly went absolutely berserk again and started growling and advancing on it in a menacing fashion, belly to the floor. Konstantin clapped his hand over his eyes, then threw himself on the floor behind him and dragged himself along on his own belly until he got close enough to grab the dog's back legs. Front paws struggling futilely, Bjårk complained vociferously to the rest of the room all the way back through the swinging kitchen doors, which slammed behind them.

Iona put her phone down. She might, she thought, she might finally have her Instagram story.

There was a moment's stunned silence. Then Hector McLinn, who ran the large, unrewarding farm that covered the western side of the hill range, grinned with his big ruddy face and started clapping. Flabbergasted, Flora turned towards him, already wishing the floor would swallow her up, but the whole thing had been such a disaster, so very awful, that there was really, in the end, nothing to do but laugh about it. Jan looked like she was about to go ballistic but just as she took a breath to start a tirade, the waiters quietly opened the kitchen doors again and started quietly beavering away to serve people food, and Flora ordered free wine for everyone from the cellar, which put them in an absolutely tremendous mood, and by the time they were seated again, there was the kind of sense – particularly as it had been so very dreadful, as Fintan carefully picked up the stag's head, and Hector, who was six foot four in his stockinged feet, went over to help him rehang it again – that actually it had been quite the adventure.

* ❄

Inside the kitchen, however, it was a different matter. Bjårk had been sent outside the kitchen door – 'he can jump in the sea, I do not care' – but instead was trying to keep out of the cold and howling wind and was whining and yipping loudly, occasionally scratching dolefully at the door, adding a strange punctuation to the righteous bollocking they were getting from Gaspard, who was managing to simultaneously scream his head off at Konstantin – and Isla for not helping, which Isla felt was extremely unfair – while also finishing off the dishes that were now going out like clockwork from the kitchen and, very shortly afterwards, coming back scraped clean, so delicious was the food. Every time the kitchen doors swung open, they could hear the rising noise of happy diners, the conversation and laughter becoming more pronounced, even as Gaspard continued to hector them with how utterly useless they all were.

Finally, furious, spent, he turned round to finish the preparations on the marmalade tart pudding – being French, Gaspard thought marmalade was an incredibly exotic and rare ingredient and used it in everything – and Isla and Konstantin were left together alone in the middle of the kitchen. Isla risked a glance at Konstantin, who was staring at the floor.

A second later, Konstantin risked a glance at her. This time, she was looking up and caught his eye. And the oddest thing happened. They both smiled; they couldn't help it.

'GET ON! CLEAN!' spat Gaspard from the other side of the kitchen and they hurried back to their own roles immediately. But neither of them felt quite so bad.

Chapter Twenty-six

It is a truth universally acknowledged that the more free-flowing the booze at a charity dinner, the more money stands to be raised and, even though it involved the sacrifice of some of Colton's wine collection, it turned out to be an incredibly lucrative night for Jan and Charlie's charity, and Jan, who had been rather looking forward to dispensing 'what a shame they can't handle that big place on their own, it's just such a pity, isn't it?' stories all over town was reduced to admitting that in fact everyone had had a brilliant time and that though the stag's head was fine, the heads of many people waking up in the morning were not in the best possible way.

The more obvious effects from that night over the next couple of weeks were found in the kitchen. It had been, it turned out, surprisingly galvanising. Konstantin realised that if he was sacked, everything was going to get massively worse for him and Bjärk massively quickly, and so he set about trying – just a tiny bit, and he wasn't very good at it (it would still never have occurred to him for example to make his own bed in the morning) – to try harder.

He practised his chopping till he found, after many bloodied fingers and a lot of strangulated swearing, that he could chop everything quickly and efficiently – if not up to Gaspard's standards, certainly a step up from his own.

* *

Iona got on it the day after the dinner. This was exactly what they needed, she figured. She'd tag it a million times. She remembered that viral video that was just a dog running around a park. This would be *much* better. And it would show off the beautifully curated shots of the hotel, and the island. She was looking forward to this.

She timed it for nine p.m., the time statistically most people were scrolling lazily through their feeds, looking for something to distract them. And she ran it all in capitals. 'OMMMGGGGGG FUNNIEST VIDEO EVER! YOU HAVE TO WATCH THIS!!!!!!' she typed, hashtagging it a million times with #funnyvideo #funnydogvideo #dogvideo #restaurantfail #hilariousvideo #manfallingover and literally everything else she had ever heard of, posting it simultaneously to her Facebook – and her mum's Facebook. Her mum was amazing at sharing all sorts of crap and had about nine thousand old lady friends around the world who also loved sharing absolute crap, so even though there was absolutely nobody Iona's age on Facebook any more, she expected it to get good currency nonetheless. And she sent it to the Twitter accounts of all the newspapers she could think of. Sometimes they had more space to fill than people realised. Iona liked Mure in a faintly haughty fashion, as she was convinced she was destined for greater things. This was just the start she needed.

Nothing. After an hour she crossly shut down her phone and went to bed.

Chapter Twenty-seven

The snow lying was such a surprise. It was usually cold enough that snow falling was rarely a problem on Mure. It was more a question of would the wind cease for long enough for it to lie on the roads, across the fields, gently papering everything in its soft and lovely gentleness.

Bramble had barely seen lying snow and, being particularly old, and also a dog, couldn't remember if he had or not, so he charged out into the lower field, rolling on his back and tossing himself around, paws in the air, like a much younger dog. Then it soaked in and he stopped liking it so much and slunk back in to dry himself off in front of the fire. It did not smell good.

The children were having such a good time up at the school that Lorna gave up on trying to get anything done, and took the two classes outside for a healthy snowball fight – no hitting in the face, no rocks in the snowballs and no putting down necks were the rules, but there were still a few tears here and there. Mrs Cook, the only other teacher at the school, already had the urn on for hot chocolate, so tears were assuaged and little pink hands and noses warmed after the laughter and exercise of the morning, and Lorna resumed reading *The Dark Is Rising*, their Christmas book, although as the room warmed up, and the hot chocolate took effect, more than a few of the little heads began to nod. It had been a long term, after all; everyone was more than ready for the two-week Christmas break. And she still hadn't heard from Saif.

* ❄

Saif, for once, wasn't thinking about Lorna. Instead, he was staring for the umpteenth time at his most recent letter from the Home Office asking him to come in for a visit. It wasn't for him: he had his indefinite right to stay. It wasn't about the boys. Which left ... what? Was it his wife?

A scientist by bent, a doctor by profession, he had been rigorously trained not to speculate, but to deduce carefully; never to jump to wild conclusions.

It was proving extraordinarily difficult.

* ❄

Up at the hotel, it was quiet. Gaspard was talking to suppliers and there was no dummy lunch service that day, and Isla knew today was the day the Christmas trees arrived – everyone on Mure knew; it was quite the excitement – so she was happy to be heading down to the port to see everyone.

She pulled on her old coat which looked jollier when she added her tam-o'-shanter and a red scarf. The scarf had been a present from Flora the year before and though she thought it was a little showy – red was such a big colour – she conceded that it suited her dark hair and pink skin, and it was made of very good lambswool.

Just as she left the Rock, she happened upon Konstantin, who was out throwing a stick across the wide white lawn for Bjårk, who was gambolling towards it in a leisurely fashion. He was rather overweight for a dog, she observed, but Konstantin tossed the stick over and over again regardless, his long arms stretching up into the air of the now bright blue sky, sending the stick far and true.

He looked boyish and, for the first time, truly carefree, not shackled to a kitchen he despised in a world he didn't understand. The hangdog look was almost completely gone.

She found herself watching him for a while. There was nobody in the hotel on this side; he obviously didn't realise he was observed and was singing rather loudly, and quite well.

Bjårk immediately sat his capacious bottom down on the snow, pushed back his head and howled loudly along to the sky.

'*IFa-la-la-la-la . . .*'

'*Aooo!*'

Isla couldn't help it: she giggled aloud. Konstantin whirled round, his cheeks bright and red, his white teeth showing.

He stopped as soon as he saw her, and his face immediately took on that closed look again and she remembered once more with horror how he had overheard her talking to Iona.

In fact, for an instant, Konstantin hadn't recognised the shy little scullery maid who hated him in this pink-cheeked, laughing girl in the beautiful red scarf, her long dark hair streaming underneath it and down the back of her coat. His first instinct was to

126

smile, then he'd realised awkwardly who it actually was, and so he set his face.

Bjårk, however, had no such compunction and bounded up to her happily. You couldn't really ever say a Mure person was frightened of dogs; there were so many dogs it would be ridiculous, like saying you were frightened of sand, but nonetheless Isla remained a timid sort as her mother had always warned her away from them. Gingerly, she put her hand out a little. Bjårk sniffed it, disappointed as soon as he worked out there was no treat in it, but nonetheless wormed his way under her hand and pushed his ears in her direction so she could scratch underneath them, which, slightly tentatively, she did.

'You're a very bad singer,' she whispered to the dog, who minded not in the slightest. 'Uh,' she said, as Konstantin still stood there. 'Sorry to interrupt. I was just heading down to the village.'

'Oh,' said Konstantin, who had a whole day free and not a clue what to do with it without friends or money. On the spur of the moment he said, 'Well, so am I.'

Isla didn't look pleased, he noticed. For goodness' sake.

'Or maybe not,' he added pointedly.

'No, no come with me,' said Isla immediately, feeling miserably aware of having fallen short with her manners. It had just flashed through her mind that if she said he couldn't come, he'd just end up walking about three paces behind her, given that there was only one road down into town anyway. But what he would he think of everyone being so excited to see a few trees? She told herself she didn't care and carried on.

The island looked so pretty though, if you were wrapped up, with the fresh snow scrunching cheerfully beneath their feet, the clear imprints of paws and bird's feet that had gone before them, and the lovely squishy shape of the ducks' footprints plopping along on duck business.

Conversation was sporadic as they neared the little port, where quite the crowd was forming.

'What's the crush?' said Konstantin. 'Has someone got the island's first computer? Be careful nobody panics when they see a moving train.'

Isla looked at him crossly, but she was so far underneath her hat that he didn't notice in the slightest.

'HELLO!' shouted a small voice. It was Ash, the younger of the island doctor's two sons, who had spent many a day while Saif was handling an emergency more or less being babysat at the café so Isla knew him well.

It was hard not to have a soft spot for Ash, who still had a limp from a badly set leg in Syria, and a desperate, confused desire never to have to go through his bad experiences again. In Ib, his older brother, this same desire manifested in a certain wariness and sullenness, but Ash had an openness to the world that made him friendly as a Labrador. On the tiny island of Mure, this was always happily reciprocated in a way that alternately made Saif happy and then worried all over again for when his darling boy had to face the real world and find out everyone wasn't quite so friendly.

'Hello, Ash,' said Isla, tousling the boy's too-long dark hair.

'The trees are coming!'

He turned to Konstantin.

'Trees are big things that grow in the ground,' he began confidently. There were, of course, very few trees on Mure; it was simply too windy.

'You put them up at Christmas time. They're for hanging lights on,' he continued. Isla expected Konstantin to be wearing his usual annoyed frown, but to her surprise he had an interested, engaged look on his face. Ash stretched out his arm as the ferry got closer.

'ALL THE TREES ARE COMING!'

He lowered his voice.

'I is going to be at the front for the biggest one.'

Konstantin looked at him.

'How are you going to carry that?'

'My daddy will. He's NORMOUS,' said Ash of his pleasantly tall but in no way enormous father. 'I will sit on it till he is here.'

'That's a brilliant plan,' said Konstantin. Ash narrowed his eyes as the ferry started to chug in in reverse.

'Don't take the biggest one.'

'I won't take the biggest one,' said Konstantin. Ash held his gaze meaningfully as Konstantin turned back to Isla, smiling.

'Do you normally take the biggest one?' said Isla.

He smiled ruefully. Konstantin always took the biggest one. 'Well . . .'

More and more people gathered as a huge pile of Christmas trees started to be unloaded onto the dock. People were trying to look unconcerned about it, and not be casting too beady an eye, all the while mentally planning exactly which one they wanted. There was a beauty at the top.

'Where are these from?' said Konstantin to the cargo loader who was ticking things off his inventory.

'Came out of Bergen last night, ken,' said the man, and Konstantin briefly wondered why the man thought his name was Ken, but still, there was something about seeing the beautiful trees, their dark green needles already tumbling out on to the dock, which made him even more homesick than usual.

'Okay,' he said, staring sadly. Flora had arrived – Fintan was still in bed – and made straight for the despatcher.

'I'm going to need the ten-footer for the Rock.'

'I wanted that!' said old Mrs MacGregor, who didn't see quite as well as she once did.

'But you live in the mill cottage,' said Flora as gently as she was able. 'There isn't space.'

'I can chop it up and have it twice,' said the old lady mutinously.

'I have a lovely five-foot tree for you,' said the despatcher. 'Don't worry about it.'

More and more people were arriving on the docks now, picking up their beautiful trees with cries and shouts. A tractor was called into service by Hamish, who loaded up the MacKenzie farmhouse's six-footer with a huge grin all over his face. Flora had harboured hopes of decorating it before Agot got home from school and put her special stamp on it, but didn't hold out much hope for that happening.

Konstantin watched sadly.

The palace at Christmas time was ridiculously overdone. Partly it was because they had so many visitors: some paying; some local schoolchildren. Grand companies held their Christmas parties there so his father pointed out the decorations made sense economically. But, deep down, Konstantin knew it was because he loved it, because his mother had loved it so much.

Trees four metres high lined the huge ornate staircase at the main entrance to the palace, with heavy green ivy wreaths winding up the delicate filigree banisters on both sides. Similar heavy wreaths were pinned perfectly along the walls, and the tree was lined with artificial lights – and also real candles lit up only a couple of days before Christmas, when just the family gathered round to exchange early gifts and eat lutefisk in preparation for the main event.

His mother had loved the traditional songs and booked the local choir repeatedly to come and sing *julesanger*. She had said it was for the visitors, who filed through the public rooms to see the palace come to life throughout December, but Konstantin had always known on some level that it was for her; she hummed the songs throughout the house wherever she was.

It had been so much ... well, he was a kid. He hadn't known anything.

It was special to live in a palace, he knew that. People mentioned it all the time. But actually, the really special thing had been having a mother who loved and adored him. He'd taken that completely for granted, not given it a second thought.

It occurred to him to tell everyone where he was from, get them to stop treating him like an idiot. But would they though? And the horror of it, thought Konstantin, if they didn't believe him or, worse, thought it was funny. Laughed at him. He couldn't bear it. Better they thought he was a drifter than an absolute loser who'd been banished by his own father. He bit his lip hard.

'Um, are you okay?' said Isla eventually, realising how quiet he'd been. Even Bjårk wasn't gambolling any more. She thought Mure looked beautiful, always did this time of year, when the lights were slung up along the lamp posts on the quay. It was just the one string, and usually something was wonky, but it was like a fairyland to Isla. It always cheered her up.

'I miss home,' he said simply. Then he looked around the docks.

'Are these all the lights there are? Is this it?'

'I like it,' said Isla.

He fell silent.

'What's home like?'

'It's amazing,' he said suddenly. 'Where I'm from, up near Bergen ... there are thick pine forests everywhere, up the mountains. You can smell the fir trees too; everything smells of pine and fresh white snow. It's dark like here but not so windy, and you can ski every day. It's not flat like this place.'

Isla frowned.

'Well, we've got the ben,' she said, referring to the hill behind the MacGregor farm, which was misleadingly treacherous to climb, leading to the spine of craggy hills up the west side of the island, that bristled with heather in the spring, but now were dull and bare.

The dock grew busier and happier. Enterprisingly, Iona had pitched up with mulled wine and hot chocolate for sale while people waited to bid on the tree they wanted. Few were the children who, on seeing another child with a cup filled with marshmallows, cream and cinnamon, didn't immediately pester their parents for one. Although more than one parent pointed out that it was absolute highway robbery, most gave in with good grace. It was a part of it, and ritual was important at Christmas time.

'Okay, six-footer, would suit flat or lovely front room,' bellowed the despatcher again. Several people stepped forward, some holding back in case there was a fatter greener tree beneath. Isla waved at Lorna who was buying two, one for her lovely little flat to sit on the table, and another – out of her own pocket – for the school. She and Mrs Cook came in on the second Sunday of advent and decorated it in secret, partly to give the children a wonderful surprise on Monday morning, as if it had happened by magic, and partly because if you invite thirty-five children to help decorate a Christmas tree, nothing good happens, and there's a lot of needles involved.

Inge-Britt sidled down lazily from the Harbour's Rest hotel. They needed a big tree, and she would only bother to decorate one side of it because really who would see the other side? And she'd have to make two trips up to the attic which would seriously impinge on her afternoon nap. Inge-Britt was a brilliant person but temperamentally highly unsuited to running a clean hostelry.

Something Flora was very much hoping to capitalise on with the Rock on Fintan's behalf.

Lorna and Inge-Britt both put their hands up for a big tree.

Lorna, however, was momentarily distracted: if little Ash was by the quayside, it meant his father, Dr Hassan – oh, who was she kidding – Saif, the man she was desperately in love with, couldn't be far behind.

'Hey, Lorna,' shouted Inge-Britt, holding up a hand to indicate that they would share catching the big tree as the despatcher moved over the ten-footer, expecting her friend to catch it . . . but Lorna's head had turned in a dream and she wasn't there to get it as it fell.

Chapter Twenty-eight

It happened very quickly. Lorna turned on hearing her name but it wasn't – was never, it seemed – the voice she wanted to hear her name from at all, and she was scanning the crowd even as Inge-Britt was asking her to help.

Ten-foot Christmas trees, even wrapped in netting, are heavy, unwieldy things, hard to get a grasp on, even if you are a tall, glamorous Icelandic girl.

'Lorna!' she yelled, but Lorna was still searching the mass of faces, looking for the one pair of dark eyes she could drown in; looking for that shaggy black hair, always in need of a haircut, that rangy frame, the golden skin ...

The tree fell straight over, heading directly for little Ash, whose damaged leg and wide-eyed demeanour meant he wasn't always as quick off the mark as he could have been.

Isla looked at it with horror as, almost in slow motion, it toppled out of Inge-Britt's arms towards the little boy until, like a flash, the tall blond man beside her dived underneath it and landed, pushing the boy out of the way, and crashing onto the cold port tarmac, with a tree smashing down on his broad back.

* ❄

'Oh my God!' Lorna dashed down at once. 'I wasn't . . .'

'I thought you'd heard me,' said Inge-Britt as they both knelt down in front of the stunned Konstantin. She shot Lorna a look.

'Are you all right?' said Isla softly, sitting down on his other side. Konstantin blinked at her.

'This is cold and wet,' he said. 'Even more than everything is here already.'

Ash was looking at the man astounded as Saif, emerging from the crowd, had rushed forward to pick him up. Lorna couldn't catch his eye then in case she found him blaming her for nearly whacking Ash on the head with a Christmas tree.

'Ash, I told you to stay out the way,' he said gently into the boy's ear, but making sure he didn't raise his voice or sound cross. How Lorna loved his voice.

'Do you want to get up?' said Isla to Konstantin. 'Or are you quite comfortable?'

'It's all relative,' said Konstantin as Saif swiftly turned to him to make sure he was all right which, apart from some gravel in his hands, and some tears to his surprisingly expensive rain-coat, he was.

'Thank you,' muttered Saif gravely. 'Thank you for saving my boy.'

Konstantin looked up at the tree, as if surprised at himself.

'You're welcome. I didn't even realise I'd done it until I had.'

'Well, you are brave,' said Saif, cleaning off Konstantin's hand with an antiseptic wipe.

'Ouch, that stings,' said Konstantin. 'So now I think that I am not.'

'Is this a cut filled with superglue?'

'Can we talk about that later?'

'Here,' said Flora. 'Have some free hot chocolate for being heroic.'

'Can I have some free hot chocolate?' said Ash.

'You were anti-heroic!' protested Flora. 'You got in the way of the trees!'

'Oh,' said Ash, crestfallen.

'Of course you can,' said Flora, feeling guilty.

'I'm sorry,' said Lorna as Saif carried her two big trees up the hill, with Ash helping from the back. He didn't say anything. It was very difficult with either of the boys around.

'You didn't do anything,' he said in his usual calm way, but his mind was far away. There was a reason he had been avoiding Lorna – deliberately avoiding her. For months. He knew it was cruel and unfair, but he didn't know how to tell her, because he didn't know *what* to tell her.

After querying the letter, he had received word through a back channel in the Home Office that there was some chatter, and to stand by, and he could think of little else. His wife had now been missing for nearly three years. It was impossible to focus on a highly demanding job as the island's only doctor, and being a single father to his two sons, and all that time having to stand by. He couldn't give heart space to Lorna, because he knew if he did, she would consume him utterly, and he couldn't, he *couldn't* let that happen. He could barely even look at her.

He can barely even look at me, thought Lorna, her heart aching.

Chapter Twenty-nine

A whole group had headed off to the Harbour's Rest for lunch. Konstantin had amazed himself that he had noticed all the things Gaspard would not have stood for in his kitchen, how far below the standards of the Rock it fell. He genuinely was surprised at himself.

Isla had slipped away to take her mother a tree; a sweet little three-footer that could sit on top of the nest of tables in the good room.

Her mother sniffed.

'Well, that's just going to shed, isn't it?'

'But it looks so pretty,' said Isla. 'And it smells good too.'

'I don't know why I bother,' said Vera, smiling sadly. 'Are you really working Christmas Day?'

Isla owned that she was, if they got the bookings.

'Well, Flora's got you run ragged, I see,' said Vera. 'I never saw you as a kitchen maid, Isla.'

'I'm not!' said Isla, stung. 'Gaspard is teaching me loads.'

'That Frenchman! I saw him in the Harbour's Rest. He looks filthy.'

Isla bit her lip.

'And those tattoos! I don't like the look of him.'

Vera didn't like the look of many people.

'You'll come though?' said Isla, trying to build bridges. 'Can't you bring a friend? I can book you in. It can be my Christmas present to you.'

'Sitting in a strange hotel eating Christmas lunch on my own? No, thank you,' said Vera, who had fallen out with her two sisters for reasons that were misty in the memory, possibly even in Vera's memory too, but which meant Isla hadn't seen her mainland cousins for six years.

'Well, maybe you'll change your mind,' said Isla. 'I'm heading back up.'

'Again?'

'We're doing a dinner service. It's going to the old folks' home. You could go and help serve it, if you like. We're doing something new; I think it's like a kind of French cake. You'd like it.'

Vera sniffed again.

'I doubt it,' she said. 'And it's *Escape to the Sun* tonight on the telly.'

And for a rebellious second, Isla really, really wished she would.

Chapter Thirty

Back at the Rock, Gaspard appeared in the kitchen, looking furious as always, a cigarette thrown out behind him. Flora had left a huge fire bucket there to try and catch them all but she didn't always succeed.

'Today!' he said. '*Tarte tatin*. With leeks from the kitchen garden. No messing. We have a million winter leeks. This rock is a good place for growing leeks. Aha, *bien*, ah *oui*, who knew? *Alors*, everyone will learn. I will need your help to make starters.'

And they spent all afternoon learning how to roast the perfect leeks in purest butter, made pastry again and again under his disappointed eye, rolled and blind-baked and wasted butter, and marvelled at Bjårk's frankly extraordinary ability to eat remnants of pastry while carefully separating out any hint of greenery and daintily spitting it out of the corner of his mouth. By the evening, all of them had made more or less presentable – and undeniably delicious – leek *tatins* sitting in tiny ramekins.

Konstantin stared at his in something like awe.

'Is that, like, the first time you've ever made something?' teased Isla quietly.

'Yes,' he said simply, still looking at it in amazement. They sat at the kitchen table and he took a bite. Gaspard's recipe was something altogether new to Konstantin, with the hollandaise sauce he'd whipped up to eat with it making it absolutely sensational. He was even more surprised when Isla, who had been looking at his coat all afternoon and getting annoyed by it, scooted over when they'd finished eating and lifted it down from the stand.

'What are you doing?'

She frowned and showed him the small sewing kit the hotel was full of. 'Do you want to do it?'

He blinked.

'You're going to sew up my coat?'

Isla went bright red. She had genuinely barely given it a second thought: she had darned for her father and was always proud of her neat stitching, and couldn't bear looking at the beautiful expensive coat with the tears in the fine material. It was mostly habit.

And partly gratitude too: Konstantin had undeniably, despite his bad attitude, saved Ash from, at the very least, a nasty hit to the head. His hands were still red and cut.

'You don't have to do that,' he said, which made her feel even worse, like a servant he was being kind to.

'Well, you helped my friend,' she said, her voice timid and shy.

Konstantin blinked again.

'You can do it if you want,' she said again.

'I don't know how.'

'You can't *sew*?'

141

He laughed.

'Of course I can't sew! Who can sew?'

'I can sew!' said Kerry.

'*Moi aussi*,' said Gaspard. 'Of course. We are not animals.'

'So, everyone can sew?' said Konstantin suspiciously. If he ever ripped anything, he tended to throw it away; he thought everyone did.

The kitchen looked back at him.

Isla would have put money on him saying something snotty and cutting, or just leaving them to get on with it on his behalf. Instead, he sat back in his chair.

'Okay,' he said. 'Teach me to sew.'

* ❄

They had a little time before the clean-up and dinner service. Gaspard went off for his daily siesta. Kerry and Tam went to clean out the chickens, a job Isla was absolutely terrified of, but they both seemed to quite like. It depended very much where you stood on chickens. Isla was scared of their beady little eyes, but she was a little scared of a lot of things. Konstantin hadn't been rostered yet in case Bjårk ate all the eggs. Bjårk tried to help anyway, but they were having none of it.

Isla retuned the radio from the shocking mid-Atlantic boy music Gaspard liked (Flora had commented drily that his good taste in food obviously had to be evened out somewhere else – his frankly horrible taste in music) to BBC Radio nan Gàidheal, and let its gentle music run through the big kitchen.

The low winter sun briefly showed its face, illuminating the clean white tiles around the walls, the shiny metal implements and the good wooden table, and she bent her dark head to his blond one and, with some swearing and a couple of pricks to the fingers (his hands, he pointed out, had never been in such a state, and she was tempted to say that his hands were so soft he should be ashamed), she showed him a simple running stitch, then a cross stitch. She made him practise on the tea towels though, wouldn't let him loose on his good coat.

'You'll ruin it.'

He looked uncharacteristically thoughtful.

'I ruin a lot of things,' he said suddenly.

She looked up at him then, and the sun caught her dark hair and made her pale eyes shine out very brightly in her face.

'Well,' she said. 'You didn't ruin the Christmas trees.'

'True.'

'And you didn't ruin the leek *tatin*.'

'Mine was by far the worst.'

'Well, I don't know ... Everyone else is a chef and I'm a baker so ...'

'It did taste good though,' he added almost to himself.

'And now you can do a running stitch!' she said and he glanced down at his handiwork.

'Oh,' he said.

'What?' said Isla, even as she noticed him smiling.

He held up his hands.

'I've sewn the tea towel to my shirt.'

Isla burst out laughing as he stood up, the towel flapping off him. He tugged at it.

'Don't pull it! You'll rip another hole in your clothes! Stay still!'

And she carefully approached him, the low sun still streaming in through the windows, and was suddenly very conscious of him, and his long, hard body through his expensive twill shirt, as she realised the kitchen scissors were in the dishwasher. There was no help for it. Carefully and deftly, as he lifted his arms, she bent towards him, snapped off the loop of thread and then neatly bit it through before pulling it out, leaving no trace.

She caught a faint scent of his aftershave too, something oddly like leather, or tobacco or something … Where on earth did a kitchen boy get all these expensive tastes? It made no sense at all.

She was blushing harder than ever as she straightened up. He was looking a bit startled too; he hadn't realised she was going to bite it. Her face so close to his, as the last of the sun shone down on her shiny dark hair, that he felt … well. It had been a while. He felt a jolt. Then stopped himself for being ridiculous. It had taken him a little bit by surprise, that was all.

'I could have got Bjårk to do that,' he said, checking the shirt again, hiding his slightly pink face just in case she could read his thoughts on it.

'Next time,' said Isla, scuttling off. 'We'd better get cleaned up.'

And in a second, she had her unflattering kitchen cap on again, and was elbow-deep in hot soapy water with the ramekins, and everything was back to normal.

Chapter Thirty-one

Isla didn't get to see Iona till later that night. She was going to mention Konstantin, but found herself oddly shy. Instead she pointed out that Iona, despite being supposedly the great social media maven, had turned her Instagram to private after she'd flirted rather disastrously with a celebrity and forgotten to turn it back on again, and so she had to run the entire piece of film again.

At first, Facebook take-up was slow but Instagram was quick. But then one of the Scottish papers retweeted it, and the radio stations started to pick up on it – and then it really started to move. By the time the numbers were clicking up exponentially and her phone had started to glow hot with the notifications, the girls were staring at each other, half in delight, half in horror.

Iona plugged her phone into the wall to stop it blowing up and texted Flora.

'Go take a look at my Insta!!!!!!!!!' but unfortunately by then it was well after nine o'clock at night which meant Flora was lying spread-eagled on her bed in the Manse, fast asleep, a television show playing on her computer screen of which she was completely oblivious. She was oblivious too to Joel giving Douglas his night bottle, half smiling, half wincing at the noisy snoring noises coming from the master bedroom.

Flora was taking too much on, and he probably should be doing more, he thought. She was the one who was meant to be on leave. Except ... he wasn't entirely sure that going to the hotel wasn't good for her. She was made to be busy, Flora. He wondered mildly if she hadn't overestimated how much she would enjoy sitting in a rocking chair.

He looked down at Douglas, who was sucking his bottle with an expression of exceptional happiness on his face. The baby drank deeply, smacked his lips in contentment and allowed himself a long luxuriant fart.

'If you had told me,' said Joel softly to the little one, 'how much I would be perfectly fine with another human being doing a massive fart in my hands, I think I'd have found it quite difficult to believe you. In the past.'

Douglas smiled dreamily as he had taken to doing at the sound of his father's voice and, as usual, Joel felt the familiar catch at the heart, laced once more with sadness that his own parents hadn't felt the same way, or if they had, they still hadn't – teenagers as they'd been – been able to look after him, protect him. Whereas now, looking down at this little face, he couldn't think of a single thing he wouldn't do to protect Douglas and to keep him safe, nor a single place on earth – he peered out into the dark night – that would be better for him to do it in. Yes, he should get back to work. Those damn lights: he was running out of time. But oh, it was better right here right now.

Under the great cold stars of the North Atlantic, all was well.

The following morning, all hell broke loose.

Chapter Thirty-two

The phone at the Rock, explained Gala, looking absolutely horrified, had been ringing off the hook since five a.m. that day.

Nobody had got any sleep until Gaspard had stormed down in a rage of swearing and unplugged it. When it had finally been plugged back in, every time they went to pick it up it was a journalist called Candice from the *Daily Post* wanting to know how things were at 'Britain's Worst Hotel!'

The papers didn't arrive in Mure until the day after publication, it taking that long to get them up there, but Flora, completely confused, opened them up online and was astounded by what she saw.

'McFAWLTY TOWERS!' screamed the headline, with a freeze-frame of Gaspard tripping over a dog and a plate in the air.

'Scotland's wackiest hotel,' the story went on. 'Left by eccentric, flamboyant billionaire . . .'

'FLAMBOYANT!'

Fintan marched into the Rock, his face absolutely puce. 'FLAMBOYANT! *FLAMBOYANT!* You know what that means?'

Flora patted him on the shoulder, but that didn't help.

'They mean gay! They're calling him a laughing stock! And me! We're laughing stocks to them! Those ... those utter bastards!'

'I know,' said Flora. 'I don't suppose ... it *might* be good publicity for us.'

'"Britain's worst restaurant"?' said Fintan. 'Run by fairies. How's that going to work? Oh, screw it. I'm going to shut it down.'

'But Colton wanted you to run it.'

'I don't care what he wanted,' said Fintan, his face white with fury. 'I don't care! I hate this and I hate them and I don't want pricks coming up to look at our "eccentric" hotel and I am going back to the farm and I am going to make cheese and be miserable and everyone else can just *fuck off.*'

Flora gazed after him in despair, quickly followed by the anxious faces of Isla and Gala peering out at her from reception.

'Does this mean we're going to lose our jobs?' Isla asked tentatively.

'I don't know,' said Flora miserably. 'I'm sure he'll calm down. It'll be fine.'

She was too cross to go and find Iona straightaway, who anyway was hiding out in her bedroom and refusing to come out from underneath the blankets. Her parents, not social media users, were completely confused. She had let her phone die because she couldn't bear the constant *beep beep beep* of more and more and more incoming messages and it growing hot in her hand but she knew she had to turn it back on because otherwise she would just be scaring her friends and then they'd start coming round and then things really would get bad. It was meant to be funny and make them popular! It wasn't meant to be 'THE WORST HOTEL ON EARTH'.

She plugged the phone in but still left it on the other side of the room, too afraid to touch it, like a spider or a red-hot poker.

Flora stalked into the Seaside Kitchen, looking for Iona. She did not get angry very often; it wasn't really in her make-up. But she was unutterably furious. Every single table in the café fell silent as she entered, which gave her a pretty good idea what they'd all been talking about.

'Where is she?' she hissed to Malik, who glanced up at her, startled.

'She hasn't come in,' muttered Malik.

'Hasn't she?' said Flora. 'Well, I can't say I'm surprised.'

'She texted me to say sorry to you.'

Flora looked squarely at Malik. 'Do you think that's how apologies work?'

'No.'

'Neither do I. Tell her to get down here.'

Twenty minutes later, a bedraggled Iona in a holey pair of jeans and a farm jumper so threadbare that it absolutely begged for sympathy emerged round the side entrance through the fire door in the back kitchen where Flora was making angry scones with chilli and Szechuan pepper.

'I'm not sure those will sell,' said Iona softly.

'Oh well, obviously you're the marketing guru,' said Flora. Iona's eyes were red. The girl was so young. Flora almost relented.

'What were you *thinking*?'

'You said get on the Instagram!'

'To make us look beautiful and wonderful. Which we are!'

'I posted loads of those too!' said Iona, pulling out her phone and showing Flora the many lovely shots – the Endless Beach in a ravishing pink sunset, the bobbing red and blue fishing boats, a heavily filtered shot of the Harbour's Rest hotel which made it look bleached out and charming rather than dilapidated.

'And did people share those?'

'Um ... not so much ...' Iona's voice trailed off.

'Why didn't you ask me if you could post it?'

'You said post stuff!'

'Iona! I have had twenty-five journalists on the phone this morning, every single last one of them asking to be comped for bloody Christmas week!'

'Well, that could be good,' said Iona. 'Maybe?'

'They want to make us a laughing stock,' said Flora. Her heart was dropping. Everything they had worked for. Everything that was Colton's legacy. 'We already are,' she added, and picked up the phone, listened for a second, then cursed roundly.

'And now our chef's disappeared,' she said.

'I'm sorry,' said Iona, cringing.

Flora took a deep breath.

'It's not all your fault,' she allowed finally. 'But Christ. What a mess.'

Chapter Thirty-three

Back at the hotel, Konstantin had wandered down into the lobby to see what was up. Phoneless, he knew nothing about what had happened. But he was still amazed. For starters, nobody had knocked at his door that morning and it wasn't a Sunday so he had absolutely no clue why he wasn't in the kitchen peeling potatoes and the skin off his knuckles while also getting yelled at.

Down in the lobby, Gala was still desperately trying to answer the telephones while Isla was standing nearby, looking concerned.

He frowned.

'There has been a nuclear attack,' he said to her. 'Everyone is dead from all the zombies. We are the only people left on earth.'

She looked at him.

'What?' he said. 'Come on, it would be cool.'

'Zombies would be cool?'

'Sorry, it's just most Scottish people ... maybe it's the lack of sunlight ...'

'Stop it! You're being so rude!'

He liked seeing the dimples come out on her face though. It felt as if ... well, to make her smile when at first she would barely look at him ... without impressing her or showing off ... Goodness, he'd been in this awful uniform the entire time. It was undeniably a nice feeling.

Even so, there was no doubt the hotel was very eerie without the usual clatter from the kitchens. Now Gala had unplugged the phone again to stop newspapers getting on to them, so there wasn't even a ring or a conversation to be had. The receptionist headed out, muttering mutinously about this not being what Uncle Mark had signed her up for.

Isla tried to explain the situation to Konstantin after she'd gone, but he wasn't really listening. Instead, he looked at her slyly.

'What?' she said.

'There's nobody here.'

'So?'

In response, he ran to the large brass baggage holder and jumped on it, then pushed himself off and glided across the wooden foyer floor.

'I've always wanted to do this!' he said, beaming. 'Come on, jump on!'

'Oh no, I couldn't,' said Isla.

'Of course you could! You're far too well behaved! I bet you never got into trouble at school or anything.'

Isla blushed. He was absolutely correct.

Konstantin came to a stop, whizzing the holder halfway round right in front of her, then jumped off.

'Come on! Your carriage, milady.'

'You are being ridiculous!'

'Quick! Quick! I can't hold the horses.'

Giggling helplessly, Isla accepted his outstretched hand up onto the holder.

'Hold on tight!'

And he rushed her across the smooth floor at high speed, then twirled her around just as she was about to hit the wall, while she shrieked with laughter, her face pink, and he reflected again how pretty she looked when she smiled. Her curly hair flew out behind her in a sheet as he made giddy-up noises and started galloping for the door ... which was where they came face to face with a very stony-looking Fintan who had been shaken by the horrific amount of social media abuse that morning. It didn't help either that he was still hardly sleeping, and so was now in an even more filthy mood about it and woe betide anyone who got in his way.

Chapter Thirty-four

'What the *hell* are you two doing?' Fintan screamed. Konstantin, who was by now towing the cart behind him, came to a halt in surprise, causing Isla to fall forwards.

Instinctively, Konstantin caught her and she found herself, equally surprised, in his arms. He held her tight just for an instant, and she felt her face grow even hotter, if that were even possible. He was tall and lean; not skinny, just slender. They were all like that, those Scandis, weren't they? she found herself thinking, then blushed even harder as his long hand brushed her waist as they both squirmed to stand upright in front of Fintan's undeniable fury.

'What the fuck is this supposed to be? A crèche? Toytown?'

Both of them stared at the floor.

'You know we're an international laughing stock?'

'Oh, it can't be that bad, man,' said Konstantin.

Konstantin still didn't have a phone so wasn't entirely clear what was going on. Even though he'd been there a month and had earned enough to get one sent from the mainland now, something strange had happened; he'd found himself not actively minding too much.

It was funny because, even though he thought of himself as someone who could take or leave social media, he realised just how much he'd used it or been on it. And, conversely, how relaxing it was not to be on it. He was, he'd realised, sleeping better since he'd come here. Something to do with hard work, he supposed, and getting up early and no booze (unless Gaspard was feeling generous), and somehow being away from everything, including the fun, also kept him away from the other things too: the empty echoing corridors of the palace, the constant sense of someone missing, the wasted mornings and pointless days, the bored indulgences; the rooms where his mother had used to walk.

It was the first time truly that he had any distance from everything, and he finally had a little time and space to himself. Not being online; not playing with his friends or tearing things up. Just a little time to contemplate the world, and a little discipline. He had found an old book in the library about wintering in the South Pole, and was engrossed in it, feeling sometimes that the person's experience wasn't massively different from his own. Peace, quiet, dark and contemplation.

So he wasn't really taking in what Fintan was saying.

But Isla . . . How pretty she had looked, he thought again, when she laughed. How soft she had felt in his arms. She was now looking absolutely terrified at the prospect of getting into trouble. It made her seem very young.

Fintan pulled out his iPad and set it up on reception, then showed them the news headlines.

Isla's knees trembled. This was awful.

Konstantin threw back his head and burst out laughing. She looked at him.

'Oh, come on,' he said. 'This will be great for business.'

'Being the worst hotel in Britain?'

'Having a very handsome dog!'

He frowned suddenly.

'What?'

'How many shares?'

It was, he had just realised, not impossible that someone he knew had seen it. Seen him. Oh well. That wouldn't mean anything, would it? Or would it?

'Forty thousand,' said Isla in awe. 'Oh my God!'

'Don't plug the phone back in,' said Fintan. 'But bloody well start behaving like professionals.'

'We're pot washers,' said Konstantin.

'I'm a junior kitchen manager!' retorted Isla, suddenly aware she sounded exactly like her mother.

Fintan ignored her.

'Well, professional pot-washers then, for Christ's sake. It's not difficult. Where's Gaspard?'

It was the first time Konstantin had realised there was no tell-tale smell of something delicious – slowly caramelising onions or fresh roasted garlic – emanating from the kitchen.

'Did you even think to look for him?' stormed Fintan. If he had been disenchanted and sad and fed up with the hotel before all this, well, now he outright hated the entire enterprise.

As the two of them shrugged sheepishly, he ordered them into the kitchen to clean up, and stormed off in search of his chef.

Chapter Thirty-five

Gaspard wasn't in his room or the library or any of the rooms of the hotel at all. Fintan sighed. Oh God, he couldn't lose his temperamental chef. Not with two weeks to go before they opened, and now with the eyes of the world on them. He couldn't get over what a stupid idea the Instagramming had been and couldn't believe he'd signed off on it.

He pulled on his hat and headed out into a wild windy day, utterly despondent. All of Colton's dreams, all of everything he'd invested in this land he loved so much – he'd entrusted it to Fintan but he'd mooched around being depressed and ignoring the business and now it was all going to be ruined because he'd just been too damn sad to do it properly.

Which made him feel even worse than he did before.

Outside, he was fully at the mercy of the elements, and the weather reflected his mood. There was absolutely no difference between sky and sea at all; everything was a tempest in grey and steely blue, the line of the horizon merely a suggestion. No ships were to be seen, just a simple single spiralling world of ferocious north Atlantic fury, the hills and the crags equally grey as the spray hit them. Gulls and terns huddled together against the tempestuous fury as Fintan walked over to the tiny pier, where seals splashed around in the shallow water, barking like dogs and looking excited at the influx of new creatures and fish the storm would land them.

Fintan ignored them. Where would Gaspard be? Propping up a corner of the Harbour's Rest was entirely possible, if Inge-Britt were even awake.

Burying his hands in his Arctic overcoat, Fintan headed slowly against the wind in the direction of the Endless Beach. Nobody would be crazy enough to go out on a day like this, surely. But then who could predict Gaspard's mood? Fintan decided to take the long way round, try and work out a little of his panic and bad temper, and hopefully by the time he reached the Harbour's Rest he would have calmed down sufficiently not to carry on yelling at everyone. He was so tired, so very, very, very tired of being so angry, of being so sad, of being so lonely.

* ❄

Fintan made out the figure from afar; it was the only black shape in the white sand with the grey sky and sea swirling around it. With the heavy hail and rain, it was as filthy a day as could be imagined. He stepped forwards a little, then a little more. The figure was trying to light a cigarette, an absurdly futile task on a day like this, or in fact on quite a lot of days on the Endless

Beach. He was cowering behind a sand dune, but it didn't seem to be doing much good. Fintan watched him. He was absolutely furious, it was clear, even from a distance, flicking angrily at his Zippo and kicking the sand in dismay.

He moved forwards. As soon as Gaspard spotted Fintan, he started screaming at him, firstly in French, then as he grew closer in English.

'What the 'ell have you done? What is this nonsense? You breeng me here; you breeng me to this place in the meedle of nowhere, and I cook for you and want to make things nice for you and you make me look eediot, eediot in front of whole world, thees is funny for you? Thees is a joke with all your friends: watch, Gaspard, 'e fall over now, is this funny? Is it?'

'It's not at all funny,' shouted Fintan back, still cross himself despite the walk. 'You think I wanted this shit to happen?'

He kicked furiously at the dancing sand around his shoes.

'You think I wanted *any* of this shit to happen? None of this! I didn't want any of this! I don't want any of this.'

Both of them this time were panting from the exertion of shouting in the pouring rain and howling gale and against the sound of the crashing waves on the shore of the Endless Beach.

'I don't want any of this.'

'Any of this?' echoed Gaspard suddenly, a taut strained look on his face, his wiry body long and braced against the wind.

And the next second they were kissing fiercely, passionately, the turmoil of the storm's hysteria reflecting their own.

Chapter Thirty-six

Saif Hassan was hurrying a sandwich in his office. It was a miserable day and he'd promised to make house calls rather than risk his older patients catching pneumonia marching over the ben to his surgery. Nevertheless, he checked his Facebook as usual. He was not a social media user and did not post pictures or forward inspirational memes or like other people's pictures of their dogs. He was simply there in case.

It was ritualistic now, just going through the motions. He had his old Syrian mobile number, still paid up and available, a dusty, ridiculous old outdated BlackBerry. It never rang. And he still had his Facebook account, with a picture of him and Amena on their wedding day as his profile and nothing else. He had absolutely no idea how to source the information as to how many times his profile had been viewed, which was lucky, as Lorna had clicked on it and stared at that photo more times than she would ever have admitted to anyone under torture.

Today, there was something. From someone he did not know. In Arabic. That was nothing particularly unusual.

Of course, it could be anything. A scam. Someone trying to rip him off, either personally or automatically: there were people who targeted clearly Arabic names in Western countries, making promises about finding relatives or tracking down bank accounts or moving money or all sorts of nefarious things. It could be any of those.

Or it could be something else. The avatar of the sender was the little Saudi Arabian Temsa7 puppet crocodile. Well, he was quite a famous crocodile. Anyone could have one of those.

But there was something about this one though. It was the favourite video of the boys when they were little. Their very favourite thing.

With shaking hands, Saif clicked on the link. His heart fell. Yup, just more spam, like it always was. GET BEST PRICE! it said. EVERYTHING HEART DESIRE PAGE! FOR NOTHING! NIZ!!! 43!!!!!

That was all. Saif looked at it. Just flotsam, floating through the internet, looking to snag the unwary, nothing out of order. The same as any other day.

But it felt different. It really felt different.

Niz, he thought suddenly, rubbing his beard. That didn't mean 'nothing'. Not in any language. And why would you put '43' next to it?

Something stirred. He remembered the book of Qabbani poetry they had had in their little apartment in Damascus. Of course, he did not have it now, but the internet could be a wonderful thing. He downloaded the edition he could find and stumbled to the page he thought would be nearest to 43 in the original text.

And, suddenly, there it was. One stanza, all alone.

لأن حبي لك أعلى من الكلمات ، فقد قررت الصمت

Because my love for you is higher than words, I have decided to fall silent.

He started. And stared. For a long time.

He wrote a note asking if it was her and sent it.

Nothing.

The next day, he tried something else and sent a poem. Then a code.

Still he received no reply.

Finally, in absolute desperation, he wrote to her straight out begging and asking her when she could come and what she would do.

The next time he opened his computer, with trembling fingers, the account had gone, vanished for ever, and it didn't matter how many times he logged on, how long he lay awake torturing himself wondering if perhaps it had indeed been a mistake, that he had been replying to spam, to some bot, that it was all a coincidence and nothing more.

Chapter Thirty-seven

The papers were still bad, the Rock's social media was still a mess and it seemed that the world was looking at them suspiciously. But to the kitchen's surprise, the following day the storm had broken, and Gaspard turned up in a ridiculously mellow mood that nobody understood in the slightest (although no one was complaining).

It was as if the previous day hadn't happened. The fight had gone out of the chef completely, the phone was still off the hook and there was music playing (back to terrible pop rock) once again in the kitchen, the clouds abating and the sun peeking through the back windows as Bjårk happily bounced around the lawn.

Gaspard had decided to line everyone up and teach them how to make poached eggs due to a surfeit in the coop.

'And *queek* and smash and in and *whoop* with the wrist!' Gaspard was hollering.

Isla had absolutely no trouble poaching an egg, as their big pans of water bubbled up and over.

Konstantin, on the other hand, was having a terrible time. He hadn't, as it turned out, ever even cracked an egg in his life, something else – there seemed to be so many things – that completely horrified the people around him. Well, in his world he was completely horrified that they'd never attended a state banquet, so there, but it wasn't the kind of thing he felt like bringing up.

Even as Gaspard called him a left-handed moron who couldn't kiss a pig, or rolled his eyes again at his ineptitude as he wasted yet another egg, there was a distinct and definite fact: since Konstantin had arrived, he'd actually learned quite a lot. Not just chopping and pot washing, although both were new skills. But he'd had to launder his own clothes, keep his room tidy and look after Bjårk, who normally got taken out by the staff once or twice a day so he didn't have to do all the more tedious bits of dog ownership like picking up poo. Now everything was on him.

For with all his faults, Konstantin was merry at heart; it was hard for him to be down for long periods of time without his natural buoyancy reasserting itself. Although the worst realisation – which made him slightly coil up in agony – was that all the time he believed he was surrounded by friends and employees who thought he was simply charming, it became increasingly obvious that in fact that was not the case at all: people were actually being paid by his father, or enjoying the fruits of the family's largesse. Here, some people liked him and some, notably Isla, very much didn't and, what was almost worse, lots of people, the entire population of the island in fact, were almost entirely indifferent to him. Back home, everyone knew who he was. Here, everyone knew who everyone else was, but nobody gave two shits about him. It was something of a headscratcher.

So. He still had absolutely no intention of letting anyone know his background, even if his first inclination had been to shout and scream about it and make a fuss till everyone let him get out of this hellhole. Now . . . he didn't mind it so much. And he was quite excited about learning how to poach an egg.

More than that: Isla had taught him – or at least let him watch – how to make pastry, keeping her hands cool and precise as she baked amazing spiced mince pies and orange cinnamon Christmas buns and warm gingerbread and they replicated their menu day after day just to be sure before sending many of the results down to be sold at the Seaside Kitchen, and the rest to the school and the old people's community centre, where they were fallen upon with gusto (and some complaining about modern new-fangled ingredients from people who thought putting anything other than salt on porridge was a spoilt affectation).

He had also learned how to make a proper sauce, and watched Gaspard in awe as he made litres and litres of stock from bones for the freezer. Isla had even let him ice a cake one day, which he made a fantastic hash of. Bjårk was happy getting long walks along the bracing front of the incredibly long beach, and he found out completely by accident that it was really hard not to start saying hello to the same people and dogs he saw every day. You could see, somehow, how this place could get under your skin. Sure, it wasn't Norway, but it was beautiful in its own way.

To everyone's surprise, their supposed boss Fintan put his head round the kitchen door. Everyone braced themselves, but in fact he was almost smiling.

'Come, come,' Gaspard was saying.

'What have you done to Colton's kitchen?' said Fintan in dismay. 'It looks like a chicken holocaust.'

'We are making the *perfect* poached egg,' said Gaspard. 'You will practise too! It needs practise! And a wrist! And vinegar! Proper vinegar! Not vinegar of Scotland. Vinegar of Scotland is for removing of the wallpaper! Here!'

He brought out an elegant glass bottle marked *vinaigre,* picked up a fine muslin and grabbed an egg.

'Okay, begin!' he said.

'What, me?' said Fintan.

'*Pourquoi pas?* Kerry, make space.'

The woman obediently did so and Fintan, unsure how to get out of it, washed his hands and stood in line.

'Crack the egg! Now, put it in the muslin cloth!'

Fintan cracked an egg and made a hoorie mess of it all over the bowl. Gaspard sighed heavily. Everyone else in the kitchen came over to watch, as the deep pan on the hob bubbled.

'You are almost as bad as Konstantin,' Gaspard remarked.

'Nobody is as bad as Konstantin,' said Konstantin.

Gaspard handed over another egg and Isla retrieved an apron to protect Fintan's lovely cashmere jumper.

This time, he managed to crack the whole thing without getting it full of shell. He then strained out the watery white through the muslin and popped the rest of the egg into a ramekin.

'Okay, what now?'

'Stir the pot!' said Gaspard excitedly, handing him the big wooden spoon. Fintan looked suspiciously at everyone looking at him, wondering if this was a joke.

'Faster!' said Konstantin, watching him intently.

'Oh yes, you're the expert,' laughed Isla and he laughed back.

Fintan stirred.

'Faster! Make a vortex! Make a hole in the water,' said Gaspard finally in frustration, grabbing Fintan's arm in his and making the water whizz round the deep pan.

Fintan breathed deeply and wondered if anybody noticed. Last night had been so strange, such a shock.

He had expected to be full of guilt at sleeping with another man; full of remorse. But it was the oddest thing. Instead, he'd felt better. Just – alive. He told Gaspard he hadn't known he was gay and Gaspard had snorted and said, 'How ees these people make a choice *comme ça*, huh? I never understand. Boy, girl, *pfuh*, I like, I like, you see?'

And Fintan did see, and tried to say '*Pfuh*' with the same amount of emphasis, which didn't come out quite right and had started them laughing and yes, it was quite something to be having sex again.

But it was *really* something to be laughing again.

Here in the kitchen, the feel of a pair of strong tattooed arms around him was like an electric shock once more, another physical defibrillation to a system that had all but shut down. He froze deliciously, could barely move his hand at all, even as Gaspard clasped his arm and moved it round and round until there was indeed a hole, or vortex, in the water.

Gaspard appeared happily oblivious to the tumult he was causing in Fintan – or at least cheerfully unconcerned as he lifted up one hand to drop a tiny tear of vinegar into it, and the smallest hint of salt. Then, as Fintan continued to stir furiously, he gently plopped the egg in and they all watched, fascinated, as the white knitted itself strongly around the yolk.

'That is not fair,' said Konstantin, whose first six attempts had gone horribly wispy with bits of unpleasantly snotty white albumen everywhere. 'Gaspard is helping him too much.'

'Yes but he's not professionally working in the kitchen,' pointed out Isla.

'Neither am— Oh yeah!' said Konstantin, briefly forgetting himself.

While Gaspard made Fintan repeat the process, Isla quick-wittedly stuck in some of the good sourdough bread to toast and within five minutes Fintan was sitting, somewhat surprised, in front of a huge plate of poached eggs on sourdough, accompanied by an enormous mug of tea.

It was the best meal he'd had in months. He realised yet again how often he forgot to eat. He was starving, ravenous. Gaspard watched him eat with a look so direct it was astonishing to Fintan that everyone else didn't realise instantly.

'I don't know what I'd do without you,' he said to Gaspard.

'Good,' snapped Gaspard with a smile. 'I should like a raise.'

Behind the two of them, Kerry noisily dropped a ton of china into Konstantin's sink, and the day went on.

Chapter Thirty-eight

Yes, yes, he'd gone off his usual standards since Douglas was born. He got that. Why wouldn't a beautiful delicious baby be more interesting than his actual job? Joel was feeling guilty in front of the computer, as Douglas napped in his crib in the corner of the room while Joel was trying to catch up.

And now he was staring at his computer in consternation. How could this be so *damn hard*? It was a few Christmas lights. But he couldn't find a damn thing anywhere.

He thought about where. In front of the school was a grassy hill with a winding path and this was always a much more attractive prospect. You could roll, tumble or simply tear down the gradient, and if you had a scooter you could attempt to steer it round the worst of the mud on the path. It was a universal option and for years the council – it was private land, but almost nobody could remember who on earth it belonged to – had lit it up. It was certainly too steep to build on so that when it got dark at three or three-thirty, this was the way to get down that guaranteed you would be covered in mud and also your shorts would probably have a hole in them. The rule about wearing shorts to school (for the boys) had been abolished some time before, but the mothers of the town, weary from darning the knees of trousers ruined on the wee brae, had revolted and insisted it be brought back, for boys and girls. So now the only casualties were a few skint knees, and the people of Mure were very much of the unfashionable opinion that you couldn't be a kid without a few skint knees.

Colton, however, had been from the USA, where you'd sue someone for letting a kid skin their knee, and he found the entire thing incomprehensible. He'd also grown up in Texas, where people started putting lights on their roofs and huge inflatable Santas on their lawns, and vast displays in every single window straight after Thanksgiving and so he felt it was a basic human right to have a bit of the same in Scotland, particularly when it was so goddam dark all the time.

So he'd left a provision for a set of lights and lighting up at Christmas – and Joel had overlooked it completely. Thanks to his sad upbringing, decorating and doing somewhere up would simply never have occurred to him.

Flora on the other hand adored Christmas. She had her cake all ready and the gifts ordered – or she normally did. Even with her being busy at the Rock they still had the tree up, hung with carefully wrapped ornaments from Christmases gone by, every year supplemented by something new – this one, from Mark and Marsha, a large D for Douglas, beautifully carved out of a dark hard wood, covered in etched leaves, that gleamed and reflected the firelight. Dougie put out a pudgy little hand and tried to stick the ornament in his mouth, nearly bringing the entire tree down, but it had been saved, and its dark green fragrance lit up the entire room. Underneath it, parcels had started to appear, which were being feverishly policed by Agot, who had to be regularly warned off them, as well as to stop pressing the buttons that made the lights on the tree flicker on and off as she was giving everyone a migraine.

But there it was in black and white: a large – very generous – budget to decorate the front of the town. Which Joel assumed meant the esplanade along the Endless Beach as well as presumably the lamp posts – what did he mean? How did that even work? Would it need planning? Would it have to be passed by the council? This was frankly a ball-ache he could absolutely do without. He was a lawyer, not a bitching ... well, whatever this job was.

He sighed and picked up the phone. Perhaps if he called Malcy, who ran the local council, they could list a stream of objections and there wouldn't be a meeting before Christmas and it absolutely couldn't be done in time and he would have to mentally apologise to Colton but it would have to be done next year.

Unfortunately Malcy was on the golf course, teeing off with some equally fat-bottomed friend, and passed the call on to his deputy, who never got anything fun to do and thought Joel was incredibly handsome.

'Oh, that's *marvellous*!' came the tremulous voice on the other end of the telephone. 'We always loved Colton.'

This was a big fat lie. They'd tried to block his hotel about four times and dumped a wind farm in the full sightline of his house just because they found him American and annoying. Who Mrs McGlone *did* like was Joel.

'Well, I'm guessing it's too late for planning,' said Joel reluctantly.

'Oh no, there's retroactive planning for the lights! We just diverted the money instead, but it's all totally allowed. Oh, this is so wonderful! When are they going up?' Mrs McGlone paused to clear her throat. 'Will you be needing ... someone important to turn them on?'

'Oh God, I suppose I'd better book someone,' said Joel.

'Oh,' came the voice. 'I see.'

'Or perhaps ... I don't know ... maybe you could do it?'

'Oh, do you really think so?' came the voice in full gush again. 'Well, I must say it would be an absolute honour! Let me clear my diary! This is wonderful.'

And she hung up, leaving Joel staring at the computer, fervently pissed off. This was all he needed.

Fortunately for Joel, as his London contacts had predicted, it seemed that every company in the world that did lights was already booked up and booked out. Except, unfortunately, Mrs McGlone had rushed straight to the Seaside Kitchen, which was regarded now as the whole island's own Instagram, and had announced to absolutely everybody that they were going to get proper Christmas lights! On the promenade! In memory of Colton, and *she* was going to do the switching on, wasn't that wonderful? I know, I can't believe they asked me, you'd think they'd want a celebrity!

Then she would give a little pause so the person would say, 'Oh, you are basically a celebrity,' which, to give her credit, most of the time they kindly did, and very soon Joel couldn't leave the house without Jonny from the fiddle band coming up and offering to play for him, or one of the kids from the school running up wide-eyed and saying, 'When are the lights coming? Are the lights coming today? Is it today?'

The next day, Joel headed up to the Rock to grab some paper-work, dodging the Murians who came out of their way to express gratitude and thanks for something that hadn't even happened yet.

Flora had contrived to find herself there as usual – this was not surprising, but seeing Joel there too was, and she beamed with delight when she saw him. 'Come eat!' she said, smiling. 'There is some good stuff going on here. We're going to show all those bastards.'

Indeed there was. Instead of the usual shouting and screaming, there was an atmosphere of quiet reverence.

'What's going on?' whispered Joel.

'Disgusting things,' snapped Gaspard, who was unwrapping something white from a pot where he had his steamer on.

'It's lutefisk,' whispered Isla, looking at Konstantin. 'He likes it.'

Konstantin was standing there, shrugging.

'What? It was just a suggestion.'

'Ten days! The fish 'as been there for *ten days*,' said Gaspard crossly.

'I didn't make you make it!'

'You said, "Gaspard, you couldn't make lutefisk",' growled Gaspard.

'Exactly!' said Konstantin, frustrated. 'So, that is the end of it.'

'That is the *challenge*!' said Gaspard.

'French people,' said Konstantin crossly.

'*Exactement*,' said Gaspard. 'French people will not eat fish that is *ten hours* old. Thees ess ten *days* old.'

Joel stared at it.

'This is going to be disgusting,' said Flora. 'It was just, we had some spare.'

'Oh, it's nice,' said Joel, completely surprising her.

'What?'

'Oh, I was out in the Midwest for a while. They eat it there.'

'Yes!' said Gaspard. 'They eat fish in America when they are thousands of kilometres from any sea. Here, we have the problem. Norwegians and *Americans*.'

They all looked at the contents of the pot. With a furious snort, Gaspard covered the white inflated fish-like substance in a thick layer of salt, twisted it in paper and threw it in the steamer.

'Thees is a *bad experiment*,' he said grumpily.

Konstantin, on the other hand, was rather excitedly going through drawers and cupboards.

'What are you doing?' asked Isla suspiciously. She was always trying to get him to make less mess, not more.

'We need bacon and peas,' said Konstantin. 'And look! I have boiled the potatoes.'

Isla blinked at this and looked into the pan he had gestured towards. He had indeed boiled potatoes – not new potatoes, just ordinary potatoes – with their skins on. There were bits of dirt floating in the water.

'I'm not sure I've ever met anyone as useless as you,' she said, shaking her head. Konstantin was crushed. He'd felt he was doing well. She caught his expression.

'Oh, don't worry – it's solvable. Quick, set the big pot on; there's some local potatoes somewhere and they boil fast. And there's some fresh lardons in the larder.'

Konstantin jumped to what she was saying and Flora gave Joel a look as if to say, look how much better we're all doing, and found it slightly amusing how excited Joel was suddenly looking about lunch.

Twenty-five minutes later, amazingly, there were mashed peas, fresh tiny boiled new potatoes covered in butter and salt, some little bits of crisped-up bacon and some sour cream set up on the old washed table, as Gaspard crossly slung down the pan of lutefisk without even putting it on a plate.

'Okay,' he said. 'I am finished with thees experiment. I am going to look for snails. Fintan, you come weeth me.'

The others laughed and beckoned him back and made him sit down as Konstantin divided the fish and Joel smiled cheerfully as the familiar salty scent reached his nostrils.

'This was about the only happy Christmas I ever had,' he said quietly to Flora. 'In Minnesota. I had to go out of state: they couldn't manage to keep us all on. It wasn't for long. They were good people.'

Flora laid a hand on his arm.

'I think that's the only nice memory I've ever heard you mention from your childhood.'

'Meanwhile Douglas already has a model railway set.'

Flora smiled and rubbed his arm.

'It's okay, isn't it?'

Joel tucked in.

'Oh, it's better than that.'

Against all odds – though Gaspard refused to touch it, like a grumpy toddler – the lutefisk was a great hit and Flora immediately made a mental note to put it on the menu. It was complicated to make, but not difficult, and the ingredients were cheap and local and authentic.

'But eet betrays all my culinary principles,' said Gaspard.

'I thought rules were made to be broken,' said Konstantin slyly.

'*Oui*, yes, *your* rules! Not *my* rules!'

Over lunch, Joel found himself explaining the lights situation to the incomers. It couldn't help but it felt good to talk to them regardless.

Konstantin thought about it.

'Oh well, surely you could find someone.'

'There are no lights to be had in the whole of Scottish mainland,' said Joel crossly. 'Or London either. They only keep enough for themselves. I cannot even begin to tell you how inefficient it was for Colton's trust to pay me to ring up all these people.'

Konstantin shrugged.

'Oh well, in Norway . . .'

'Oh yes, in *Norway* you eat things that are rotting and you screw reindeer,' said Gaspard, who had at least managed to drink the eau de vie Konstantin had found in the dusty back of the bar, insisting that lutefisk could not be enjoyed without a tiny shot of it.

' . . . well, anyway, there are always a lot of lights up north because you know – twenty-four-hour darkness. They keep a lot of spares. We're nearer there than London.'

'But I don't speak any . . . oh.'

Joel took off his glasses.

'Seriously, you'd help?'

Nobody had ever asked Konstantin for his help before. It was a strange situation. He considered it.

'Would it get me out of scrubbing lutefisk off the metal tins?'

'*Non!*' said Gaspard. But Konstantin offered to help anyway, which was something of a new sensation, but a pleasing one.

Of course, he'd theoretically done good things. Normally, it

177

had been Konstantin's job to turn up and stand at his father's side for anything important and ceremonial. He had absolutely hated it; it had been the most boring thing ever. Endless speeches and people thanking people for other things and congratulating them and *wah wah wah*, it just went on and on. All normally while standing outside in the freezing cold.

Now, as he made the calls up to his homeland, he realised why people got thanked for doing this kind of thing for absolutely no money. Because it was frankly a total pain in the arse. Still, it was better than scrubbing – lutefisk, it turned out, was an absolute bastard to get off a pan – but still a massive timesuck nonetheless, particularly when trying to get manpower and goods to a remote inaccessible island nobody had heard of or could pronounce or spell.

Again and again, he tried different companies and got the same results. Too late, already booked. On the hotel computer, he did – just once – quickly google himself in Norwegian. A picture came up of him looking absurdly drunk with two models draped over him and a gossipy headline in *Se og Hør* saying 'No sightings of the Playboy Prince ... is he in rehab?' and he winced and turned round quickly in case anyone at the hotel had seen it. Thank God they didn't read the Norwegian papers. He had been briefly outraged, wanted to say of course he wasn't in rehab – but the real story of course was worse, and oh my goodness, the last thing he needed was everyone to know he'd actually been banished. He'd shut the web page and decided to go back to blocking everything out from the outside world. It was actually rather easier to do that on Mure than he'd realised.

Finally – at last! – he found an old artist who said he could maybe help out. He lived in the north and worked with light and was willing to come over to Mure – at great expense, but

Konstantin never noticed expense and fortunately Joel's budget was generous – and 'see if the space worked for him'.

Konstantin had asked if the space often worked for him and didn't receive much of an answer, but it was the best he could do. The artist insisted in flying in for a morning and out again, by which time apparently his artistic sensibilities would have taken in all they needed to know.

'I need to charm him,' Konstantin announced to the kitchen. 'He needs to want to make one of his creations here.'

'I thought it was just hanging lights on a lamp post,' said Isla.

'Me too,' said Konstantin.

He was much more crestfallen than he would admit. He was used to impressing people fairly easily, something about himself which had somewhat evaporated in the last month, and now feared that either the artist wouldn't care or he'd tell the papers, neither of which was ideal.

'I don't know how to impress him. And he's only here for breakfast.'

'You could make croissants,' said Isla. She meant it as a joke, but Gaspard came skidding across the kitchen like he was on roller-skates.

'You make croissant?' he said, his lip curling. Isla couldn't help it, by habit she trembled slightly under his gaze.

'Um . . . Flora showed me once.'

'You do it?'

'Well, I . . .'

'*Aha!* I knew it. Do not lie of croissants!'

He turned to stalk away.

'I am not lying of . . . about croissants.'

The only reply was a contemptuous sniff.

'Okay then! We'll do it!' said Isla, surprised at herself.

'You cannot pronounce the word, 'ow you do it?'

Isla couldn't believe where she found the courage.

'You'll see,' she said.

'I will see,' said Gaspard, but there was hope as well as disdain in his voice. 'Pot boy, he help you.'

'I'm sure I can do it by myself.'

'No. You watch and learn.' He pointed at Konstantin. 'Or if ees rubbish, you can forget.'

Which is how they found themselves, before the artist Gunnar arrived, up at four o'clock in the bloody morning – Isla resigned; Konstantin astounded – coming out of the freezing dark and into the warm, still kitchen in what felt like the middle of the night.

Gaspard had refused to let her use Flora's recipe and left his own instead. Spread chilled butter. Then roll it into the dough she'd started the night before. Then fold over the dough. Then chill. Then do it again. And again.

'This is ridiculous,' she said, looking at the enormous mound of butter. 'How does anyone ever have the patience to do this? I forgot it was such a pain.'

'No, it's a croissant,' said Konstantin, trying to figure out the coffee machine and hoping if he did it badly enough that Isla would just take over and do it for him. She didn't get his joke either. He straightened up.

'Don't people make croissants every day?'

'Yes,' said Isla. 'Insane people.'

Outside, an owl hooted. It was so early and dark and odd to be in the night kitchen, they both half-smiled, Isla immediately stopping herself in case it looked like she was smiling at him on purpose.

They shared out the dough between them and tried to smear the cold butter over.

'"If anything gets warm it is ... *poubelle*",' said Isla, carefully reading off the instructions. 'What does that mean?'

'It means you put it in the bin,' said Konstantin without thinking. Isla glanced at him.

'You speak French?'

Konstantin shrugged, annoyed he had given himself away.

'Ah, hardly any.'

He certainly didn't mention he also spoke Swedish and German.

'I mean, why are you working here?' said Isla. 'You obviously hate it.'

'Well, seeing as you have already judged everything about me, I don't think I have to answer that question,' he said as they each carried on with the butter, then put the layer into chill for twenty minutes in the fridge. A silence descended.

Isla got up and made coffee. Konstantin was delighted.

'So, tell me what's great about Mure, then,' said Konstantin, sipping the coffee, which was excellent.

'You really want to know?'

'No, but I've got to wait twenty minutes and I don't have any credit on my phone.'

Isla sniffed.

'Well, you obviously just haven't been paying attention.'

'I have,' said Konstantin. 'But the wind keeps blowing my hat over my eyes.'

Isla almost smiled.

'Well. It's got the most beautiful views everywhere you go. It's just a wee island, but when you stand on the ben, it feels huge. You feel like you're nowhere near anybody, but if you want company, then everyone is pleased to see you, or at least will be happy to have a chat. You're safe wherever you go. Nothing bad is going to happen to you as long as you don't fall in the harbour.'

'Does that happen often?'

'When I was wee,' said Isla, smiling despite herself, 'I heard that someone had fallen off the gangway to the ferry and the selkies took them and I was *so terrified*.'

'Did you know them?'

She shook her head.

'It was always someone's friend's cousin who was visiting from the mainland. Then my mum said she'd been told that when she was small, and her mother too, back when it was the old boats. I think it's just something they tell children to keep them away from the water.'

Konstantin smiled.

'What's a selkie? A drowned person?'

'Not quite. A seal person that would take you to play with you. And sometimes they would send a seal back in your place who would be good-looking but weird.'

'We have something like that too! The King of Ekeberg. He hated his own children, so he would swap his for yours. So if you woke up and your child was different . . .'

'That's strange,' said Isla, 'that there's different stories about changeling children.'

Konstantin shook his head. 'I don't think so. Most cultures have them. I think it's how they explained autistic children before science.'

Isla hadn't thought of that before.

'Goodness,' she said, thinking of the legends of the children, so beautiful but so strange behind their seal eyes. 'That's so sad.'

'Well, it comes on at about that age . . .'

He stopped himself.

'It's not always sad though, is it? Just different.'

Isla thought of Flora's train-obsessed big brother Hamish, who

182

had never been able to leave home or really be trusted going down to the shops by himself, but was adored by everyone.

'I suppose you're right,' she said. 'They must have been so frightened though.'

'Oh, I think people are very frightened now,' said Konstantin. 'They think it's an evil doctor with an injection.'

'They do,' said Isla, pondering. 'Gosh.'

The ding on the timer slightly startled them both from speaking about changeling children under a dark and freezing moon.

Together they jumped up and re-buttered and folded their dough companionably twice more, chopped it up into twelve triangles and rolled them, then popped the trays in the hot oven and refilled the coffee machine.

'This can't be good for you,' complained Konstantin. 'This is a heart attack amount of butter. Why aren't the French all dead?'

'Because it's good butter,' said Isla soothingly. 'That's the other great thing about Mure: everything we make here is pure and local. There's a cow, there's some rain—'

'Quite a lot of rain!' added Konstantin.

'—and some grass, and salt from the new local salt pans, and there you are.'

'Okay,' said Konstantin, breathing in the warm scented air. 'If that tastes as good as it smells, you'll absolutely have convinced me.'

This time he brought Isla a coffee, and they sat together, and he let her tell him all about the myths of the land – the princess who stepped onto the iceberg to escape the Vikings; the witches who ran ships aground – and he told her about the trolls of the great dark forests; and the elves that came to give strange gifts in his northern homeland. Then finally the croissants rose up, warm and steaming and light as a feather – absolute miracles – and they added, to their giggling shame, even *more* butter, and ate one which was too hot, and then another because frankly they couldn't help themselves. They were so airy; crunchy on the outside, yielding and miraculously light underneath and the most ambrosial things Isla thought she'd ever tasted. The smell even drew Gaspard down from upstairs, who entered the kitchen with his eyes closed, saying:

'*Vraiment?* It cannot be true. I am in Lyon, *non?*' which was as high a compliment as he could possibly give.

They had to hide them to keep them for the artist and Gaspard suggested they both get up and make croissants at four a.m. every day and of course they chorused 'noooooo!', but they were possibly nonetheless both a little disappointed that he didn't insist.

* ✳

It was fairly obvious who the artist was as he stepped off the tiny plane into a howling snowstorm. He was wearing pink and purple trousers, for starters, and very in-your-face glasses. He scowled, even as they took him to a cosy corner of the lounge and plied him with coffee and croissants. Which he declined.

'I need to see,' he said, just as they were hoping the snug setting and lovely food would be enough to convince him. 'Show me! Let me walk.'

Konstantin put the croissants back in the kitchen with stern instructions to people not to eat them, whereupon Gaspard picked up one in each hand and defiantly took a bite out of each. Konstantin rolled his eyes and walked out with the artist, who spoke little English.

They stomped off down the road together. Gunnar didn't ask Konstantin anything about himself, which was something of a relief, but instead he pointed out various things Konstantin hadn't noticed at all before: the contrasting colours of the little buildings along the harbour; the way the sun moved across the water; the speed of the shadows. He obviously saw the world in a different way to most, and he took his time, ambled and glanced around at everything. Finally, they made it to the little hill outside the school and he stood and hummed.

'No,' he said finally. 'My work has drama. Scope. This is too limited. People will not like it. This place, you know. It is *cosy*.'

He said this as if it were the biggest insult he could think of.

'Well, it's nice,' said Konstantin, feeling suddenly defensive about the island.

'Exactly. *Nice*,' Gunnar growled, pushing up his trendy spectacles.

Konstantin's heart sank. He'd been sure if he could get him here the deal would be done. And he'd promised Joel, who seemed to be rather impressed by him, thinking that he was quite a grown-up person. And he'd promised the kitchen. And now he'd just look like a stupid idiot that couldn't handle anything. He sighed.

'Well, you could make it amazing.'

The artist shrugged.

'Why?'

'EXCUSE ME,' came an imperious voice on its way to school. Agot came out deliberately early to find the best iced puddle, and these two were right in the way.

'THIS IS MY PUDDLE.'

Konstantin eyed up the child who eyed him up straight back. He had the uncomfortable feeling she had the measure of him, after the last puddle incident.

'I think it's everyone's puddle,' he said.

'No,' said Agot. She took off her little fur-lined boots and proceeded to scoot across the thin ice in her socks.

'You can't skate in your socks.'

'YOU can't.'

She proceeded to hum 'Bolero' very loudly to drown them out, doing her best to pirouette around the ice with varied results.

'You have wet socks,' said the artist in thickly accented English.

'Your glasses are stupid,' said Agot without pausing.

'Sorry, she's a very rude island girl,' said Konstantin in Norwegian. Agot fixed him with such a look that he was almost sure she'd understood him.

Gunnar ignored him.

'What would you build?' he said. 'If you were making something for Christmas?'

Agot looked at him like he was an idiot.

'An ice rink.'

'I do not do ice rinks.'

Agot sniffed as if to say *so much for you then*.

The artist smiled. Then he stood back. He looked at the little girl, then up at the top of the hill and back down.

Agot's friends (and/or terrified acolytes) had come running up behind her and the artist walked left and right, looking at them and the hill and at them again. Agot put her soggy feet back in her boots and marched off without giving either of them a backwards glance.

'I suppose they're pretty tough up here,' said the artist, almost to himself.

They watched the little crowd weave its way to school, kicking, shouting, laughing, throwing snowballs, tumbling down, scrambling back up again. Parents didn't need to walk their children to school on Mure, although some did, of course. It was safe and close by for almost everybody. They made a merry sight in their red sweatshirts and hats.

'Hmm,' said the artist. 'Okay. Okay. I can do it.'

Konstantin felt himself break into a huge grin.

'Really?'

'Yes. For the children. Yes.'

Gunnar took out his phone and started taking lots of pictures of the site from all different angles.

Konstantin could have skipped.

'Would you like a croissant before you go catch your plane?'

'Christ, no.'

Chapter Thirty-nine

'So, just to get this straight,' said Joel, who felt a headache coming on. 'You don't actually know what's turning up?'

They were down at the docks two weeks later to pick up the light installation. Gunnar had worked quickly but hadn't answered any of Konstantin's emails about what he was actually doing, or how big it would be. They needed a power source on the hill, that's all he knew. Joel was trying to pacify Mrs McGlone, who was getting slightly worried about what Malcy would say.

'He's an artist,' said Konstantin in the hopes that this would prove enough. Innes was standing by with his truck, as was Colin the policeman, and they watched the ferry dock in some nervous anticipation.

It hadn't occurred to any of them that they couldn't possibly have such a group of people together loitering on the wharf on a work day without arousing frantic amounts of chit-chat and suspicion, and indeed a lot of people gathered in the Seaside Kitchen to keep an eye on them.

'Who is that new chap anyway?' said Mrs Brodie suspiciously. 'I'm just saying: he's a bit of a ride and no mistake.'

'Elspeth!' said Flora reprovingly. She glanced out of the window. Nobody, she ever thought, was handsomer than Joel, ever. His curly hair, his horn-rimmed spectacles, his long, muscular body . . . She sighed happily. But yes, sure, the blond stranger was cool too, if you liked that lanky Scandi look.

'He's a ride,' said Mrs Brodie again, and the Fair Isle knitting group looked up to see who she was talking about, then vehemently nodded as one before going back to their intricately patterned wool.

'He hasn't been in here?' asked Flora, confused. Most people popped in sooner or later: it wasn't as if Mure was falling over itself with different places to go.

'He's a pot boy,' said Mrs Brodie. 'He must be skint.'

'Working his way round the world maybe? Student?'

'That's an expensive coat he's got on. And shoes.'

'Doesn't stop people wanting to work.'

'Well, maybe scouring out all those pots will give him some proper muscles,' said Mrs Brodie, all but licking her lips.

'Mrs Brodie! That's quite enough.'

Lorna came in for a coffee.

'We're talking about who's a ride,' said Mrs Brodie, but Lorna looked at her without quite taking it in. Flora pulled her aside.

'Are you okay?'

'He's been called in,' said Lorna in a low voice. They both knew what that meant. 'Home Office.'

'Oh shit. What now?' said Flora, genuinely worried. Not just for Lorna, her best friend, nor for Saif, whom she liked very much.

She was slightly scared that the doctor would leave the island and they'd be without the best one they'd ever had. It was a helicopter ride to get to hospital so she was much happier with a baby and her father getting ever older knowing she had Saif to call on.

Lorna shrugged.

'They won't ever tell you. He has to go in to find out.'

'Are you talking?'

She nodded.

'Yes. But he doesn't know any more than me. And he's terrified.'

Flora patted her shoulder.

'Are you?'

'Yes.'

Flora bundled up the largest piece of gingerbread she could find, added an extra shot to Lorna's coffee and sent her on her way. Meanwhile, the rest of the Seaside Kitchen was trying desperately to pretend they weren't still spying on what the men were doing.

'Maybe they're landing a new car!' said one. 'Maybe it's a Christmas present for someone!'

'Who for?'

'Maybe it's you, Flora. That rich lawyer of yours.'

Flora snorted. They absolutely did not feel rich. Joel had given up all of his lucrative practice to work for Colton's charities, and was paid to reflect that, and there had been no money to spare for maternity leave.

'It's the lights,' she said and everyone nodded happily.

'Already?' said Mrs Brodie. 'That's efficient.'

'The children are going to love it,' said Mrs MacPherson.

'And I'm going to love watching the men put them up,' said the inexhaustible Mrs Brodie. 'Oh, and that reminds me! Pay up for the Loony Dook!'

There was a lot of good-natured grumbling at that. The Loony

Dook happened every Boxing Day. Two pounds to charity, then you had to run in the sea in your swimming trunks. It had become bizarrely popular, even though everyone dreaded it and there were numerous rumours of pneumonia. The Loony Dook was a tradition, and that was that.

* * ❋

There was box after box, all vast. Everyone looked at each other anxiously. There was also a collection of typed A4 instructions as to how to put it together. Unfortunately, they were all in Norwegian.

'Um,' said Konstantin. 'Okay.'

'Can you put this stuff together?' said Innes.

'I can read the instructions,' said Konstantin. He looked really worried. 'Oh God,' he said. 'I'm sorry. I might have completely messed up.'

He stared at his shoes and looked very young all of a sudden.

Innes shrugged.

'Ach, you read 'em out and we'll build it,' he said. 'I'll text Hamish.'

Konstantin's face snapped up, amazed.

'Really?'

'Have you never built anything?' said Innes. Konstantin had had more than enough of 'have you never' questions, so instead of really answering he got stuck into helping the others lift the incredibly heavy cases into the van – where they all hung out of the back as the space was tight – and they headed back up to the Rock to build it, waving merrily at the ladies of the Seaside Kitchen as they passed by.

The men all met again after work, at nine p.m. when much of Mure was already asleep. Charlie joined them too, as well as Hamish, who was getting very excited about the welding equipment.

They started setting up in one of the Rock's old garages, which was fully equipped with brand-new tools that had mostly never been used. Konstantin read out instructions and watched in some awe as the practical men of Mure started welding and bolting everything together, except for Joel who was practically useless – his eyesight was horrendous, but at least he was good at holding things still.

They had to throw open the big doors of the garage as the object started to take shape. It grew bigger and bigger, and everyone was getting so excited they barely cared about the cold wind blowing straight in off the sea. Everyone had gloves and hats on and was toiling away with stiff old-fashioned metal bolts and tiny Allen keys. It was like a vast Lego kit, and they were secretly all having a brilliant time, even though they complained about the crappy freezing weather and the bloody buggering metal bolts.

Finally, just before midnight, the team stood back. It was done. The light from the garage didn't show much any more. It was completely blocked out by the towering edifice, which they'd had to move outside as it had grown.

'Bloody hell,' said Innes, whistling through his teeth.

'Is this really going to work?' said practical Charlie.

'It certainly cost enough,' said Joel, studying the diagrams in the instructions with some care.

'*C'est énorme!*' said Gaspard, coming out to have a cigarette. It was indeed, and was going to have to be set in a dug-down hole onsite and secured with concrete, yet another thing that was news to Konstantin. But throughout all the hard work, he had translated, explained, made tea and even learned how to use a spanner and a wrench. The others laughed at his uselessness, but to Konstantin learning something else new – something useful, and practical – was miraculous, even if Hamish had to do everything again after he'd finished, just in case something fell off and killed someone.

It was four metres tall – about fourteen feet – and when they stood back, they gasped.

What they had was a huge, beautiful, smooth-faced metal contemporary angel, designed in a gorgeous shiny steel. When you turned the central crank, a vast pair of wings, too wide for the garage, came out and spread for what seemed like miles. They hadn't even plugged it in yet, but it was, Konstantin couldn't help thinking with a smile, going to blow everyone's tiny minds.

'I'm not sure these are the fairy lights people were expecting,' said Charlie.

'Good,' said Joel, who thought it was rather fine.

'Shall we give it a shot then?' said Konstantin, pink-faced with excitement.

Joel carefully moved towards the plug socket and put in the European pin adaptor.

'Okay!' he said, and pressed down.

Every light went out for four square miles.

Chapter Forty

Meanwhile, back on the south side of the island, where the lights were still on, in the old manse, Saif Hassan was staring at his computer and wondering how on earth he had ever believed that he had come to Mure for a quiet life.

There was no doubt that his children were thriving here, even though that sometimes made him a little sad: they could be Scottish now, British if they wanted, but their Syrian culture was falling away, day by day, however much he tried to interest them in their own background and keep up their Arabic. Frankly, he was working too hard and was often too tired to remember so he spoke to them in English more often than not.

And Lorna. He hadn't expected to fall in love. The idea of it was so far beyond his concept of what life would be like after Syria. Just surviving had been the priority for so long: making it into Europe, claiming asylum, resitting his exams, being sent to the end of the world. Then when the boys came home, dealing with that; trying to heal their trauma, even if it meant that their memories of their homeland were dropping behind them like a scene glanced from a passing train.

And now he was staring at something on his computer, shaking, trembling. Because everything was about to get a lot worse.

By the following afternoon, he was in Glasgow, back at the same horrible Home Office police building he'd been to the last time when they thought they had found his wife, and it had turned out to be somebody else.

He had told Lorna he'd been summoned, but that he didn't know why, and she had longed more than anything to go with him although they both knew that that was impossible. So he had got on the plane, and she had gone to school as always.

* * ❄

One of the good things about being a primary school teacher, she'd always thought, more grateful than ever to have the job today, was that it left simply no time or mental space for pondering or mulling over things.

Children didn't care what was going on in your private life. Children had absolutely no idea that you actually had a private life, in fact. Even though they lived in a small community, the little ones still gawped when they saw her out and about at the post office or the grocery store, as if she lived in the school stationery cupboard.

No matter how upset or worried you were, you had to come in and smile, and you would instantly be distracted by Horace McGill's underpants mysteriously appearing on the outside of his trousers after PE, or Ruby's poster paint incident, or getting everyone to put their hands on their heads or correcting maths while simultaneously preventing a muddy scuffle over the vast toy elephant, so big you could ride it, which Fintan and Colton had kindly donated the Christmas before last and unfortunately was so much better than all their other handed-down toys and games that it caused World War Three at least twice a week.

So she threw herself into school life as usual, trying not to think about what was going on in Glasgow, four hundred miles to the south.

Except of course Ash was in her class and every so often she'd look up to see him eyeing her anxiously. He sidled up after break.

'My daddy is away.'

'I know,' she said. She was always concerned about giving Saif's boys special treatment. The problem was, what if – as in Ash's case – they patently needed special treatment? And it was wrong not to give him a bit of extra fuss, even if she was absolutely terrified of giving herself away or stepping out of line. Why, why, why was it all so complicated?

'But he's coming back soon?' she replied.

Ash nodded.

'Soon,' he said. 'I don't like it when he's away.'

'I know,' said Lorna. 'But you like Mrs Laird, don't you?'

'I like sausage rolls,' said Ash. Mrs Laird, their babysitter, was one of the great bakers of the island, and she did indeed make a mean sausage roll.

'Well then,' said Lorna. 'It won't be for long.'

'It will,' said Ash gloomily. 'I'll be sleeping. BUT. I won't really be sleeping!'

'I am sure,' said Lorna, putting out the Copydex at which Ash's expression perked up a bit. When you were seven and Copydex was coming out, you knew it wasn't extra maths. Even a down-hearted child could be perked up momentarily by some Copydex.

'I was thinking,' said Lorna, pragmatically changing the subject, 'would you like to help me hand out the glitter?'

'GLITTER!' Ash almost forgot himself. 'YES, I WOULD.'

'Okay then,' said Lorna, as the bell went for the end of break. 'And, Ash,' she added, as he took the little plastic canisters containing the tantalising shiny dots of silver and gold, red and green, which were going to decorate their Christmas pictures, which in their turn would wallpaper the entire entrance of the school.

'Uh-huh?' he said, turning the glitter containers upside down and back again, enthralled.

'Your dad isn't going to mind you waiting up for him. Not at all.'

'LOOK! AGOT! I HAS GLITTER!' Ash was already shouting as his partner in crime came charging in, pink-faced from outside. Immediately, Agot pulled up, furious.

'I DO GLITTER. I HELP.'

'Just let Ash do it, Agot, please,' said Lorna, who was so fond of lovely laid-back Innes and didn't know quite how to break it to him that his beautiful daughter – and her best friend Flora's beloved niece – was a stealth hellion.

'NO, I HELP!'

She made a grab for the red container, and Ash instinctively jerked his hand back which meant he shook the lid off the container and the glitter went into the air. A huge 'Ohhhhhh' came from the other children streaming back into the classroom, in awe and excitedly sensing a row in the offing.

'I DID NOT DO THAT!' yelled Agot immediately. 'THAT WAS ASH!'

And Ash's face screwed up, ready to cry, and Lorna had to dash forwards to sort it out, and, well, it was an effective distraction. She supposed.

Chapter Forty-one

It was another day in Glasgow – did it ever stop raining here? Seriously? In Mure, high up to the north, the rain blew in and it blew out again. Glasgow was undeniably beautiful as well as vibrant and noisy and fun. But it felt like it was in a sunken valley for ever under a grey cloud. He suspected if you ever asked a Glaswegian, they would defiantly declare that they liked it that way.

But also he had never been there for anything other than fairly rotten news. So that probably coloured things too.

'How is it going?' said Neda in her usual no-nonsense way. She had a heavy caseload – well, who didn't in social care? But Saif was a bit of a special case. She'd managed to place many refugees with other Syrians or people who spoke Arabic at least. Saif had had to manage entirely by himself, at first without even knowing whether his own children were alive. In fact, he had not only managed but was also clearly thriving (even if he would not call it that, his patients adored him and he was a more treasured member of the community than he knew). He was one of her successes and she was proud of him. Therefore, this was harder than ever.

'You need a haircut,' she added.

'I know, I know,' said Saif. There was a female hairdresser rather than a barber on Mure, and Saif had been somewhat reluctant. It was just habit, he knew, but even so. Neda had a neat flat-top that always looked tidy.

'There's a Turkish barber just down the road,' she said. 'You could pop in afterwards.'

Saif nodded numbly. After what? he wanted to ask, but he knew Neda couldn't tell him, even if she knew herself. It had to be done under the proper circumstances.

They were in the same secure, dull, ugly low building, with the same signing-in process and military personnel wearing the same grave expressions. There were the same long corridors and bad coffee and the tedious administration of the state, of inconvenient persons and complicated caseloads, with tired human beings trying to work out a way to be fair to one another, to live with one another when they weren't given enough money or political support always to be kind.

Saif knew he should be grateful to his adoptive country – and he was, he absolutely was, of course. He and his children could be in a horrible refugee camp, or conscripted, or dead by now. But the very act of having to feel constantly grateful could somehow also feel like a burden and he wasn't sure how he could express that. A rich country trying to be parsimonious and magnanimous at the same time was a painful thing to witness.

He was led into a small room and a man who looked like

he didn't normally wear a suit cleared his throat. Without pre-amble, he opened a plain brown file and took out three large photographs.

He turned them round to show Saif. Time slowed down.

In many ways, Saif told himself he'd been waiting for this, or something like this.

But, he discovered, he had not. For this was beyond imagining.

Chapter Forty-two

They had managed to wire the sculpture up to a generator to get it to work, but there was no doubt that it was going to have to get wired into the council main if they weren't to fuse the entire island.

'What's it going to look like?' said Innes. 'A disco?'

'How much wattage does it suck up?' said Charlie.

Konstantin looked absolutely blank. He had totally no clue what they were talking about.

So the next day, while Saif was heading to Glasgow, Innes had gone down and had a word with Colm the councilman or, to be more specific, to donate a couple of very good fat hens to Colm the councilman as a sweetener. That's not to say Colm wouldn't have been immediately amenable but is to say it might have cut through a bit of the red tape involved in waiting for the next council meeting, and a debate, and having to deal with Malcy, which nobody liked if they didn't have to. Sure enough, Colm lent them the skeleton key to open the supply on the promise that they'd do it carefully in the dark and not tell anyone, and that only Hamish would do it and if they all killed themselves they weren't to come running to him. Flora was furious because Innes had nicked two of the best layers, and the demand for eggs in the Seaside Kitchen and the Rock combined was absolutely massive, didn't they ever think, and Innes looked defiant and very like Agot whereas Hamish hung his head, but it didn't matter, it was too late now and this Big Special Project better be very worth it, said Flora.

The boys could hardly wait until dark though. They even (and Flora rolled her eyes like you wouldn't believe) got all togged up in balaclavas and scarves over their faces. She pealed with laughter when she saw Joel with his best Burberry cashmere pulled up.

'You are kidding! This isn't a heist.'

'Legally,' said Joel in his studied way, 'it absolutely is a heist. We're hacking into the council electricity supply.'

Flora frowned.

'If you get killed, I will absolutely kill you.'

'Roger that,' said Joel, looking at her, and she laughed again and kissed him full on.

'What was that for?' said Joel, confused.

'Joel Binder. Since I have known you, I have loved everything about you. But I don't think I've ever seen you have much fun.'

Joel frowned.

'Except . . .'

'Yes, except for that,' said Flora. 'But there is more than one type of fun.'

'It's freezing out there and I might get electrocuted,' said Joel.

'Yeah,' said Flora. 'But you're still having fun.'

Chapter Forty-three

Saif had stared at the pictures for a long time. He hadn't been able to believe what he was seeing. It didn't make any sense at all; he felt like his brain was broken. A part of him thought if he could shut his eyes – if he could close everything off – then this would go away. He could unravel everything, travel backwards in time, leave this country, go home, start over. A cold sweat crept over him as he remembered Amena suddenly, caught a glimpse, could almost smell the familiar scent of bougainvillea, the traffic fumes in the warm night and cooking from the other apartments across the courtyard where they lived, the air heavy and orange. He remembered her walking Ibrahim up and down, singing Arabic lullabies to his baby.

The person in this picture . . . he stared and stared.

It was Amena, yes. It was her. He couldn't deny it. But it couldn't be. The figure was straight ahead, staring into the camera. She looked older but her beautiful eyes were still just like Ash's, the long eyelashes flicking off towards the side; mother and son were so very similar.

But this woman ... who was and was not Amena. She had her arm through another man's. On her left hand glinted a wedding ring, and it was not the ring of coiled silver that Saif had given her, had brought from Beirut, bought on a medical student's meagre salary. This was a thick dull band that could have been gold or could have been a brass curtain ring for all he could tell.

And underneath her long traditional robes, far more conservative than anything she had ever worn when they had been together, was the round swell of a pregnant belly.

He pushed the photograph away.

'No,' he said. 'It's not her.'

'Are you sure?' said the commander persistently. 'Take another look. It's not like last time, when we simply didn't know. We have good intelligence that this is who she is.'

Saif could barely lift his shaggy head; he couldn't let his tear-filled eyes even focus on the picture.

'I do not understand what this means,' he croaked.

Quietly, the man placed another picture on the table. She was there again, but this time standing next to someone: a man with a generous moustache and a small beard. He was dressed plainly but he had a large gun and a sword hanging from his belt.

'This is from a little earlier,' said the man. 'We believe ... we think that it's a wedding photo.'

Saif stared at her face.

'But she is already married,' he said numbly. Neda put a comforting hand on his shoulder.

'There are forced marriages,' she said. 'You understand this?'

But Saif was staring at the wedding photo again and again. The woman in the picture was smiling.

Tea was brought and the situation outlined, although he could hardly take it in, none of it. It appeared that Amena Hassan née Abboud had remarried a Syrian freedom fighter two years after the disappearance of her husband and sons.

Which led to many problems. Not least who the freedom fighter was believed to be fighting for.

'We cannot ... In the situation it would be extremely difficult to extricate her to the UK. In the current political climate ... I'm afraid it could get extremely awkward.'

Saif looked up and stared straight into the officer's eyes. The man was not unkind, he knew. This was a profoundly bitter truth.

'She ... is ... a ... Daesh ... bride,' he said as carefully and calmly as he could manage. The man merely nodded.

'But her two sons are here. You would deny her her sons?'

Again, the man did not speak.

'If you can make a positive identification ...'

'*What?*'

Saif's eyes were brimming over with misery. His first thought was could he go back and find her. But what was there to go back to? The war wasn't over. Who knew what kind of hellscape was happening in Damascus? Who knew what effect it would have on his children, his entire world? How could he pull them out of their wonderful environment, their fabulous school and, most important of all – more important than anything in the world – their safety?

Mure might be small, chilly and out of the way. But, oh my goodness, it was so safe. Nobody would be harmed. Nobody would be pulled out of bed by soldiers. There weren't any, unless you counted the occasional Russian nuclear submariners who secretly resurfaced from time to time and emptied the grocer's of vodka, but Saif didn't count those, seeing as all they wanted to do was drink vodka and chat up the café girls.

His children were safe. What could be more important than that?

Well. Their mother. Seeing their mother. What child would not brave the whole world to be in their mother's arms?

But what if there was another baby already in her arms?

Chapter Forty-four

It didn't take long at this time of year to wait for it to be dark, but they had decided, through some unspoken agreement, that they really needed to wait until everyone had gone to bed and so the men all skulked about, Hamish unable to stifle his giggles. A farmer through and through, it was extremely unusual for him to be up and about after nine o'clock at night.

The great metal sculpture was hollow, otherwise it would have been completely unliftable – but they were still going to have to somehow get it to the hill and set it in concrete. It weighed an absolute ton and they sweated and panted as they loaded it onto the island's only flat-bed truck, which belonged to Anndra the builder who fortunately had four stout children of school age, so he hadn't needed much persuading: it was a dang sight easier than having to fly them all to Inbhir Nis to see the Christmas lights. Now all they needed was a Santa. Politely, nobody mentioned to

Anndra that, with his rotund belly and fine beard, he was almost certainly the best specimen they had.

Isla came out with hot toddies for everyone, partly because it was freezing and she could see that they were obviously up to something, and partly because everyone else in the hotel was insane with curiosity as to what they were up to so it had fallen to her to try and wheedle it out of them.

'No chance,' said Konstantin, rushing up to meet her. 'Stay there!' he commanded, then came up behind her and put his hands over her eyes.

'Don't look! Hold the tray still! You can't see!'

'Don't be ridiculous,' said Isla, but she stood stock-still nonetheless. It was the oddest sensation, feeling his long smooth hands in front of her eyes, sensing his tall presence behind her. She found herself trembling slightly. It was the cold, had to be. Of course, he wouldn't be thinking anything of it; he was only playing. On the other hand, he stiffened too – she was sure of it – for just a second. She thought she felt him quiver, and in an uncharacteristically timid manner, he paused.

Then he said, somewhat tremulously, 'Come on, everyone, take your drinks! And don't let her see it!'

'I want to see it!'

'You can see it when it's ready.'

'That's very unfair when I've made all the hot toddies!'

'I don't care! Turn around.'

Reluctantly, his arms making sure she didn't stumble, she turned around and looked up at him. Her tray was empty now; he held the last two glasses and handed one back to her.

'Can you come and find me when I can see it?' she found herself asking him.

'Immediately,' he said without hesitation.

And just for a second, under the freezing dark starlight and the moon halfway through its travels to the east, they looked at one other, her small head tilted upwards towards him. And they looked at each other, and Konstantin felt something quite unusual. It was, he thought, not unlike the feeling you got when you saw a little bird, or a kitten – something very fragile, very innocent, that you had to be very careful not to touch or disturb.

It was the oddest thing: before now, he'd barely given his sinkmate a second thought. But now he saw her eyes wide open, looking up at him, a frightfully appealing look on her face.

'Oi!' shouted Hamish, and she broke free.

He watched her thoughtfully as she took the tray back up to the hotel. She kept her promise not to turn around.

*　*　❄

They had taken the wings off the sculpture again but it was still a monster. They strapped it down with guy ropes, and finally Innes started very carefully backing out of the driveway of the Rock, the others jumping around the outside, making sure it didn't wobble too much. Then, very gingerly, Innes did a four-hundred-point turn, and headed off, trundling down the headland away from the lit-up hotel, and on towards the village.

Sure enough, they didn't meet another car on the way down the road. One day, Joel thought, he'd like to think that there would be many people coming up here to stay at the Rock, to enjoy its beautiful surroundings and peace and quiet – with only twelve rooms, they would never get crowded.

There would always be all the space, fresh air and tranquillity for anyone who decided to go there, the kind of peace of mind he himself had found. Well. Who knew? And this ridiculous project of Konstantin's might even help. He eyed the young blond man. For a spoilt rich kid, he was doing surprisingly well. His father would hopefully be pleased.

As he watched, Konstantin finally figured the statue was safe enough on the back of the truck and, with a giddy run, threw himself and his long legs onto the bed next to the sculpture, beckoning Bjårk up behind him.

'So long, suckers!' he yelled cheerily, looking very young all of a sudden. 'Enjoy your walk!'

Innes suddenly turned the wheel briskly and he nearly fell off (Bjårk, with his low and hairy centre of gravity, was completely fine), and a long leg went up in the air. Normally, this would have peeved him as he hated to look foolish in front of people, especially when most of him were always telling him how cool he was. Somehow, here it didn't matter so much. Hamish was laughing so hard it looked like he was going to fall over himself, skidding on the icy ground. And, half of them walking, the other half riding, they all made it down to the village, although they made such a commotion that they frightened the cows in the surrounding fields.

At the foot of the hill that led up to the school, they stopped. The spot they'd chosen was as well positioned as they could make it, the most important thing being not to beam in anybody's window all night and send them completely insane.

The buried connection was about halfway up the hill, round

the back of an old barn, so they weren't in much danger of bothering anyone. Innes had already had the hole dug – causing much interest among the children, including many who wanted to bring spades of their own and 'DO DIGGING' which was hard enough in the frozen ground. He told them it was farm business and to be on their way. It being after school, when most children are in absolutely dire need of a large snack and a sit-down before going out to play again, this more or less did the trick, except for Agot of course, who stayed 'DOING HELPING' and shooing off any other children who came by, saying only she was allowed to help as it was farm business, which was actually quite useful.

Now, the concrete mixer was churning away, and everyone was incredibly excited. As well as the headlamps from the flat-bed, they had some storm lanterns to light everything so they could make sure the sculpture was straight as they carefully winched it down, hand over hand, into the hole. Then, when everything was as plumb as it could be, and the wires were fixed, they got out of the way and let the concrete cascade down into the hole.

They stood back to admire their handiwork. There was no doubt about it: the thing was huge. It would change the face of Mure for ever; you'd have to saw it apart to take it down.

'Oh my God,' said Innes.

'The council people do know it's four metres high?' said Konstantin, feeling a bit worried, though of course it was far too late.

'No,' said Joel. 'Because you wouldn't tell me what was happening.'

'Yes, but did you tell the lady today?'

'I told her it was four . . .' Joel let his voice trail off.

'I'm not sure,' observed Innes, 'that she ever got metric.'

There was a pause.

'You mean she thinks it's four *feet*?'

'That,' said Innes slowly, 'is a distinct possibility.'

They all looked at the concrete, now rapidly hardening.

'Oh, come on,' said Konstantin finally, mischief creasing his features. 'Let's just plug it in anyway.'

Chapter Forty-five

'Bloody hell' is rarely something you want to hear your pilot say. Fortunately, it was rather muffled, even in the tiny space of the minuscule prop plane that acted as a rural bus between the far northern islands, with its eight seats and rather rudimentary noise insulation.

Saif didn't need to hear it because he'd been entirely sunken in a misery so deep and vast that the black endless sea and sky outside did nothing but mirror his mood.

In fact, before he realised what had just been said and snapped to attention, a tiny bit of him considered that if the pilot was saying the plane was about to plunge into the sea, well, that wouldn't necessarily be the worst thing in the world. It would at least bring an end to the maelstrom of thoughts tearing up his head. There was one idea so horrifying and upsetting that he banished it from his mind immediately, astounded.

But he had thought it nonetheless.

He wrenched his mind away from all the dark thoughts swirling inside him, and blinked several times.

They were descending which meant that they were nearly here. The tiny airstrip in Mure was manned by a husband and wife team who also ran the post office, so there was absolutely nothing they didn't know about every single soul on the island.

Normally, from the left-hand set of portholes you saw exactly what you'd expect to see – a tiny mound, like an extenuated comma in shape, with lighthouses dotted all round it to protect passing shipping, and lights clustered on the whole on the south-east corner, where the village was, tiny pinpricks of warmth in a vast dark ocean, homely and comforting. It was somehow a tiny bit awe-inspiring the way human beings could thrive and prosper so far away on such a tiny spot of land, so far out at sea.

But tonight it wasn't like that. It wasn't like that at all. Just behind the main streets, on the hill that led to the school was ... Well, what the hell was that?

Saif and the other travellers, a birdwatching couple from Nova Scotia who had excitedly tried to engage him in Gaelic, and a young smartly dressed woman on her own, all peered out of the left-hand side of the plane until the co-pilot came back and told them to stop craning on one side and balance it up again.

'*Obh obh!*' said the older woman, and Saif could kind of see her point: it looked like the island was on fire. A great big shaft of light was beaming straight up in the air, leading down to a vast white shape below.

'Is that hazardous?' he asked the co-pilot, who frowned.

'Well ... it's *vulgar*.'

Saif stared at it. He had been lost in contemplation, trying to remember every single word of every bit of the conversation back in Glasgow.

'Why hasn't she been in touch?' he had said chokingly. 'I still have the same number. I'm on Facebook. I'm on Red Cross and Red Crescent.'

The man had looked strained.

'There might be a few reasons,' he said awkwardly. 'If she's in a refugee camp, she may not have access.'

'Anyone can borrow a phone.'

'She may ... Her husband may not allow her access.'

Saif's eyes squeezed together.

'Who would not let her contact her own children?'

'Someone who did not want her to have had another family,' said the man kindly but plainly.

Saif shook his head.

'Or,' said the man, 'she understands the situation all too well and doesn't want to make life difficult for you.'

Saif frowned.

'What do you mean?' he said. And then he looked up. 'I got a strange message that didn't ... I thought it might just be coincidence.'

He explained and the man shrugged.

'Well, she knows the status of jihadi brides in the West. She knows that it would be nothing other than disruptive to you. That the British government would be unhappy, would not let her enter the country. May not even let you stay. It is possible she is counting on her silence ... keeping you safe.'

And Saif had been quiet for a long time after that.

He leant his head on the plane window again.

It was – it couldn't be – but it seemed to be a vast angel built of light. He couldn't help but stare at it. An angel of light. Mikael, the archangel of Mercy.

He squeezed his eyes shut. He was a doctor, a man of science. He was not the kind of person who believed that angels would suddenly appear, suddenly manifest, just to personally help him out of a predicament. That made absolutely no sense at all. Of course not.

Nonetheless, when he had left Mure that morning – he had dropped the children at school – he knew beyond the shadow of a doubt that there had been absolutely nothing on the hill in front of the school, except for the little tree lanterns that were slung there every Christmas. And now . . .

Saif stared on, absolutely hypnotised. It grew bigger and brighter as they drew closer to it. It was completely other-worldly.

'Bloody hell,' said the pilot again. 'Ladies and gentleman, I'm just going to . . .'

There wasn't another plane for hundreds of miles. He took a little detour, just to take a look. The co-pilot took a photo, but it came out like a mad, massive UFO, which was even worse. They flew low to see it, but it made no more sense close up than it did from the air.

Except that it was beautiful.

It was visible from the airfield, right across the other side of the island. It was almost certainly visible from everywhere else, possibly including space.

Billy and his wife Effie who ran the airfield ran out to meet them as the plane taxied to a standstill.

'We've had everyone on the line!' they exclaimed breathlessly. 'Pilots and everyone on the radio are going absolutely ballistic.'

'What on earth is it?' asked the birdwatchers

'Apparently,' said Effie. 'Apparently it's our Christmas decorations.'

The young woman who was disembarking started taking loads of photographs. She'd taken a few out of the side of the plane, but they bounced back off the thick glass and didn't show anything except a blur. She did, though, have a sense that there might be more to this story – her editor wanted a scoop on the 'worst hotel in Britain' and in these days of reduced budgets and straitened newsrooms, it was normally pretty difficult to find enough money to send a reporter out. But she'd convinced him that it would be worthwhile and here she was, a zillion miles from God knows where, with one mission in mind – find the worst hotel in Britain.

Chapter Forty-six

There was absolutely no chance Mrs Laird could have kept Ash and Ib in bed even if there wasn't a large commotion about the now awakened town with various people walking the streets at unfortunate hours to see what on earth was going on up the hill.

Even without that, they were never relaxed when their father went off the island, which he only ever did if it absolutely couldn't be helped.

Ash's eyes were looking particularly wide as he ran into his dad's arms. It hurt Saif to look at him. So like her. So like Amena. Ib too. It was as if being away for just a day had made him see them anew: he noticed once again how much they had both filled out; Ib especially had taken a stretch. He was going to be tall like him. Ash possibly not. Saif knew infant malnutrition could lead to growth issues. But Ib was looking tall and strong. Amena would probably never see him look like this, never see him so big.

How could he bear it? How could she not be desperate to see them? Or perhaps she was. But there she was, married to another man. Pregnant. His head told him of course that she might clearly have no choice.

But hadn't . . . ? The smile.

Of course, smiles could be forced. Of course.

And then again. What if she truly believed they were dead? What if she had spent two years as wretched as he had? What if she'd known the boys were lost, assumed the worst? What if she had grabbed at any brass ring of happiness, at any morsel?

After all, wasn't that exactly what he'd done with Lorna?

But he had his children; and if he had not, he wouldn't have been able to . . .

Well. Would he?

But it wasn't the same.

Wasn't it?

He buried his tortured face in the hair of his youngest boy.

'*Abba! Abba!* There is a spaceship and we MUST GO SEE IT,' Ash said with some urgency. Agot was – madly, in Saif's opinion – allowed to use her father's mobile phone and had apparently woken the entire house ordering them all down there even though it was very late on a school night and five degrees below zero.

Ash was already pulling on his fur-lined boots.

'OFF WE GO TO SEE THE SPACESHIP!' he said in a way that showed he was pretending to be very confident about something happening in the hope that that would help it happen.

'It won't be a spaceship, stupid,' said Ib, who absolutely had to be contrary, but it was a weak effort on his part: he was obviously as desperate to see it as Ash was, not least so he didn't miss out on the playground conversation the next day.

Mrs Laird rolled her eyes.

'I think quite a lot of people are going out to see it,' she said.

Saif sighed. On the other hand, what was the alternative? Going to bed to lie for hours and hours, fiercely awake, thinking of Amena every second of the night, letting every possibility – terrible and worse – run through his brain? Explain to the children that their mummy was alive, but she had another family now?

It hurt like a physical pain. He might as well walk it out.

* * ❄

It was freezing outside, a windy night with snow bouncing around lazily and more – much more – forecast for coming in.

The boys were beside themselves at getting up in night-time, long past bedtime, as if the normal rules were forgotten. And how exciting too, once they'd got jumpers and padded jackets and hats and scarves and socks and wellingtons all on over their pyjamas, to leave the house, each with a hand in their father's (normally Ib didn't like being seen out and about holding hands with his dad, it absolutely wasn't cool in Primary 7, but he was making an exception for tonight and Saif was deeply and profoundly grateful for it).

Everywhere, doors were opening as they walked down the street to the village from the old manse, and excited chattering – and some very disapproving chattering – could be heard here and there. There was loads of noise as overexcited child shouted to overexcited child and more and more joined the parade. Agot came charging up to Ash, and they did their usual bouncing up and down dance for when they saw each other out of school – they were truly the best of friends.

'IT ME!' shouted Agot. 'It an angel. Like me!'

Agot was playing an angel in the nativity play. Lorna would like to have said there was no nepotism in it and in a way that was true. Agot was so unbelievably irritating about how much she wanted to play the angel Gabriel that it was easier just to let her – it wasn't a big part like Mary – rather than deal with the aggro everyone would put up with if she was denied. On a very deep level, Lorna knew this was a bad lesson for Agot to learn, that by being a monstrous pain in the arse she'd get whatever she wanted. On the other hand, Lorna had a full class, a mountain of paperwork, a school to run, an unhappy love affair to obsess over and plenty of other children as well as, it appeared, a space rocket materialising just in front of the school building, and Agot wouldn't be her problem for ever, so this one she was just letting fly.

'They built a statue of you?' said Ash wonderingly. He thought everything Agot did was marvellous.

'I THINK SO.'

'I don't think that's you, *mo ghràidh*,' said Innes fondly.

'YES, IT IS ME,' said Agot, with a happy sigh. Then she frowned. 'I NEEDS MY ANGEL COSTUME.'

Innes rushed on ahead when he spied Flora to avoid having to get into that precise conversation.

'What the hell is it?' he asked her.

Flora was eyeing it up and wondering why people kept asking her as if she knew everything rather than, for example, Joel who was standing right beside her and had actually built the damn thing.

Standing back, however, she decided that she liked it. She couldn't deny it. It was too absurdly huge and she couldn't imagine how much electricity it would use – thank goodness for the wind farms – and she knew some people were going to complain about it and possibly the civil aviation authority would ask them to take it down.

But it was undeniably a huge, bright, beautiful, shining angel that had appeared in the middle of the village. And she liked it as that.

'What do you think?' said Joel.

'It's insane,' said Flora. 'But . . . in a good way.'

'Do you think?'

Flora gestured.

'Look how happy the kids are!'

And, sure enough, there was row upon row of excited upturned faces, and a large *oooh* went out when the wings were extended.

Konstantin had his head thrown back laughing. Someone had put some music on so he bundled over and stuck on Christmas carols, to play through a speaker, fiddling with Spotify until it was playing 'Silent Night' in Norwegian. He bellowed it loudly and Isla looked at him, suddenly overcome.

She had thought he was such a callow, ignorant boy; rude and snotty and unpleasant. But to build this angel was such an unforced, ridiculous thing to do. He couldn't be so up himself after all; it was just lovely. And now he stood there handing out shots from the bottle of aquavit the importer had left him, beaming broadly even if anyone made a rude remark about the Mure Angel, not minding in the slightest. He pointed out the shiny bits for the smaller ones, agreeing solemnly with Agot that it was absolutely definitely a statue of her. She was wearing the angel costume now; someone must have given in.

Watching him, Isla felt her heart lurch suddenly. She realised that now they were out of the confines of the kitchen she was actively a little jealous: Iona was buzzing around; so were lots of girls, in fact. All the teasing that she had pretended not to listen to, or had brushed off . . . Well, suddenly she felt slightly annoyed that he was spreading it around, chatting to everyone. She was used, she realised, to having Konstantin to herself.

And as she looked at him, tall and silly and laughing in the bright light, as excited as any of the schoolchildren standing around, she realised something.

She liked him.

She liked him a lot.

Oh God. She liked him and his stupid blond hair and his ridiculous dog and the way he couldn't get up in the morning and the puppy dog look he gave her when he wanted her to do something for him.

At first she'd found him pathetic, unable to do anything.

But he had worked with a will and dealt with his failures with good grace. He was improving every day. And he had definitely done this: this was all him. An achievement that was just him. Spoilt losers couldn't have managed this.

As if sensing what she was thinking, he glanced up and caught her eye.

She couldn't help it: she absolutely beamed at him. His face jumped almost comically and a smile split his own face. He gave her a querying 'thumbs up' and she replied with a double thumbs up and got rewarded by that grin again.

She looked so pretty, he thought. Not overdone and Instagram-ready like so many of the girls he met at parties, with four inches of make-up and eyebrows plucked and stupid duck lips, wearing expensive clothes and talking about how bored they were with everything.

She was pink-cheeked and clear-eyed, her skin like roses, her lovely thick dark hair blowing around her, and her long scarf and

223

coat concealing ... Well, who knew? It would be like unwrapping a parcel.

Even as the commotion continued all around him, he didn't drop her gaze. In response, she took a step towards him. The light was flaring out behind him; it was quite, quite dazzling.

He was quite, quite dazzling.

She took another step. His face had changed; was nervous now. His mouth was closed, a faint smile playing around his curled lips. God, thought Isla. He was so handsome. Had she really not noticed before? Or had she thought, Stupid handsome tosser?

Probably that one. She didn't think he was a tosser now. Not at all. She thought of those long hands and long fingers and suddenly felt a shiver go down her. This was something ... this was something. She was sure of it. She took another step.

Perhaps, thought Konstantin. No. He already knew she didn't like him. She'd made it quite clear. Although ... he licked his lips nervously.

Normally when he met women – and he met a lot of women – he had a lot of bolsters behind him like his money and his name. Most girls he met knew exactly who he was, and absolutely fancied a shot at him.

In those situations, he'd probably be drunk, and everyone else would be too, and it would just be a natural progression. The girl would do much of the chasing, and he'd be more or less happy to go along with it. For a little while at least.

This was different, and so very new and strange.

He was standing in front of Isla with nothing – a kitchen boy, really, with no name and no money and not much except a dog who seemed to layer mud wherever he went. He hadn't been charming with her, or deliberately flirtatious. Quite the opposite.

She knew him. She hadn't liked him ... at first. But now ... here she was, stepping forwards towards him – and he had nothing at all. Could he have changed?

He felt a tug at his sleeve and glanced over, assuming it was Hamish wanting reassurance about how brilliant the statue was.

Instead, it was a blonde woman with a pointed chin whom he didn't recognise.

'Uh, hi,' he said, cross at being distracted.

'Hi there!' said the girl, exposing very white teeth. 'I've heard this is your doing! Wow. Amazing. Candice Blunt. *Daily Post*.'

* * ❄

As the children yelled and capered in front of the angel and Lorna started to massively downgrade the amount of her lesson plan she was going to get through the next day, she saw him.

Of course, she'd known the boys would want to come down. It was obviously part of the reason she was here in the first place. There was no point in lying to herself. She glanced around. Flora was looking at her in concern, which was ironic seeing as it used to be Flora as the one in the dodgy relationship while she was trying to be sympathetic. Now Flora was up in that beautiful house with a man and a baby while Lorna was . . .

Well. No point in feeling sorry for herself: it helped nothing. To her surprise, Saif edged towards her. Perfectly normal, just the village doctor having a brief conversation with the headmistress, business as usual, who could possibly suspect? And if they were up to anything they certainly wouldn't be talking out in public like this, would they? No. So.

Nonetheless, she retreated a little into the shadows out of the great light the angel cast.

'Hello, Lorenah,' he said in that low gravelly voice she loved so very much.

'Um, hi,' she said, as usual as casual as she could make it, which wasn't very. 'Has this got anything to do with you?'

'No,' said Saif. 'But it explains all the electric shock burns in the surgery.'

'Seriously?'

'Oh no, I am joking.'

Saif didn't usually have to explain to Lorna when he was joking. Everyone else, yes. But sometimes it felt like when everything was falling apart, joking was all he could do.

'It's ... I rather like it,' said Lorna.

'I saw it from the sky.'

She nodded.

'How was it?' she asked in a voice of infinite tenderness.

He stopped short, realising suddenly he was about to burst into tears if he talked any further. They could not be casual; they could not just chat about this.

Flora came over. She sensed something was up.

'You guys okay?' she said brightly. 'I can watch the boys for half an hour if you like.'

'We just ... need to talk,' said Lorna, glancing at Saif's stricken face.

'Sure, whatever,' said Flora blithely, pointedly looking away. But Lorna couldn't worry about that just now. She glanced at Saif who understood immediately – and could not stand the crowd for much longer anyway – and he slipped away to the entrance to her flat, just behind the museum, down in the town. There were no other inhabitants of the building. Nobody saw him, and the flat was, as always, unlocked.

Chapter Forty-seven

Lorna found him there, sitting in the front of the fire, his face buried in his knees, his hands clasping them to his chest. He looked like a statue: he wasn't rocking, or sobbing, or anything – almost anything else would have made Lorna feel less nervous about him than she did.

She poured them both a little whisky and waited.

Eventually – because they never had time, ever – he managed to raise his head. But he was still staring into the fire, and would not look at her. She put the whisky in his hand and he took a small sip then put it down and let out a huge sigh.

Her heart was pounding in her chest. A tiny bit of her – even now, even so – leapt at the simple fact that he was there, in her room, in front of her fire. The physical fact of him, to which she was so ridiculously and absolutely addicted. He was in front of her. Perhaps this was him telling her, telling her that he had decided – of course it would be sad – that he had made his decision, that they could be together . . .

The fact that this was absurd, unlikely, difficult . . .

Well. Difficult things happened all the time.

She almost couldn't bear it. To sit still and wait for him to speak. Finally, she gently touched his shoulder, and his flinch cut her like a knife.

'Amena,' he managed finally, and Lorna's heart dropped like a plummeting lift. Of course, it wasn't him telling her things would be okay. Of course not. She bent over in pain. Soon, there would be nothing left of her; just a Lorna-shaped skinsuit she would have to carry for the rest of her life.

'They . . . they found her?' she found herself saying. He nodded, tears coming to his eyes now, and still stubbornly, defiantly, he would not look at her.

She stroked his arm very gently, even as she felt as if she was being carved out by a cruel knife to the gentle sound of nothing but the softly crackling fire and the distant 'oohs' and 'ohs' of more and more villagers coming to see the unearthly light.

He nodded, still burying his face.

'She's . . . alive?'

Again the nod. But why was he so . . . ?

'What is it, Saif?' she said gently but firmly, drawing on all her years of dealing with recalcitrant children or shy little ones. 'Tell me what it is.'

Candice Blunt was confused. She'd arrived only to find no cabs, no transport, no nothing except the airport manager who had offered to give her a lift somewhere.

She'd informed him she wanted to go to the Rock – without

228

saying why, which was that she was down for the *Daily Post* to write an exposé on how dreadful it was – but he explained that it wasn't open for paying guests yet and dropped her at the Harbour's Rest instead. Which was, she had to admit, a bit peeling round the edges, and the glasses were a bit sticky, but the welcome from a large, friendly Icelandic girl was warm, the drinks were generous and her bedroom was absolutely vast and overlooking the sea. There wasn't that much to complain about.

She headed up to the scene of a commotion on the sniff for a story. She needed to justify this. One hit piece might not be enough.

It was freezing up here, good God. Her smart London mackintosh wasn't going to cut it at all. No wonder all the locals looked like they were going to join the British Antarctic Survey. The wind sliced through her and she narrowed her eyes. How the hell could people live here?

It was actually slightly spooky, all of them gathering around a vast lit-up statue of an angel. At least, she *thought* it was an angel; it was hard to tell. Modern art, she thought. Her readers absolutely hated modern art or anything that smacked of fancy concepts. If it had public funding, that would probably be another excellent take on things. 'Island wasting tax payers' money on crazy modern art' was definitely an angle that would work with this.

She asked the first person she met who was responsible, and was nodded towards a tall, surprisingly good-looking blond boy who was laughing and looking at something over by the foot of the statue. Her eyes narrowed. He looked familiar but she couldn't quite put her finger on it. Nonetheless, her journalistic instincts were tingling. She marched up to him confidently.

'Hi there! I've heard this is your doing!'

At first, Konstantin found it hard to break Isla's gaze. Why, he was thinking, had he not noticed before? How lovely she was. How sweet and shy and ... just so different from the people he knew.

'Candice Blunt. *Daily Post.*'

The blonde girl standing next to him was looking cross. He noticed she was wearing expensive high-heeled boots that could not have been less suitable for walking up a Mure hill at midnight. She stood confidently next to him, in no doubt she was about to claim his attention.

'Yes?' he said reluctantly.

'So is this your doing?'

'Well, I had a lot of help.'

'And the council funded it?'

Konstantin wasn't really listening; he was looking for Isla, but she'd disappeared back into the crowd. He frowned.

'The council?'

'Yes, the council.'

Konstantin shrugged. He knew they'd had something to do with letting them have the space.

'Sure,' he said, and Candice smiled happily.

'Wow, amazing,' she said, jotting it down in her notebook. 'You must be very proud.'

'It's a great thing,' said Konstantin. 'It needs brightening up, *ja?*'

He meant, of course, the space as it had been before the Christmas lights had been switched on. This was not what it sounded like to Candice.

'Well, it's a pretty dark, cold, miserable place,' she said, looking round.

'Hmm,' said Konstantin. Isla had disappeared from his line of sight. Where on earth had she gone?

'And what's your name again?' Candice wrote it down, spelling it carefully. He gave her his first name, not his second. That was suspicious too. 'Scandinavian? What brings you here?'

'I'm just working in the hotel.'

'The new hotel?'

'Yes. Excuse me, I have to go.'

'Perhaps I can come talk to you there tomorrow? And can I just take a picture of you next to the . . . ? That's right,' said Candice, bringing out her camera. She caught Konstantin mugging, and sent it immediately to the pictures desk. They had people on there who were world experts at recognising faces. If it rang a bell with anyone, then chances were she could figure it out.

Chapter Forty-eight

'But who ... who is she married to?'

Saif shrugged.

'And they think he's ... a jihadi? A terrorist?'

'Perhaps.'

The silence sat between them. This was absolutely ridiculous, thought Lorna. She was a primary school teacher from a tiny village in the Scottish islands. She didn't get mixed up with horrific political situations in the Middle East.

She looked at Saif's head, still bowed. Nobody did, she thought. Nobody asked to get mixed up in this. But war could come and burst through the gates of peace; it could crawl in any window, sneak under the cracks of any door, just when you thought you were safe.

And they were safe. They were.

But oh – Amena.

'Will they let her come back?'

Saif shrugged again.

'Do you want her to come back?' she asked more quietly this time.

He let out a muffled sound that was more howl than anything else.

Lorna drew closer to him and encircled his waist with her arms, sitting behind him, her knees either side of him.

'There, there,' she said.

'I have to get back to the boys.'

'Not yet, my love,' said Lorna, so quiet it was almost a whisper. 'Stay a while.'

He took hold of her hands and lifted them to his face, which was wet with tears; kissed them gently.

She shifted round to face him so now she was sitting crouching between his knees. Helpless, looking into his face, she felt suddenly overwhelmingly filled with desire, desperate to feel his strong arms around her, gazing into his dark brown eyes, the feel of his long body jolting against hers.

She moved closer towards him.

'Stay a while,' she said again, and he closed his eyes and rested his entire face in her hair, breathing her in, trying to surround himself with her, the only thing that made him feel better. She moved even closer towards him until he entirely engulfed her in front of the flickering firelight.

'Darling,' she breathed, and moved in to kiss those sad, soft lips.

He pulled away, furious with himself, with the world, with everything, shaking his head vigorously: stood up. She stood up too, looking at him.

'You can be angry,' she said, their two bodies still touching, her voice cracked and hoarse. She barely recognised herself. She had never been so desperate for someone; never in her life. It was absolutely crazy what he did to her, what he did to her body.

'You can be angry. It's okay. You're safe. You're with me.' She looked straight at him, full of desire, and said what she wanted out loud. 'You can take it out on me.'

He understood her meaning in a moment and grasped her, his arms pinning hers to her side, staring fiercely down into her eyes and suddenly pushing her hard against the wall. He kissed her fiercely, and she felt his long, lean body tightly pressed against her, every inch of him, and she felt herself melt into his hardness, push herself frantically against him, felt her breathing quicken and the blood rush to her head.

Then, furiously, he swore at himself in Arabic, shaking his head, tearing himself away, breathing heavily, clearly aroused.

This was not the kind of man he was. This was not the kind of man he wanted to be.

'I'm sorry. I'm sorry. I'm so sorry.'

He half walked, half stumbled out of the flat, leaving Lorna breathing hard, also furious and desolate, behind him.

Chapter Forty-nine

Isla's mum was awake when she got back.

'What's all that nonsense going on there?' she said accusingly.

'It's the Christmas lights,' said Isla happily, even though she had taken fright when Konstantin had been distracted – of course he had, she told herself. Of course he'd wanted to go talk to someone else. Some gorgeous blonde she'd never seen before. She had scared herself, so had bolted.

But also, the intensity of it. The sheer hugeness of it had startled her; made her run off like a rabbit. This wasn't like getting drunk and pulling a Russian sailor. Or getting off with Nobby Parsons at every school disco for long enough that eventually they were kind of technically going out anyway even if they didn't have much to say to each other and Nobby spent most of his life playing FIFA, talking about FIFA and trying to explain FIFA to her.

This was completely different. He was so handsome, so fun, so full of life and ideas and nonsense. And tonight . . .

She wanted to clasp the idea to her heart, turn it over, enjoy thinking about it. Her mother was looking out of the window sourly.

'Bloody waste of money if you ask me.'

'Well, I think it was Colton's money,' said Isla gingerly, which only made her mother sniff harder.

'You'd think he'd have something better to do with it than wasting it on that nonsense.'

'I think he's done lots of other good things too,' suggested Isla nervously, but only got another sniff. 'I'm going to bed.'

'Nobody will get any sleep with that thing buzzing and giving off electricity,' predicted Vera, who was half right: people got no sleep for many different reasons.

*　*

Lorna sobbed her heart out on her empty bed, once again feeling as if she was born to be ridiculous and to suffer. Love was meant to be something that people simply found, they found people they liked and they settled down. Look at Billy and Effie. They just seemed to rub on okay, have a bun together every so often, watched their children grow.

Had they ever collapsed fully forward onto the floor in despair of their love for one another? Had they spilled a river of tears; or yearned so hard that they were driven half mad by a confused and furious lust?

Perhaps they had.

Saif grabbed the boys by the hands. They were cold and ready for their cosy beds, and a kiss on the head and the absolute peace and security that they, he thought bitterly, had had to wait so long for, that had been so hard won.

And now what? He stood for a long time at Ib's bed, watched the stern little face relax and untangle in the sweetness of a child's dream. Could he bring in more disruption? Another man even. Another man.

His blood ran cold. What if she wanted to take them away? To live with her new family.

But no. Not his sweet Amena. Not his wife.

But she was not his wife any more. And could anyone truly still be sweet after a war? After believing they had lost their own children?

Puzzled, he clicked on his own Facebook once again. He had left the post there, even after he stopped checking it pathologically, religiously, all the time. Why, why had she never looked for him? Never found him? Was she being held, married against her will? It was still there. But nothing more. He pulled down the poetry book, looked for answers, found none.

But she had looked happy. She looked happy in the photograph. She looked happy. How could she be happy?

Fintan lay awake, still worried at his betrayal of Colton, which had happened again – even if Colton wouldn't have minded, not in the slightest, had told him a million times that he was still young, that he had to get back out there.

Even so, it felt wrong. It felt like cheating, even if it were cheating on a dead person.

Konstantin couldn't help it, he was excited. For the first time in a while, he missed his phone. He'd liked to have looked up some pictures of her. Remind himself. But what should he do? The problem was, it was near impossible to ask her to something, given they had to stand next to each other at the sink all day long. What if she said no? Why had she run away?

He was so used to just having women show up like taxis. Whereas with Isla ... She was so quiet and shy, he was going to have to tempt her out. He wasn't even sure she liked him.

Although, that smile ...

Fintan glanced downwards. Under his arm, Gaspard slept the sleep of the dead, a heavily tattooed arm pulled over his eyes, his legs kicked out in front of him, fast asleep and utterly content in his own inked skin.

This was comforting in itself. Fintan thought back to their conversation earlier. He had tentatively asked Gaspard what he was getting out of this and Gaspard had looked incredulous at the question, then launched into a very complicated discussion about salmon heading upstream which Fintan hadn't entirely understood – 'ze feesh, 'e ees home, yes? But the water eet ees *always moving.*'

'So is this a good thing?' Fintan had ventured.

'*Bien sûr*, of course! Day by day, this is good, this is fresh, this 'as clear eyes.'

'Do you mean me or the fish?'

'Today, you.'

And just watching him, feeling his warm body, Fintan gradually drifted off.

Chapter Fifty

The Seaside Kitchen was insanely busy from the second it opened, with the Mure Angel still lighting the dark up on the hill behind it.

'It's a scandal,' said Mrs Brodie.

'It's grand, ay,' said Cuthbert McSquib, whose farm had only got electricity in 2002 so he thought seeing the Mure Angel was a bit like what going to New York must be like.

Already lots of people had taken pictures of it, and Iona could only assume that when it got light there'd be even more of them. She sold endless coffees and made a happy note to get out the angel cake cutters again to make gingerbread angels. She had a hunch they'd go down well.

The Angel already had a crowd of spectators around it by dawn, and as Iona watched it did the most amazing thing. If you went to the south-west side of the structure, you could watch the very first of the sun's rays hit it. And as they did so, they bent and refracted in the clear perspex inlay in the wings – and a huge rainbow spilled out the other side.

There was an audible gasp from the children and even some of the adults who were watching, eyes open. Iona had to yell at them to get out the way so she could get a good shot, which she did, proclaiming herself the 'official photographer'. When you moved someone into the right position, it looked as if a rainbow was dancing off their head. The rest of the front of the statue glowed shining gold. It was undeniably magnificent.

Malcy arrived with the rest of the council to close it down at 9.05 a.m.

* ❋

It was absurd, thought Flora at home, that it was actually easier than usual, in the middle of everything else she had going on, to throw Agot a nativity party. They had had one every year since the year dot: her own mother had held them for them all and gradually the entire village had very much co-opted it as an annual celebration. Flora would have felt remiss for the MacKenzies not to carry on the tradition but this time she outsourced it to the Rock to cater, figuring she might as well get a little recompense for her time and effort given she was doing Fintan's entire job. He had been less tearful recently, she thought, but perhaps more thoughtful. As usual, any attempt on her part to get him to open up or talk about things or plan for the future was met with furious disdain.

Anyway. She popped in to find the kitchen at the Rock for once in perfect harmony. They were churning out scones and

241

chopping sandwiches and terrible French pop music was playing but the atmosphere on the whole seemed playful. She still wasn't a hundred per cent sure they should have a dog in the dining room but she'd leave that for another day.

'Drop them off around three-ish?' she said. 'And please do stay.'

Konstantin snuck a glance at Isla. A party. It seemed like a pretty good opportunity, even though she had been pink and nervous all round him that morning.

Because, in fact, she had been so pink and nervous around him all morning, (although she was wearing lipstick, which was new) – this was also a good sign. Then she noticed him staring at her lipstick and vanished and the next time he saw her the lipstick had gone. That was a bad sign. Or was it? He wished it was just a little easier, like with the girls he knew when he lived in the palace. Or had it been, though? He couldn't remember when he'd last felt so excited, so alive about something. The butterflies were in his tummy absolutely; he couldn't wait for three o'clock to come. His scones were light as air all of a sudden. He couldn't quite believe he now cared about the fluffiness of scones but they reflected his mood and he ran around the kitchen like a puppy when the first lot came out, insisting everyone taste one and grinning his head off.

Isla had disappeared into the bathroom and was leaning her head against the cool wall tiles. How could she have been so stupid? He had spotted she was wearing lipstick straightaway, and he'd looked like a wolf licking his chops. Oh God, was she making a terrible mistake? Was this a ridiculous thing to be doing? What if . . . what if he just wanted to get off with her then sod off back to Norway? He talked about Norway enough, didn't he? He would be desperate to get back there. He wouldn't want to be in a hotel kitchen for ever – look how he'd organised the statue. He'd want to be with someone like that blonde girl.

She looked at herself in the mirror. He was slumming it. She knew it. He was bored, and looking for a dalliance. Of course he was. Then he'd go back to one of those nine-foot blonde Scandinavian girls. It didn't matter how often Iona had told her that her dark hair and green eyes was witch colouring, and beautiful. She was still five foot nothing in her stockinged feet, and all circles from her round face, curly hair, round breasts, round bum, short legs. Her mother had once called her Chorlton, which she hadn't understood until she was much older, but had stung deeply ever since even when her mother had said, don't be so sensitive darling, I'm only joking.

But here was her dilemma: if he was only messing about – and he almost certainly was – she still really, really liked him. *Really* liked him. So what would be the harm in going for it?

She'd asked Iona in several frantic late-night WhatsApp chats so her mother couldn't overhear but of course Iona had a very straightforward attitude to all of this and firmly believed she should get off with him – at the very least – regardless.

'Life is long,' she had said, wise with her twenty-odd years. 'Do you really want to look back in ten years' time when you're surrounded by ankle-biters and your tits are hitting the floor and nobody ever even looks at you and you've got a mum-tum and a long stare and you stay in every night with sick on you like Flora. Do you really want to look back and think, well, everything sucks but thank *God* I never got off with that really hot bloke that Christmas but instead spent Christmas entirely by myself?'

'When you put it like that ...' said Isla weakly. 'But what if he only wants to take advantage of me ... ?'

'Take advantage of him!' said Iona, knowing Isla's weak spots irritatingly well. 'Think of it as practice!'

'Oh, I don't ...' said Isla. 'I don't know.'

'Well, I do,' said Iona. 'He looks like he'd be massive fun. All that energy, for starters.'

Isla squeezed her eyes shut. Even to think about him like that . . .

'Oh goodness,' she said.

'Well,' said Iona. 'That's what you want him to get you to say.'

So Isla had put on make-up and curled her eyelashes and washed her hair even though that was pointless as it had to be scraped back, and she'd seen him looking at her again and now it was just overwhelming. Could it . . . could it really be happening? She wiped the lipstick off. Then reapplied it. Then wiped it off again. Then absolutely fell out with herself: this was ridiculous.

She thought about her mother always warning her about putting it about or showing off.

Oddly, this was the thing that steeled her resolve. She was an adult, not a child. And her mother's rules didn't seem to bring her much happiness. It was nearly Christmas, there was a party to go to and a handsome man outside who wanted to take her. Did it have to be more complicated than that?

'Yes,' whispered her treacherous, terrified brain, but she resolved, just this once, to ignore it. Sometimes, being an introvert, it just got too much. That was all.

She reapplied a very thin layer of lipstick indeed, and blotted it so it was almost – but not quite – gone, and forced herself out of the bathroom and back into the raucous warm, cheery kitchen, where even Gaspard, who was firmly of the belief that scones were not patisserie and never would be even vaguely acceptable and were they a sandwich or a cake or *quoi, c'est quoi?* was tucking into one of Konstantin's, piling it high with local elderberry jam.

She smiled tentatively.

'Okay!' said Gaspard as they loaded up the trays to put them in the van. 'Thees ees a party for tiny children and old people and I do not know who are the crazy people who leeve on this island so far from the theatre because it is 'orrible and cold, you know, it is a bad, bad island.'

He stopped himself suddenly, completely distracted. Outside, without anyone realising, it had started to snow again. The whole world was a blur.

Delighted, everyone ran to the windows.

'Look how beautiful that is,' said Konstantin.

'Like home?' said Isla, a little nervously. He turned, delighted she was talking to him again.

'Not a bit,' he said. 'But I like it anyway.'

'But!' said Gaspard, who hadn't finished. 'It is still a party. Next week, we start and we open. But today, you should be happy and have fun.'

And they all rushed to the door and started pulling on their hats and coats, almost as excited as children.

Chapter Fifty-one

Meanwhile, up at the school, the nativity was unfolding with its usual quota of tears, attention-grabbing and stupefied confusion, typified this year in Conal Feachan of Primary 1 standing stock-still facing out at the audience throughout, one finger stoically up his nose as his horrified parents desperately tried to mime him removing it, a feat which only caused him to root around slightly harder.

Agot was having none of this.

'I BRING TIDINGS OF GREAT JOY,' she announced, looking less like a miniature witch and more like a fairy, her hair blow-dried for once rather than full of knots or grabbed back in fierce braids that made her eyes water. Its near white blondness rippled behind her like a wave; it was a true beauty.

Her full costume, ludicrously over the top, made her walk self-consciously and, having been entirely convinced that she was the star of the show, it took a lot to get her to stand behind and not in front of Mary, an affronted Effie-Jane McGhie. She and Agot would end up as lifelong enemies, Effie-Jane decided, clutching the doll and trying to catch her grandfather's eye around Agot's enormously wide skirts, not realising that Agot already hated her with a deep and abiding passion because she got to hold the doll. Agot had argued furiously that the angel should bring the baby Jesus doll FROM GOD IN HEAVEN? YOU KNOW? GOD? IN THE SKY? pushing even kind Lorna's patience beyond endurance, and was therefore still making the most of her time in the spotlight.

Being at the front of the stage, she glanced at Conal Feachan, shepherding manfully still with a stout finger up his tiny nostril.

'I IS ANGEL GABRIEL. STOP PICKING YOUR NOSE,' announced Agot to gales of laughter from the crowd. Realising this would be a terrible spur to Agot to show off even more, Flora nudged Innes crossly, only to see him laughing along with everyone else – his daughter could do absolutely no wrong in his opinion – and so it was down to Lorna to give her 'the look' that finally sent her to the back of the stage where she could join Ash who, after last year's debacle, when he'd played an innkeeper and Saif had got extremely upset about the wearing of tea towels, was safely playing a sheep. Ib, thankfully, was now too old to be in the nativity at all; he was in the choir, mouthing the words so he didn't have to sing along as he was twelve now and this was patently baby stuff and absolutely ridiculous.

Saif was planning on giving it a miss. Everything was too near the knuckle this year – work was still work and he had more than enough on his plate – but at the last minute Ash's heartbreak that he might not be there had more than overcome his fundamental objections, and faced with an empty surgery – it was amazing just how much better everyone seemed to feel on the day of the MacKenzies' famous nativity party – he had closed up early and slipped in at the back, desperate not to attract attention. He made sure, though, that Ash could see him. The little boy instantly waved frantically, and Lorna fatally turned round to see Saif, then cursed herself for doing so.

She couldn't help remembering this time last year, when they had kissed for the first time. She knew he would be thinking about it too and swore to herself. She had thought things were complicated enough last year. This year it was a million times worse.

She focused back on the nativity play.

'The wise men arrived from afar,' said the narrator, stolid Jimmy Donaghy. Good for him. They were going to get this thing done and dusted, then there were carols to sing and people to gouge for some very weak mulled wine, then everyone could go . . . she peeped out of the windows. It was nearing three thus it was practically dark and yes, there it was. Lit up again, you could make out the top of the Angel's head over the crest of the hill. It was still surrounded by people, as it had been all day. But she loved it. She thought it was beautiful, even more so now as the snow settled all around.

Agot was refusing to take off her costume because people kept saying 'Hello, Angel Gabriel' when she went up to them and this suited her very well, especially as Effie-Jane had had to take her Mary costume off so ha ha to her, an emotion that lasted right up until Effie-Jane smugly emerged from the girls' toilets in the stiffest, pinkest party dress Agot had ever seen. It had sequins that changed colour when you pushed them over *and* an underskirt *and* a unicorn on the front and Agot was instantly furious again at having to wait till she got home to change into her own party dress, which was not pink and did not have a unicorn on it. It was silver and had a bear on it and she had absolutely begged for it the last time her mother had taken her to the mainland. She bitterly regretted that now.

But everything was forgotten as the children finished their final song – as ever, it was 'Paiste Am Betlehem', the Gaelic carol that could and did make the entire hall weep, then of course 'Caledonia'. And then the children, bolting their juice and biscuit, burst out of the school, screaming and yelling and delighting at the nearness of the Christmas holidays, at another exciting event ticked off the countdown to the most exciting day of all, their senses getting near hysterical as they met the snowflakes swirling in the playground as well as – most exciting of all – the incredible new Angel that had appeared from nowhere to light their path.

As if of one mind, they all dashed towards it. After Malcy's failure to get the thing taken down that morning – the concrete had come as quite the surprise – he was convening an emergency meeting so by the time the children got there, some loud grown-ups were already standing in front of it muttering things like 'planning' and 'you just can't barge in like this' and 'completely illegal' and somebody was noting things down on a clipboard and someone else was muttering crossly into a telephone but of course as far as children are concerned anything and everything grown-ups are talking about at any time is irredeemably boring and to be completely ignored at every conceivable opportunity, so this didn't worry them in the slightest, and as the snow came down they danced ever closer, stunned by the Angel's size and beauty.

Taking a detour, Konstantin had been unable to resist going to sneak another look at his creation. He still couldn't believe they'd pulled it off. He absolutely loved it. Isla was walking beside him, making small talk, occasionally sneaking glances at him from underneath her Fair Isle bonnet. Once their gloves brushed in the cold air and she had flinched, and he hadn't been able to tell if it was the good kind of flinch or the bad one.

Now, seeing all the children there, he ran up to the sculpture more or less like an overgrown child himself.

'Do you like it?' he called out confidently. Isla smiled; he wasn't the least bit nervous talking to anyone. Of course, she had no idea how many trips he'd had to make with his father to children's hospitals and schools.

'Now, in Norway we have a song we sing going round the Christmas tree,' he said. 'It is called "Jeg Er Så Glad Hver Julekveld". Do you know it?'

They children all laughed and shouted, 'NOOOOO!'

'Oh,' said Konstantin. 'Is there a song you know that would be good for running round a Christmas tree?'

'There's "O Christmas Tree",' said Effie-Jane, flouncing out her petticoats. Although she was only five, she thought that Konstantin looked like the prince in *Frozen*. Okay, that prince had turned out to be bad, but he was still a prince, so she had decided to like him anyway.

'THAT'S A REALLY STUPID IDEA,' came an angel's voice from somewhere nearby but actually rather more people were agreeing.

'Okay then,' said Konstantin, keeping a weather eye on the grown-ups. He knew exactly what they were trying to do and it was very much in his interests to stop this happening, and showing them how much the children loved it could surely only help.

'Now if my glamorous assistant will join me . . .'

He meant Isla, and he held out his hand. She could barely believe it, but she stepped forward and took his hand, and then the hand of the child next to her, until everyone had linked hands all the way around the great sculpture. The adults were either pushed out of the way or reluctantly made to join in. Konstantin smiled like it was all a coincidence.

'Okay then!'

He whispered to Isla. 'I do not know this song. Please quickly help me with this song.'

Isla smiled prettily.

'Okay! *O Christmas tree, o Christmas tree . . .*'

She sounded a little tremulous at first but the sweetness of her voice singing the old melody soon broke through, sounding clear as a bell in the white afternoon, and it wasn't long before the children joined in.

'*How lovely are your branches . . .*'

'Oh!' said Konstantin in delight. 'I know this!' and instantly joined in in a lovely German baritone: '*Wie treu sind deine blätter!*'

The children immediately laughed at him and he winked and they all carried on:

'*O Christmas tree . . .*'

'*O Tannenbaum . . .*'

Two of the older ladies with grandchildren in the show arrived and joined in loudly and querulously, '*O Chraobh Na Nollaig!*' and now they really had a party. Once they got to the end of the verse, they started going round the sculpture and nobody apart from Isla really knew the second verse anyway so they just did the first one again, and then again as they got faster and faster until they were whizzing round and round the brilliantly lit statue, singing faster and faster at the top of their lungs, and finally collapsed, all of them, giggling in the snow.

Which more or less started a snowball fight, which Konstantin and Isla got out of the way of as quickly as possible.

'I thought you would be good in a snowball fight,' observed Isla as they marched down the hill, leaving it to the parents to intervene or join in depending on personality.

'I am,' said Konstantin gravely. 'Too good. I would kill every single one of those children.'

Isla started laughing – she couldn't help it – as they trudged up the stony lane towards the MacKenzie farm. The van from the Rock was already parked there and Gaspard was looking at them crossly for not being there on time to help set up.

'*Venez, venez*, the love birds, come on,' he grumbled, and suddenly neither of them could look at the other.

Chapter Fifty-two

The village descended on the scones and cakes and sandwiches like a plague of happy locusts. Hot mulled cider sat in pans on the hob, and people opened bottles and passed around whisky while the children ran riot over the farm, barely disturbing the beautiful, sleepy cows who eyed them in passing without interest and went back to nosing about the snowy grass.

Flora took one look at Lorna, who came in late as ever after she'd closed up the school, and instantly poured her a very large drink and dragged her into Flora's old childhood bedroom, now full of coats and scarves.

'Tell me everything,' she said, and unable to help herself, Lorna told her everything.

'Oh my God,' said Flora when she'd finished.

'I know,' said Lorna.

'I mean, that's just . . .'

'I know.'

'On the other hand,' said Flora, 'it means you haven't done anything . . . technically wrong.'

'Apart from sleep with a bigamist,' said Lorna gloomily. 'No, hang on . . . a bigamist's husband.'

'You don't suppose it means . . . ? Does it mean he's free?'

'I don't think,' said Lorna, 'he can ever be free.'

And her voice cracked.

Konstantin grabbed another two mugsful of the delicious hot cider and went and found Isla in a quiet corner of the kitchen. It wasn't exactly private, but people were more or less heavily involved with eating and drinking and discussing whether the weather would keep the boats away – deliveries being increasingly important this time of year, as were trips to the mainland for everything you couldn't necessarily get on Mure which was, to be entirely fair, quite a lot of things. But Gaspard didn't like them hanging about for too long, and soon sent them into the little lean-to pantry at the back to start washing up, and they rolled their eyes at each other but somehow, even washing up, Isla thought, was kind of exciting when it was with someone you desperately wanted to wash up next to.

Isla also thought it was a good chance to ask him more about himself, but he skilfully deflected every question.

'No – tell me about you.'

She shrugged.

'There is nothing to tell about me. Well, I was born here. In the house my father was born in and his father and so on.'

She smiled.

'And is your father still there?'

Her face changed immediately.

'No,' she said. 'He died. When I was small.'

Suddenly he had her full attention.

'How small?'

'Eight,' she said, the very memory of it wanting to make her roll up into a ball all over again. The grief had lessened, of course, a bit. But one of the massive benefits of living on Mure was that everyone knew her, and everyone had known Roddy too, and liked him very much. And she never had to explain or tell anyone why she was so quiet – she didn't used to be – and she didn't have to explain how her world had been torn apart, because everyone understood.

She hid her face a little, carried on drying in silence. She didn't want to see his pitying face.

But when she looked up, his face wasn't pitying at all. He was nodding.

'I was thirteen,' he said, his voice sounding slightly strangulated.

'Your dad?' said Isla.

'My mum. Cancer.'

Isla nodded. They were both quiet for a little while. It was somehow oddly relaxing to be able to tell people who understood. Because most people went 'Oh, I'm so sorry; that must have been terrible' which of course was true but they didn't feel it, didn't *really* know what it was like to have your world cracked in two.

'How was your mum?' said Konstantin.

Isla bit her lip. She had to defend her mother. She knew other people had had harsh words for how bitter Vera Donnelly had turned, and how she'd taken it out on the wee lass. She wasn't stupid. And she would never ever have spoken to anyone on Mure about it, not even Iona.

But somehow, in the presence of someone from somewhere else – someone who understood; someone who, for all their annoying ways, was clearly and very simply kind – she felt something she hadn't felt for many years.

She wanted to talk. She wanted to speak.

'Very . . . very difficult,' she stammered. Konstantin nodded and didn't say anything, waiting for her to go on.

'I think,' she said, 'she was so very angry at him for dying. He died young, didn't leave us with much. And it was just me. I think she might have taken it out on me. I don't think she meant to,' she added.

'Do you look like him?'

'Apparently, yes,' said Isla drily. 'But not in a way she likes.'

Konstantin nodded again, adding more hot water to the suds.

'Yeah,' he said. 'They come out in all the ways they hate. It hardly seems fair, does it?'

'I can't help my stupid dad's face,' said Isla, then laughed suddenly. 'Sorry, that sounded so furious.'

'I get it.'

'Uh-huh.'

'And I like your face. Very much.'

There was a very long pause after that as a flustered Iona dried and re-dried a cup because she had forgotten what she should do with it.

Konstantin found himself staring at the suds.

'My dad sent me away,' he said.

'You're kidding.'

'I think he got sick looking of me. I think I was quite annoying.'

'He sent you here?'

'Well, I had to go somewhere. First away to school, then when I still wouldn't be what he wanted ... he sent me here ...'

'He turned you out?'

Konstantin shrugged.

'Oh God,' said Isla. This was her worst fear: that her mother would just tell her to go. Because where would she go?

'Well, it could be worse,' said Konstantin. 'You know, I like the mince pies you have here.'

'Oh my God,' said Isla. 'I can't believe ... No wonder you were miserable.'

'I sometimes think,' said Konstantin, 'that my mother was my only protector.'

'Yes! My dad, he just thought ... he thought I was great. He thought everything I did was kind of cute and funny ...'

' ... even when I was naughty ...'

'Sometimes I think he liked it when I was naughty. Like we were ganging up against my mum ...'

'Yes! We were a gang and then ...'

There was a silence and suddenly Isla looked at the hurt and the pain in his eyes whereupon, without realising it, he slammed his hand down hard and it splashed into the water and sent white soapy bubbles everywhere, including onto Isla's nose. She looked at the mess for a second and he looked at her, worried about her reaction.

The next second, she too had splashed in the water, her hand sending great big gouts of foam up onto his hair.

Surprised, he laughed and immediately splashed back and in two seconds they had gone from feeling miserable to laughing almost hysterically and having a massive foam fight.

As he rubbed some off her nose while trying to get some more of the foam down her neck, she found herself suddenly, willingly, drawn closer and closer to him, and she reached up a finger to wipe the big dod of suds off the tip of his nose and he took her hand, gently this time, and put it on his cheek, looking at her, his blue eyes full of intent, his hand large and soft and warm. Colour flooded to her cheeks, but she did not turn away, instead turned and gazed up at him, eyes wide.

He looked at her trusting face, eyes which were wide open, and got such a start. He brought his other hand up – still damp, but that didn't matter – took her little heart-shaped face in it, tilted it up towards him as she moved closer to him, and a little more, and more again without either of them taking their eyes off each other. Of course, there was noise from beyond from the party – fiddles and Nollaig songs – but here in the little back utility room, it felt quiet suddenly, and everybody else seemed very far away.

Infinitely slowly, Konstantin bent his head towards hers, while she found herself almost involuntarily creeping up on her tiptoes to meet him; the space between them grew smaller and smaller and she found her eyes closing as she bent herself into him . . .

'Konstantin? Konstantin?'

The voice was loud, harsh and English and they both immediately and guiltily jumped apart.

Chapter Fifty-three

Squeezing her hand tightly, Konstantin turned and vanished into the kitchen, not wanting whoever it was to spot them like that, put two and two together and make . . .

. . . well, four, he supposed. He smiled to himself and glanced back. Isla was still staring at him, a smile also playing round her lips, those huge eyes staring at him. Christ, she gave him such a charge.

Candice noticed straightaway, her journalistic antennae quivering, and she made a beeline for the pair.

She leaned over to Isla.

'You don't mind if I borrow him, do you?' smiling and showing very white teeth.

Taken aback, Isla frowned.

'Um, no, why would I?' she said, her voice a bit shaky.

'Oh, just looked like you were getting cosy! Not surprised, such a handsome chap!'

Candice couldn't help stirring, and she was pleased to see Isla's face fall at the thought of being obvious.

'Oh, I'm only teasing you,' she added meanly. 'It's clearly nothing. Now come with me, you gorgeous hunk.'

She threaded her arm through Konstantin's.

'Lovely to see you again.'

It was Konstantin's turn to frown. They were hardly friends. He turned round to see Isla, but she was busying herself at the sink, desperately trying to hide her blushes had he but known it. Meanwhile, Candice was holding out her iPhone as if she was taping something.

'Listen, I just wondered how you felt about all the controversy about the statue?'

'What controversy?'

'From the council? They want it pulled down? Don't you think it looks like another calamity for Mure?'

'They want to pull it down?!'

Indeed, it hadn't taken Candice much time to talk to the people around the statue who were complaining, and she certainly didn't encourage them, no, not at all. But she might have asked them a little bit about didn't they feel very let down that nobody had properly consulted the council and didn't this rather overrun planning and, well, what were they going to do about it and wasn't it a disgrace?

'It is a disgrace.' Malcy had nodded solemnly, being slightly bewitched by how pretty Candice was and failing to notice that three of his granddaughters were running round the statue cheering and dancing.

She continued her investigation: were they going to have a special committee meeting to figure out what they were going to do about it? They were, of course. The men in particular liked to look tough and decisive in front of the exceptionally pretty young woman from London. Candice was amazed. This couldn't be going any better. Had none of them had any media training whatsoever?

But she still suspected she had a bigger prize on her hands. For a fishing expedition, Mure was certainly turning out to be absolutely chockful of useful things.

'So,' she said, turning all her attention towards Konstantin, who still looked worryingly distracted. Perhaps he was gay; there were a lot of gay men up here, she'd heard. On the other hand, if he was who she thought he was, then that wasn't what she was hearing at all.

'So you must miss Norway living here?'

Konstantin squinted. Why was she asking him all this stuff?

'Oh sure,' he said. 'But it has its compensations.'

'It looks like you're cutting quite the swathe through the local girls!'

Konstantin eyed her suspiciously.

'What?' He really should get back to speak to Isla.

'How long are you thinking of staying in this life?'

It was an oddly worded question and if Konstantin had been paying closer attention he would have asked for clarification or had his suspicions about what exactly she was after. But he was desperate to get back to Isla, finish what he started. A smile played across his lips.

'Not long then?' said Candice pushily.

'What? No,' said Konstantin, and they both turned round, interrupted by a noise at the door.

'Where is that Scandi fellow?' someone was shouting.

The room turned round. Flora barrelled up, cross that people were making a commotion at what was meant to be, excuse me, a children's party.

It was Malcy.

'We're having an emergency council meeting,' he said. 'You need to come and explain yourself.'

'It's eight o'clock at night,' said Flora furiously.

'That's why it's called an emergency meeting.'

'Also, I don't want to go,' said Konstantin.

'Well ...' The man hadn't really been anticipating this. 'You have to.'

'I don't. You're not the police.'

'You have to come and explain yourself.'

Konstantin waved his hands.

'Yeah – no, thank you.'

Joel stepped forwards, along with Ewan the police officer who rarely had anything more to do than direct lost tourists. Ewan was looking slightly nervous.

'Excuse me?' said Joel. 'I'm this man's lawyer.'

'I don't need a lawyer!' said Konstantin.

'... and I'm the lawyer for the money spent by the Colton Rogers Foundation,' went on Joel smoothly. 'This is something you'll have to take up with me in the morning.'

'Yeah, also you can't walk into people's houses like that,' added Ewan. He screwed up his face. It had been a while since Tulliallan Training College, after all.

Malcy looked about in consternation. He was used to being pretty much the most important man on Mure, and wasn't used to being spoken to like this.

'Well, we'll sort it out tomorrow then.'

'I'm afraid we got permission from the council,' said Joel. 'So it's going to be a bit of a fight.'

'You have to take it down.'

'We have to do nothing of the sort,' said Joel.

'And it's beautiful,' said Konstantin crossly. 'You just have absolutely no taste. Which is why you are wearing those trousers.'

This was a bad move. Malcy was very proud of his tartan trews and wore them proudly to every smart occasion, which included the nativity play as far as he was concerned. He turned a very dark red, turned on his heel and walked out, leaving the party slightly giggly and hysterical, the children running about wondering what had happened and Candice, who had filmed the entire thing, absolutely delighted.

There was a bit of quiet. Konstantin turned to Joel.

'Seriously, I don't think ... we need a lawyer?'

Joel shrugged.

'I don't think the council budget could afford me. So hopefully they'll just have to let it go.'

Around them, the party was clearly winding down and Flora was quite happy to see everyone go.

'*Allez, allez!*' Gaspard was shouting, hurrying Isla out to the van with great trays of pans, empty except for the odd spare crumb. Everything had patently been an absolutely massive success.

'Still, you should probably go to the meeting,' said Joel, unaware he was taking up valuable time Konstantin would much rather be using to chase Isla. She glanced back at him.

'We could offer them a—'

'*ALLEZ!*' Gaspard was shouting. 'Let's go, Konstantin! Isla, you can go home, chérie.'

Everyone had gone.

With a desperate look at Konstantin, then at a beaming Candice,

Isla slowly started pulling on her coat. Konstantin desperately wanted to go to her, but how could he in a slowly emptying room with everyone looking at them both?

'Um, see you tomorrow,' Isla said, feeling her voice pathetically weak, as she went on her way.

Konstantin dashed out of the back door of the farm and round to the front where Isla was tramping away down the hill through the low-lying snow. The stars were gleaming overhead and it was absolutely freezing.

There were, to his utmost frustration, too many other people all heading the same way back into the village: sleepy children being carried piggyback, nodding over their parents' shoulders; buggies with babies wrapped up tighter than parcels; some people singing and breath showing everywhere on the frosty air. From up on the hill, the statue was lighting all their ways back home; a kindly glow over the moonlit hills. Konstantin's brown furrowed again. How could they say it was horrible?

But he had to catch up with Isla. Normally in day-to-day life it would be nothing to shout at her, seeing as they worked together and knew each other. Nobody would think anything of it. Already she'd been engulfed in a crowd of people she knew.

But somehow now, everything had changed. He felt if he said her name – or, even worse, shouted it – the entire village would stand and stare and he could not, absolutely would not be able to do what he wanted to do, which was take her in his arms and kiss her till he couldn't kiss her any more.

Meanwhile, Gaspard was calling his name from the farmhouse behind him. He thought about it for a second, then thought, to hell with it, it was only a pot-washing job, and, feeling faintly sinister for a moment, ran off down the hill behind her.

Chapter Fifty-four

It felt all kinds of wrong, following a woman, but Konstantin just wanted them to be alone, that was all.

He wondered where she lived and what it was like, but he didn't have to wait long to find out. Up the second of the high cobbled streets in the village, behind the main street and the docks, Isla, her friends carrying on, stopped at a pretty little cottage painted bright pink, with light glowing in the windows

It was a small house, but cute as a button and Konstantin smiled when he saw it: it suited her. Small and adorable, like a little mouse's house.

He meant to stop her before she got home, and he could see her glancing around – for him? – but just as he was trying to work out a way to make himself known without startling her, the door flung open, revealing a tiny, furious-looking woman.

'What time do you call this?'

'Mum,' said Isla patiently in that pretty voice he liked. 'It was the MacKenzies' nativity party. You were invited! You should have come!'

'Waste of bloody time, parties.'

'Well, anyway, I was working—'

'Yup. As usual treating you like a bloody skivvy. You're meant for better than this, darling.'

'Mum . . . can we talk about it later . . . ?'

She sounded conciliatory and soothing. And tired. He could see what her loss had done to her; to them. He thought of how his father had tried to do the right thing; had tried to be kind and how he, his only son, had let him down. He found he had a lump in his throat.

'Did you bring me anything to eat?' Isla's mother sounded demanding.

'No, but I can make you an omelette if you like? We've got eggs.'

'Go on then. If you're not tired?'

'No,' said Isla, sounding exhausted.

And the door closed shut, and Konstantin turned away, sad for all the little things.

Chapter Fifty-five

The next morning, despite the threat of Mure civil war over the statue, and Christmas being four days away, Konstantin felt better. He was up early, playing with Bjårk, frolicking in the snow.

He contrived to be out throwing a ball on the side lawn near the entrance Isla always came in despite the fact that it was both pitch-black and minus one degree which, if Konstantin could handle, Bjårk was very much not a fan of. Still, he had a plan that involved hot chocolate and some early baked Norwegian ginger *boller* he'd put on before he left. He was ridiculously proud of himself: just a couple of months ago, the idea that he could just go in and look up a recipe and then make it would have been as alien to him as flying in the air. It was amazing, he thought as he had left them to rise, that of all things he would like doing in his life, working in a kitchen would be one of them.

But it was more than that. After a life entirely devoted to

pleasure and fun, with as few difficult or intrusive things to do as he could bear, having to actually stick to things, and get up early to work on dull repetitive tasks until he got good at them – this was all very new to him. There was a physical satisfaction in it that he had simply never known before and he was genuinely astonished.

He was therefore in a happy frame of mind when Isla slipped through the side gate, and got quite the fright when Bjårk bounded up to her, barking in a way that suggested GET ME OUT OF THIS FREEZING NONSENSE IMMEDIATELY. She smiled, tentatively at first – there was a bit of her, once she'd had the dressing-down from her mother, that had wondered if she'd possibly dreamed the entire thing, or at the very least built it up own her own head.

But now, seeing his blond head tilting towards her, she couldn't help but smile.

'What are you doing out here? You're nuts!'

He shrugged.

'Oh, this is nothing to Norwegians.'

'I don't believe you!'

She bounced up to him, smiling, her eyes streaming with the cold. He reached out his gloved hand and took hers, then glanced around in case anyone could see them, something she couldn't help noticing. For once, she put her insecure thoughts about other people – in this case, very much Candice – to rest and tried to let herself enjoy it. He was here now. Wasn't that enough?

'*VENEZ, VENEZ!*' a voice hollered at them from the kitchen door. '*Pas de* flirting in my kitchen please!' it shouted loudly and they giggled at one another and slipped into the luxurious warmth.

It occurred to Isla suddenly that Konstantin of course actually lived in the hotel and had his bed upstairs. They were ... well, more or less in his house. She blushed at the thought of it. Of course not. It was impossible. They were at work. Konstantin glanced at her, wondering what she was thinking. He needed to get away from the hotel; it was ludicrous given that his bed was upstairs. That was definitely a problem in somewhere so small: he could hardly take her to the Seaside Kitchen on a date.

Which left the Harbour's Rest, he supposed. Well, maybe if they found a dark corner, the sticky glasses wouldn't be quite so noticeable. Yes. They could do that later. It was a great shame, he reflected, that they couldn't go to one of the official rooms in the hotel, because he couldn't think of a more romantic place to take a girl, as the snow swirled outside the little dock, and the big picture windows and the toasty central heating and the vast blazing fire . . . a little of Gaspard's hidden stash of Bordeaux and everything would just be so nice.

Well. Alas. That absolutely wasn't going to happen. So he was pretty short of options. A picnic wasn't really on the agenda either.

'Um,' he said as they were standing side by side again, both of them giggling at nothing and concentrating very hard on listening to the radio. 'Um, so . . .'

This was ridiculous. The confident Konstantin of a couple of months ago had entirely disappeared. He wondered for an instant if it was possible that the previous Konstantin had been . . . a bit irritating and full of himself?

Isla couldn't keep her voice calm. 'Yeah?'

Please, she thought to herself. Please let you not be about to suggest that they go upstairs. Please don't have plans for something absolutely sordid and not . . . She was building it up, she knew. She had feelings for the pot boy. But at the end of the day he was still just a boy, a normal boy who . . . well. She held her breath.

'Um, would you like to go for a drink at that strange place on the harbour later?'

Isla could have burst with joy and relief. She knew she was supposed to play it cool and act like she wasn't bothered, but she was so happy, she couldn't keep a thing from her face.

'Um, yeah all right,' she said, trying to damp down her own smile, which was immediately matched next to her.

Chapter Fifty-six

To Flora's amazement, there were more and more bookings; she had asked the patient Gala to go through the system with her one afternoon. She liked to think, possibly entirely optimistically, people could see past the silly headlines into the lovely rooms, the delicious dinners and the fabulous peace of the place. She wondered if they couldn't necessarily remember the story and had just booked because of the hotel itself, that the name had stuck in their heads. She hoped the latter was true. Christmas Day and Boxing Day were full. Then they would close for a few days, before opening to an absolutely full house for Hogmanay. There would be a band as well, and a full ceilidh. If people couldn't enjoy that, she thought to herself, well, there was not much she could do about it.

Tonight was their last dry run. They were feeding all the people who went to the community day care centre – the very oldest residents of Mure and their carers. It was just a good chance to give the kitchen a last dress rehearsal with the waiters in place, and make sure they were good to go for the big day. Flora couldn't deny it: she was excited.

'This is getting ridiculous,' Joel had said as she had collapsed into bed the previous evening, as exhausted as only someone doing someone else's job with a six-month-old could be. Joel never had any trouble sleeping, and it made Flora jealous. Flora never knew how before he'd met her he had rarely slept more than four hours a night, jittery, anxious. Coming to Mure was the first time he'd slept all night in his adult life. The sweetness of the fresh, cold air and the sheer ability to relax had transformed his life so entirely he got embarrassed even thinking about it. Waking up once or twice to pick up Dougie still hardly felt like a hardship of any kind.

'I know,' groaned Flora, staring at some spreadsheets that were swimming in front of her eyes. 'Innes says this should be easy to read but I don't think Fintan even opened the message.'

There was a silence.

'I mean, I can't *sack* him,' said Flora. 'It's his hotel.'

'But you're doing everything! It's not right! You should be enjoying your baby!'

A bolt of fear went through Flora's heart. Did he know?

'I am!' protested Flora, even as Douglas was tugging on Joel's fingers. 'I do! I love the baby.'

'Uh, yeah, I know,' said Joel, baffled.

Flora's eyes strayed back to her email.

'I'll get him in tomorrow. If he can pull the old Fintan charm on the old ladies, that will be good for business.'

The old Fintan charm hadn't shown itself for quite some time, but you could live in hope.

'Have I told you,' said Joel, 'how absolutely amazing and fabulous you've been and how proud of you I am?'

'For opening "the worst hotel in Britain"?' grumbled Flora.

'Oh, that's all over and done with now,' said Joel, putting Douglas to bed and pulling her close to him.

He was completely and absolutely wrong.

Chapter Fifty-seven

Candice couldn't believe it. Sometimes, life depended on luck, she knew, and in this case she liked to think that she'd made the luck on her own.

She stared at it again. Amazing. She'd talked to her friend on the picture desk, who was just as an obsessive a reader of *Hello!* magazine as she was, and they'd tracked back through the pictures, knowing he was Norwegian and – tadah! With a bit of help from Google Translate, they'd been able to easily put together 'Tragedy of Young Norwegian of Noble Descent' with lots of pictures of his amazing castle, and stories of the death of his beautiful mother.

Then, under his full name, racy tabloid-y stories of his dating models, pictures of him falling out of nightclubs and a tabloid nickname (the Party Prince). There was also a small gossip item about him, speculating at him missing at Christmas parties and wondering whether he was in rehab, as well as links to his social media accounts which proved the matter beyond doubt, and were also full of ridiculous pictures she could easily pull, with him shooting deer and posing next to Ferraris. It was absolute gold. It was patently clear he'd been banished.

She had his quotes about Mure and how he couldn't wait to go; she had pictures – as well as the freeze-frame pulls from the video – and now it was up and absolutely ready to fly. This was brilliant. She was going to get promoted for sure. It had absolutely everything: money, good-looking people, nobility, tragedy, shame and – her readers' favourite thing – someone being punished ferociously. It couldn't fail. They'd have it up by the evening, clickbait of the finest order.

She emailed off the final copy, waiting for the page mock-ups with satisfaction. Then she headed out to get the last flight of the evening. God, she'd be pleased to shuck off this crap-hole and get back to London. How could they handle being so far away and stuck in the middle of nowhere? It was absolutely freezing all the bloody time and there was nothing going on. Although to be fair, that statue wasn't bad.

Anyway. Her work was done. She was out. She packed her neat little wheelie bag and headed through the snow to the airport.

Chapter Fifty-eight

For once, the night of 23 December, everything went flawlessly at the Rock. Well, as flawlessly as a dinner for quite a lot of extremely old people can go. There was some delicious lobster bisque, much of which made it onto the white starched tablecloths, and the waiting staff – many of whom were young recruits who knew or were related to most others there – found themselves doing more cutting up of the beef than they might have expected during a normal service, and the noise levels reached an absolute cacophony, even without the nice album of Christmas carols being played which they took off pretty sharpish. The vast tree was beautifully decorated in scarlet and gold, crowned with a huge golden star and gently twinkling lights. The salmon was delicious; the goose was tender and pink, and crispy on the outside.

Fintan didn't actually even bother turning up at all, to the point where Joel was going to go round the farmhouse and yell at him (or, more realistically, get Innes to yell at him) but *apart* from that it was great. There was the fact that Mrs O'Brien got stuck crying in the toilets because old Seoras, whom she'd been secretly in love with since 1954, and who had been widowed the previous year, on account of which she had gone all the way to the mainland to get her hair done and her make-up done professionally in Debenhams which had been all right when she'd left but had got somewhat blown about on the ferry back, leaving her with mascara halfway across her cheek and a definite slipping effect, but nobody had told her about it until she went to the bathroom – they'd all told her she looked lovely, which she might if you didn't have your glasses on but when you could see properly she clearly looked like Haggis McBaggis and anyway, Seoras was already cracking on chatting to that blowsy Julie McSquire who had always been a bit of a one and here she was again, getting away with it, when she'd loved him for sixty-five years, so surely – *surely* – she had dibs.

That took a lot of talking down. But *apart* from that, it was flawless. Ish. Flora was a little concerned that a lot of raspberry juice from the light-as-air cranachan was adding to the lobster bisque and red wine on the tablecloths, making it look a little as if they'd been hosting a large selection of grizzly bears, but surely the laundry could cope.

In the kitchen, however, all was sweetness and light, apart from them having to occasionally turn back sweet Mrs Piper, who had a tendency to wander, but everyone looked after her and was used to seeing her around and about, except Gaspard made the mistake the first time of giving her a biscuit, which meant they saw her seven or eight times. The carers from the old people's home were doing a brilliant job, but they only had so many hands and, to be fair, they worked very long hours in what could be quite a challenging environment, so it was only right that they got a glass of champagne and some good red wine on a very rare evening out and entirely explicable that they might slightly over-partake and okay, it wasn't ideal that one of them had had to have a very small spew in the toilets but other than *that*, it was flawless.

Flora briefly thought she might sleep standing up. She found herself eyeing up a spare wheelchair in the corner of the room and wondering if anyone would mind if she borrowed it for half an hour.

But to Isla and Konstantin, young and full of energy, and merry and excited and wildly, possibly on the brink of, well, who knew what, the evening flew in an exciting rush of suds and assembling food and washing up and dancing to music and giggling with each other and when you were with the person you wanted to be with more than anyone in the world, work didn't really feel like work at all.

Chapter Fifty-nine

'What do you mean?'

Candice banged her hand down on the top of the desk, which wobbled as it wasn't a real desk, just a table set up in a small room.

Billy, who staffed the airport, looked up at her kindly. He was used to having to give this kind of news, but normally people were either accepting, if they were local, or genuinely quite pleased if they were tourists, that they were going to have to take another day or two of holiday.

'I'm afraid the plane can't land tonight. Cross winds.'

'What do you mean?' Candice asked again.

'Well. We have a wind from the north, aye, and a wind from the west and they've kind of got themselves in quite the tizzy—'

'No, I mean, how can I get back to Britain?'

'This is Britain, you know, even though it's actually closer to—'

'No, I mean, is there another plane tonight?'

Billy laughed.

'Well, no. There would be but because of—'

'—cross winds. When's the next plane?'

Billy shrugged.

'Well, the weather forecast is no' ideal, so it isn't.'

'Can I get back on the ferry?'

'Well, you can ask them.'

'When?'

'In the morning. They leave pretty early, you know.'

'I don't care,' said Candice furiously. She had a big Christmas planned at her new boyfriend's mother's house in Fulham. His mother was absolutely terrifying, really a horrible scrawny old bat, and she had a lot of shopping to do to make a good impression. And she needed her nails fixed and her roots done, and she ought to have had plenty of time for this if she hadn't been chasing this stupid story. She'd like to tell herself that Dan loved her for her; he wouldn't care two shits if she had her nails done or not. Nobody on this island, she'd noticed, cared about that kind of thing; nobody had their nails done.

But she couldn't be entirely a hundred per cent sure that Dan didn't put quite a lot of store by his mother's opinion, and she had a reasonable suspicion as to what Dan's mother thought nails should be like, and it wasn't being chipped while standing in a ridiculous blizzard banging on a wobbly desk in the middle of absolutely bloody nowhere.

'Now, you have a place to stay? You can always sleep at our place,' said Billy kindly. More than a few people had slept on his sofa after an unfortunate mix-up or other. It was very much part of the job. Candice sniffed. Oh Christ, how on earth was she meant to get back? She missed the old glory days of newspapers she'd read about, where people would hire helicopters and whatever it took to get them on a story. As it was, she would probably have to go back to that grubby Harbour's Rest, which she was sure was far worse than the place she'd been sent up to do the actual exposé on.

'No, thank you,' she said snottily. 'Can I ask you to contact me if a plane *does* decide to visit?'

Billy nodded as cheerfully as he could. Generally, people didn't behave as rudely as this on Mure, and he wasn't completely sure how to handle it.

Candice had already turned round. She suddenly remembered with a sigh that she would need to get the island's only taxi back, and the driver had been nosy enough the first time. And she was going to have to call Dan. This was going to be tricky. Very tricky indeed.

Chapter Sixty

Isla tended to keep her make-up out of sight at home as her mother would always have something to say about the cost, and about it being a little tarty. She wasn't anything like old enough to have been to the dinner, Isla thought, but even there you could see groups of friends, ladies chatting with each other and having a laugh and even discussing having a knees-up as the party had carried on into the bar. She wished so dearly her mum had people like that.

But tonight, having cycled at top speed down the hill from the Rock into the village, and jumped into the shower, she was in too much of a hurry to be too bothered about what her mother thought. Even though they'd agreed to meet at the Harbour's Rest following her shift and even though he still had to mop the floor and after all, where else was he going to go and what else was he going to do, she still nonetheless felt slightly that if she were late

when she got there he'd be gone. Ridiculous. Like he was something out of a fairy tale, a puff of smoke. But still.

She put on her prettiest dress which she'd bought for dancing
at Colton's wedding the year before, and never got to use since.
It was palest pink satin, pretty as anything and far too thin for
the weather.

'Where are you going?'

'I'm going to meet a friend for a drink.'

'Who?'

'Doesn't matter. Just a friend.'

Isla felt daring and nervous.

'That lipstick looks tarty.'

'Good,' said Isla. Her mother looked taken aback.

'Don't answer me back,' she said.

Isla rolled her eyes.

'And don't you roll your eyes at me. Are you going out to see
some lad?'

'Maybe,' said Isla.

'Is he good enough for you?'

'For *once*,' said Isla. 'For *once*, would you let me be the judge of
what is good enough for me?'

There was silence. Isla felt terrified. But she wasn't going to
be the conciliatory one for a change, the one who tried to make
everything better.

And she went straight back out of the door and onto her bicycle,
her hands trembling, before she could even turn around and see
her mother's face. Mrs Donnelly was all the while still holding
that damn teapot.

Chapter Sixty-one

There weren't really opening hours at the Harbour's Rest. Inge-Britt generally closed up when everyone was done, which could be very early in the winter – and in January she closed altogether and went to Iceland to sit in volcanic hot pools. More than once, the people of Mure had suggested clubbing together to fumigate the place while she wasn't around – she normally left at least one fire exit propped open by mistake so it wouldn't be a problem to get in – but it hadn't happened so far.

In the summer, by contrast, when it didn't get dark till midnight, often people got rather carried away and could be found carousing until the early hours, which were also broad daylight, so everything could get a touch confusing.

At ten p.m. on a December night, however, the cosy bar was warm and welcoming, full of jolly-looking locals celebrating Christmas or farmers having a quick pint, this being their quieter time of year before the havoc of spring and lambing. As usual, they were talking about the disastrous work of farming, but nobody minded so much as there had never been a year ever where farmers hadn't been talking about the disastrous work of farming.

Isla felt incredibly self-conscious as she walked in in her best dress. What if he wasn't there? What if he'd changed his mind? What if the bar was full of everyone she knew and they all had to watch her being stood up? Why couldn't there be at least one place to go where she didn't know every single person on earth? Normally, she'd found that such a nice, comforting thing about living in a small community. Tonight, it was utterly unbearable.

She had texted Iona en route, particularly to tell her the big news that she was thinking of moving out! Iona had been on at her to do this for ages, had visions of them sharing a flat together, but she'd known Isla would never leave that awful mother of hers. Iona's own mother was a riot, they would happily share a bottle of Prosecco on a Saturday night watching *Strictly* together.

Isla glanced around the room. And her heart leapt as she suddenly forgot everyone else looking at her and saying hello, for there wasn't a soul on Mure who hadn't known Isla since she was a shy, wide-eyed bairn, and barely a heart that hadn't broken for her when good gentle Roddy had passed and left that mainland harridan to mother her. For there he was, sitting in the corner, looking more handsome than ever – he needed a haircut, and his blond hair was looking floppy and falling over his eyes which, it turned out, was exactly how Isla liked it – and he was already getting up, patently absolutely delighted to see her. A few of the older farmers smiled wryly at each other. Young love.

But Isla and Konstantin only had eyes for each other. They came towards each other and stopped just as he was about to grasp her hands, both giggly, each pink from rushed showers; the wintry chill, the excitement.

'Um, hello,' said Konstantin, his eyes dancing. He glanced towards the bar and, winking broadly, Inge-Britt went to the slightly iced-up freezer and removed one of Mure's very few bottles of actual vintage champagne. Isla's eyes widened.

'How can you afford . . . ?'

'I have saved all my pot-boy wages,' said Konstantin, shushing her. 'And this is the only thing I could find to buy on the entire island.'

He ushered her to the corner table, specially wiped down for the occasion with an almost-new cloth, and Inge-Britt, smirking only very slightly, which was good of her under the circumstances, brought over the bottle and two glasses with some ceremony.

Konstantin was used to being watched pretty much everywhere he went, so he was completely oblivious to Isla's blushing awkwardness, but once they'd had a little fizz, everything seemed to settle down. They were in the very darkest corner of the room, where finally they could talk.

'What's happening with the statue?' asked Isla anxiously. She'd passed it on the way down and thought it as beautiful as ever.

'I don't know,' said Konstantin pensively. 'The council is really cross, I don't know why.'

'But people will come to see it! It'll be like the Angel of the North!'

'I think so. I think they're just cross we didn't ask them first and it didn't take five and a half years to get through nine committees and we didn't have a big ceremony and let them all make a very boring speech each.'

Isla thought for a moment.

'Well, couldn't we?'

286

'What do you mean?'

'Couldn't you name it after them?'

Konstantin blinked.

'You could call it the Malcolm Marsali Aoghas Fraser William Effie Angel,' said Isla, tidily ticking off the committee members on her hand. 'Put Malcy at the front: he's the biggest arsehole so he's the most likely to be happy if he's first. And let them all make a speech. Isn't that how Joel got it through in the first place?'

She smiled suddenly.

'They could do it at the Loony Dook!'

'In front of everyone naked?'

'They're not going to be naked, Konstantin! That's your stupid country! Here everyone is wearing breeks.'

'Getting in the sea wearing wet clothing on a winter's day is the stupidest thing I've ever heard,' grumbled Konstantin.

'No, you're right, nothing better on a small island than everyone being familiar with everyone else's genitals,' said Isla, rolling her eyes. 'Breeks are fine.'

Konstantin looked pensive.

'Well ... I mean ... it might be worth a shot ...'

'Have a grand opening. They'll have to make the speeches short, otherwise everyone will freeze to death.'

Konstantin grinned.

'Actually, Joel wants me to meet them. That might not be a bad idea.'

'I think it's a very good idea.'

'Yeah,' said Konstantin. 'Making people feel important.'

Isla looked at him mistily.

'You ... make me feel important.'

'Well, because you are,' said Konstantin. 'You're the most important person I've met here. You've saved me loads of times.'

Suddenly she was very conscious of his hand on the table and found hers moving towards his, just a little. Once again, she had that oddest sense she only had when she was with him, that nothing else in her life mattered in the slightest.

Konstantin looked towards her, smiling. She was just so very lovely.

'We could ...' she said, amazed at how bold she was about to be. But she suddenly, and very fiercely, did not want to do some of the things she very strongly now wanted to do in the full glare of the Harbour's Rest.

'You know, we could maybe take that champagne up to the Rock,' she said rather quietly.

'Are you kidding?' said Konstantin, smiling. 'If you'd told me that, we could have just stolen some of theirs.'

But he saw from her face that she was indeed serious, and he stopped talking and gravely proffered his arm. She emptied her glass for Dutch courage, then took it.

Just as they stood up, there was a commotion at the door.

Candice had bumped her expensive bags crossly back up the black painted steps of the Harbour's Rest. This was absurd. She needed to get back to London and she was trapped here. It was cruel and unusual, like a punishment for breaking a fantastic story. Ridiculous. And Christ, here she was, trapped in this hell-hole.

She left her bag in reception in the mistaken belief that there would be someone else to take it up for her, and stared at the empty desk (although she noted there were keys hanging up behind it, so hopefully she'd get a bed for the night – the possibility of that not happening was just too awful to contemplate).

She would head into the bar, she decided, order a large G&T, check if the story was up yet and then and only then decide what to type to Dan. Oh God. It had taken ten months to even get him to this point, of inviting her to have Christmas with his mother. And now she was not going to make it and if there was a way that could be interpreted as not an actual snub, she had absolutely no idea what it was.

On the other hand, she was nothing if not goal-orientated. She clopped over to the bar in her heels, her feet absolutely freezing from standing in that ridiculous barn they called an airport. She pushed open the doors, feeling the not unwelcome whoosh of warm, slightly fuggy air hit her, and strode inside. Oh good, Isla and Konstantin were right there. She wandered up to join them, her face taking on a curl that might pass for a smile.

'Hellooo!' she said, sitting next to Isla. 'So, how does it feel, I have to ask ... to be dating the runaway prince?'

'The what?' said Isla, completely and utterly confused.

In answer, Candice took out her phone, beaming.

'I'm just going to tape your reactions,' she said and watched as Isla stared at Konstantin then back at the scrolling page in disbelief.

PLAYBOY PRINCE SLUMMING IT
IN BRITAIN'S WORST HOTEL

She blinked. There was a huge photo of Konstantin wearing some kind of weird military uniform with medals on it next to the pic of Gaspard falling over with Bjårk.

Britain's Worst Hotel, the Rock on the tiny island of Mure, will be further 'rocked' by the revelation today that their kitchen junior is none other that Konstantin Sundt-Knagenhjem, the playboy son of one of Norway's richest and most aristocratic families . . .

Beneath this there was a picture of Konstantin looking drunk and frazzled at a party, surrounded by scantily clad models.

Isla's hand flew to her mouth. What on earth was happening? She scanned the following paragraphs, as phrases leaped out at her –

'I'm not going to stay long in this life . . . I really miss Norway.'

And:

'Mure is a dark, cold miserable place . . . it needs brightening up.'

It made reference to his illegal 'eyesore' (a direct quote from a 'senior council source' who spoke of planning to 'pull it down as soon as they had the chance'), and talked about how he had been banished from Norway for his appalling behaviour:

Close friends have been asking when he's coming back from his time with the 'little people', so they can all have fun again.

So what is next for the Island of Calamity when the Prince finishes his little session of 'slumming it' with the locals? – he's been reported as 'cutting quite a swathe'.

And to her horror, there was a picture of him with Isla, taken on Candice's traitorous iPhone, Konstantin looking handsome, her wearing the ridiculous kitchen hat, looking pathetic and hungry and utterly stupid.

Isla jumped up, just as someone burst through the saloon doors. It was Iona.

'Have you seen this *shite*?'

She pointed at Konstantin.

'You bloody bastard! You leave my friend alone. And *you*!'

It struck Candace forcibly that she'd have much rather been circling into Heathrow about now.

'Just doing my job,' she said smoothly. Isla went up to stand next to her friend, who put a supportive arm around her.

'Look at the two of you,' said Iona. 'Well suited. Come on, Isla. Let's leave them to it.'

And she helped her speechless friend out of the door as the rest of the bar looked on. They hadn't had quite such an entertaining evening since Wullie Stevenson had got his false teeth stuck dooking for apples at Hallowe'en and scared the living death out of all the children by taking them out, apple and all.

Chapter Sixty-two

Isla stumbled out into the snow with Iona, her thoughts blurring.

Oh, she was such an idiot. He was slumming it. Literally flirting with her because she was standing right next to him; he couldn't even be bothered to take a look around the island. She was right there; she would do. Her face flamed brighter than ever as she remembered the pictures of Norwegian supermodels and actresses and of him at premieres and parties. Oh God, how could she have been so dumb?

As if. As if she would ever have been more than a plaything for someone like him. And worse than that; he was obviously horrible. Imagine being sent away by your own father. She thought back to her fight with her mother. Oh God. Everything was so awful.

And she had been about to ... Her blood run cold. Would he have made fun of her with all his rich Norwegian friends when he went home?

So much made sense now. His lack of phone. His obviously decent clothes. The way he had absolutely no idea of the value of money. Even the stupid bottle of champagne, now sitting nearly empty on the corner table.

Iona didn't even pause and took her straight to her house and opened up a bottle of whisky.

Chapter Sixty-three

Lorna sat at home by herself, staring at the box and wondering whether to wrap it. She was going to the MacKenzies' on Christmas Day, so she had a massive pile of presents for them including far too much for Agot as usual, even though she knew fine well spoiling her didn't help.

But she had one gift – very small, something easily concealed, nothing anyone would ask about. She had hummed and hawed and wondered about it but in the end had decided now what did she possibly have to lose?

They hadn't been in contact at all and she had absolutely no idea what was going on with him, but the boys, she noticed with some satisfaction, seemed happy and well; they hadn't become withdrawn or difficult. Ash was looking forward to Christmas as much as any of them; Ib was still out there in the most freezing weather kicking a ball at playtime with his chums. If there had been some major upset

294

at home, she'd have seen it through the behaviour of the children. Teachers always did. So nothing had changed. Yet.

She wanted to take him a gift. But she knew she shouldn't. If he was free, she'd have seen him.

She walked out into the swirling snow, past the Angel. Looking at it made her smile. It was amazing how quickly it had become part of the landscape. She rather loved it. It gave her light and courage somehow and suddenly, feeling the parcel in her pocket, she became emboldened. She would wrap it and take it to him. She made a mental note also to turn up to the emergency council meeting on Boxing Day to make sure to add her voice, and give her support to the people who wanted to keep it.

She got almost as far as the surgery, then turned round and went home again. Maybe tomorrow.

*　❆

Iona for once didn't start gabbling, but came over and put her arms round her friend.

'I'm sorry,' she said. 'I honestly didn't realise. I didn't know you liked him so much.'

She poured two large measures of the medicinal whisky she'd found downstairs.

'I miss you,' she said simply.

'I miss you too,' said Isla. 'If you'd been about, I probably wouldn't have made such a fool of myself.'

'You haven't made a fool of yourself! He's a dickhead!'

In response, Isla pulled down the top of the pink dress an inch, exposing a bright red bra strap, something she'd ordered specially from the mainland.

There was a moment's silence, then both girls burst out laughing, Isla's bordering slightly on hysteria.

'Oh lord,' said Iona. 'Well, he's missing out.'

'You'd have steered me clear, told me to leave him alone,' said Isla.

'No, I wouldn't,' said Iona. 'I think he's a ride. I'd have been even worse. I'd have been with him a million times by now.'

Isla let out a big sigh.

'I really liked him,' she said. 'What an idiot.'

'Why?' said Iona. 'He looked really cut up about it.'

Isla sniffed. 'Yeah, he'll just have to get off with a million super-models. Or that stupid journalist.'

'She *is* stupid,' said Iona, and she refilled their glasses.

Isla glanced around Iona's little bedroom, filled with Highland dancing trophies and old pony books. Not unlike hers, in fact.

'He had no interest in involving me in his life at all. I was just a bit of fun.'

'Well,' said Iona defiantly. '*We* are going to have fun.'

'What do you mean?'

'There's a flat coming up on the high street. Mum wants to move Piotr in. I miss you; you miss me. We *could* rent it together.'

'Oh!' said Isla. 'But I'd have leave Mum.'

'You're going to have to leave her some time!' said Iona. 'She was always trying to push you to university or something anyway. "Don't you think you could do better, Isla?"' Iona made a passable stab at Vera's voice. Isla sighed.

'She means well.'

'But it makes you miserable.'

Isla shrugged. 'It's just not my day.'

'Don't be daft. You're famous and in the paper!'

'For being an idiot!'

'We'll have fun, I promise. Come on. It's Christmas, Loony Dook, Hogmanay, Burns Night, Valentine's and then it'll be spring and all the tourists will be here, and you can enchant one of them to fall in love with you and they'll stay for ever and all will be well, because we'll have our own place and you won't have to skulk about to get a lumber!'

Isla couldn't help smiling at that.

'You're such an optimist.'

'That's because we live on top of the world. Stay over?'

She was already pulling out the little trundle they'd used when they had sleepovers at eight and nine, talking excitedly about *How to Train Your Dragon*, and at thirteen, talking the same but about Justin Bieber and the fourth-year boys, and now it was strangely incredibly comforting that here they were again, looking for the spare toothbrush, trying not to wake Iona's mum, hushing each other, giggling and, to her great surprise, Isla slept.

Chapter Sixty-four

Konstantin did not sleep. Quite the contrary. As Candice stood at the bar, he considered going after Isla, but remembered Iona's ferocity and considered it a good idea not to. He was also very, very pleased he didn't have a phone: the last thing he needed right now was to hear from his father about how he had somehow managed to bring even more disgrace on the family. Oh God. That was hellish in itself. It would be everywhere.

He'd just ignore it all. Presumably Gaspard wasn't going to fire him – or even if he did, he thought defiantly, he knew how to wash pots now. He could find another job. Go out and seek his fortune. It hadn't been bad here, not at all.

In fact, he thought sadly, he'd been enjoying it. Learning how to do something properly for the first time in his life. People liking him – really liking him – for himself, not for his money or his ridiculous house. He thought back to the camaraderie of the barn when they had built the statue; the patience (albeit laced with shouting) of Gaspard, taking him from knowing nothing to being actually reasonably useful. He'd been looking forward to the Christmas service, the first time to really stretch themselves at full mettle; to make a roomful of disparate people happy and warm and content. It seemed to him a rather fine way to live your life.

But now everyone was going to despise him, thinking he was just using their island to play Marie Antoinette, to pretend to be poor.

He hadn't felt poor. But he felt every stare in the bar, every aggressive glance as more and more people read and whispered about how he'd brought the island down.

In fact, here came the first person now. He stiffened, ready to defend himself, or if he couldn't, at least take it.

It was Innes, who he'd built the statue with.

'Well,' said Innes, in his slow careful way, 'I see you've been shaking things up a bit.'

Konstantin winced.

'I'm sorry,' he said.

'What about?' said Innes. 'I don't care that you live in a castle. Looks nice, if anything. And the statue is brilliant, so screw them.'

'But this might be really bad news for the hotel.'

Innes snorted. 'I wouldn't care about that either. I don't think Fintan wants anything to do with it and it's killing Flora. I'd be happy if it fell in the sea.'

Konstantin smiled.

'I like the way you think.'

They chinked glasses.

'How is Agot?' asked Konstantin. 'Does she still hate me?'

Innes sniffed.

'She hates everyone who tells her she can't skate.'

'Have you got her ice skates?'

'There's nothing to skate on, is there? All the water here is salt! Eilidh sent for some from Aberdeen but they'll be wasted.'

'It's a bad Christmas for everyone,' said Konstantin, and they chinked glasses again, sadly.

Konstantin smiled at his kind friend, then got up and made his lonely way out into the dark, miserable by how unhappy he had made his lovely little Isla; the look on her face had cut him to the quick and he missed her. Everything was in ruins.

'Come on, Angel,' he whispered in his native tongue as he walked by the great figure beaming out brightly across the water. He trudged up against the wind to the northernmost point of the island, towards his little eyrie at the Rock, looking forward all the way home to having Bjårk's shaggy company. 'Now I need a miracle.'

It then occurred to him that he would have to make an offering to the Angel before he could receive anything, which was a strange thing to think, but it crossed his mind nevertheless. It was something to do with this place: the interdependence; the kindness of the people.

It struck him forcibly that it was 23 December, the start of celebrating Christmas back home in Norway. The last few years had been stiff affairs, with long dinners of lutefisk and ribs, often with worthy charity leaders of the region.

But he remembered long ago when Christmas was still the most exciting thing in the world, when his mother made a treasure hunt through the palace for him and all the local children, excitingly wrapped gifts in every crevice. He remembered her singing, her happy pleasure as she went to parties, looking and smelling magnificent. The palace had been filled with what felt like thousands and thousands of sparking lights.

Christmas was on 25 December here and nobody had so much as known to mention that tomorrow was actually the real thing for him. Nobody knew.

And of course he hadn't heard from his father. He wouldn't, now he'd brought down even more disgrace on the family name.

He had gone to Mure; he had done everything he had been told to do. He could even grudgingly accept that his father was right. And now he had been forgotten.

It hurt enormously.

On the empty road, as the Angel faded behind him, he had never felt lonelier in his entire life; like the only man in a world that had turned very, very cold towards him.

Chapter Sixty-five

The next day was the prep day for Christmas, and Isla, waking up with a sore head, had arranged with Gaspard that she would come in early for the first shift so she could leave early and wouldn't overlap with Konstantin. When Konstantin came down the stairs later, he was slightly terrified not to see her there, even after Kerry reassured him she was just working an earlier shift, which wasn't ideal either.

Chopping and prepping in a cold kitchen wasn't remotely as much fun without his companion by his side. Konstantin had the sinking feeling that nothing would. He vowed to go find her after he'd finished. Explain to her . . . Or at least try.

But it wasn't all false, that was the problem. He had hated it here. He hadn't wanted to stay.

Until he'd met her. But would she believe that? He thought again of those awful pictures of him and the models. Okay, he'd thought it was pretty funny at the time. But that wasn't who he was now, not how he felt, not at all. Isla was special. He just needed to figure out how to show that.

* ❋

Lorna woke, determined to do better today. Or at least to finish it.

The surgery was empty, many people miraculously finding their symptoms improving as they prepared to stay indoors for a few days fortified by Quality Streets, telly and the fire on. Jeannie was tidying up and trying to ignore the many, many boxes of chocolate that had landed there – Saif was ridiculously popular, but he didn't want to take the sweets home, seeing as he neither had a sweet tooth nor had ever got used to the amount of sugar Scottish children ate, and being keen to spare his own children a similar fate – which littered the place up. Jeannie had been pressing boxes on people as they'd come in for being 'good customers' but unsurprisingly that had gone down very badly indeed so she was going to swing past the community hall.

'Oh, hello, Lorna,' she said shrewdly, looking her up and down. There was patently not a thing wrong with the pretty teacher. 'He's not here.'

She realised immediately she'd said the wrong thing.

'Dr Hassan, I mean,' she said, using his surname, which nobody ever did. 'He's just finishing up his last rounds before the holiday, topping up prescriptions, that kind of thing.'

'Of course,' said Lorna, her courage suddenly deserting her. She couldn't bear looking foolish in front of Jeannie: was terrified of giving herself away. Jeannie likewise couldn't bear the fact that she had guessed after seeing that Lorna went away every time Saif had booked leave, so she busied herself with paperwork. Then something occurred to her.

'Everyone's been dropping off doctor presents! Have you got one too? Is it from the school?'

'Uh, yes,' said Lorna, grateful for a way out. 'Sorry . . . we should have got you something.'

Jeannie gestured drily to the piles of chocolates. 'I'm fine, thanks.'

Lorna smiled.

'Oh yes.'

She also had plenty of boxes piled up, along with some really not very helpful personally made artwork from children and – thank God – a bottle of island-made gin from the kind family at Rubhan Taigh, who had to make up for their five naughty red-headed chaps somehow.

Saif sat in the car in the shadow of the car park, watching her leave. It took everything he had not to jump up and run out. He saw the sadness on her face as she left, her hands deep in the pockets of her long studenty coat, the red hair under a black velvet cap that made her look so young, so lovely, so undeserving to be so sad when happiness was always circling and never in reach.

He wanted to run to her, grab her, who cared what the world saw.

He looked again at his phone. At his Facebook. Nothing.

When he finally got back in, Jeannie handed over the little parcel from Lorna with a kind look that bypassed Saif completely. He held onto it as he went home, heated up the lasagne kind Mrs Laird had left for him and tried completely unsuccessfully to calm down a highly overexcited Ash. There would be presents tomorrow, then they were booked into the Rock; Flora wouldn't hear of them having Christmas on their own and had absolutely insisted. Of course, it wasn't entirely unselfish: she wanted the place filled with people she knew would appreciate it, plus Ash could keep Agot distracted which could only be a good thing.

He looked at the sparkly tree in the corner, smiling again at the joy Ash had got out of it. Sighing as it marked another year without . . .

Well. He had driven himself crazy for so long. And she now . . . Had she had the baby? She must have. Or perhaps that photograph had been old; perhaps that child was growing up. Did he look like her other children? he wondered.

After the boys were finally asleep, he sat downstairs, feeling the silence weighing heavily on him.

He wished, more than anything . . . Well, what did he wish for? He was in love with two different people. One who was there; one who was not and could never be again. But the latter was still his wife, his legal wife. Sworn to him before God. Mother of his children.

He held Lorna's parcel in his hands, found himself opening it, his heart heavy. At first, he couldn't quite believe what he was looking at. It wasn't possible.

It was the same – the exact same edition – of the book he had looked up online the previous week, for the message that may or may not have come from Amena.

This couldn't be true. It couldn't be real. How could she know? Could she have sent it? No, of course not, how could she have known about the crocodile? How could she have known? And Nizar Qabbani was a very famous poet, of course he was. Of course.

It was a coincidence, that was all.

The volume was beautiful, after all: gold and bright blue.

There was a bookmark in it, placed as if it could almost have been put in at random. But he knew, of course that it had not been.

Letter from Under the Sea

If you are my friend
Help me to leave you
Or if you are my lover
Help me so I can be healed of you
If I knew
That the ocean is very deep ... I would not have swum

Saif sighed heavily. He got up and stared out of the window. Just at the very edge of his vision, he could see the beam of the Angel statue light up into the sky. He looked at it for a very long time.

Then he picked up the phone.

☆ * ❄

In the deep quiet of Christmas Eve there were still clusters of drinkers in the Harbour's Rest, mostly the young people home from the mainland to see their families, laughing loudly and boasting madly about their new lives in Inverness, Aberdeen, London or Edinburgh, while in homes mums and dads wrapped presents and lost the Sellotape and begged excited children to sleep and cursed themselves for hiding gifts months ago and forgetting exactly where, and checked anxiously again to make sure they had enough roast potatoes and attempted to make their mothers-in-law comfortable in their bed while they struggled to arrange themselves on the pull-out sofa, and tried to hide the sherry from Auntie Morag who got a bit maudlin this time of year which was completely understandable what with everything she'd been through but even so for the sixth year on the trot it was really bringing everybody down and oh my God did you see that thing on the *Post Online*, what on earth were the MacKenzies going to do? Families rolled on at Christmas with the mixture of the sad and the sublime, and several hardy fellows made it to midnight mass and the Reverend Janey gave a lovely sermon about never making the perfect the enemy of the good which wasn't strictly speaking in the Bible but she always found it a very useful sentiment at this time of year anyway.

Nobody noticed a small red-headed figure slip out of the flat door tucked behind the tiny museum, hop into the little hatch-back, creep up the back road to the old manse (Reverend Janey *much* preferred her modern flat next to the church with its triple glazing and gas central heating), park round the back rather than out the front and steal softly to the back door, where she did not have to knock, because someone was waiting for her, had been waiting for her for a very long time, who said nothing but pulled her in, the warmth of his body and the dark sweetness of his eyes and the quiet beating of their two hearts and shared the deepest gift two people can share.

Chapter Sixty-six

BANG! BANG! BANG!

'IT IS CHRISTMAS AND EVERYTHING IS TERRIBLE!'

Flora and Joel had woken up very early of course, to check on Douglas, and they had brought him into the bed and exchanged gifts, which were in Joel's case the most stunning diamond bracelet for Flora because he thought she deserved something beautiful and she nearly cried because she wanted to wear it to more exotic places and Joel said, 'As soon as you knock sense into Fintan, I am taking you to the Bahamas' and then she burst into tears again because she couldn't imagine a day when that might be the case and that made her sad all over again even as she assured Joel she loved everything. She gave him a Folio Society bound set of Dickens' novels, which she had correctly thought he might like.

Then they had attempted to give Dougie his gift – a beautiful rocking horse – but they both realised that he was far too young to get Christmas at all in any way so they were completely wasting their time, though to his credit he made a fair stab at eating the tail, which was fairly impressive.

They had loaded up the car with food and gifts even though they were going less than a kilometre. It wasn't really walking weather anyway: the snow had settled and it was treacherous for buggies. There was no doubt about it though: the Angel was an incredibly helpful beacon. It was amazing, Flora had thought, loading the boot, how quickly she'd got used to it, always checking to see where it was – you could see it from almost anywhere. It was absurd, she knew, to feel like it was looking out for you, looking after them all, huddled together on this little rock. But it made her smile to see it.

Everyone was already up in the farmhouse, Eck by the fire with his morning tea, Hamish running up and down excitedly and buzzing about the new train set they'd all clubbed in for, Innes and Eilidh sighing and trying to calm down Agot who was banging spoons very hard everywhere and saying:

'EVERYTHING IS TERRIBLE!'

'It's not terrible!' said Flora, giving her beloved niece a big kiss. Agot instantly wriggled away.

'IT'S A TERRIBLE, TERRIBLE CHRISTMAS!'

Flora looking enquiringly at Innes.

'She is being the brattiest brat in the history of terrible brats,' he said quietly as Eilidh poured coffee. Eilidh looked like she'd been having a very stressful morning. 'Would you like another kid? You've already got one; it shouldn't be too much trouble.'

'Most people wait till after eight a.m. on Christmas morning to try and give their children away,' said Flora. 'Oh dear. We have some lovely presents for you, darling!'

'IS THERE ICING SKATES?'

Flora blinked.

'No . . .' she said. 'There *might* be Shopkins.'

Agot sighed and her chin trembled.

'I HAAAATE Shopkins.'

This is something of a change from her letter to Father Christmas,' whispered Flora.

'I know,' said Innes.

'When she loved Shopkins more than anything on earth.'

'I know.'

'Seriously, you don't even have to keep her, you can sell her to pirates,' said Eilidh, looking a tad too longingly at the champagne Joel was unloading into the fridge.

Agot looked around at the roomful of adults, then ran out.

She had gone to Flora's room, her favourite, because it still had Flora's old Highland dancing trophies and ribbons. Agot had just started dancing but Flora had still found her on occasion holding up Flora's gold medal and announcing, 'I would like to thank everyone for this award.'

Flora followed her now, leaving Joel to start breakfast while Eilidh cuddled Douglas and made lots of cooing noises about how nice it was to remember what it was like to have a lovely baby.

Agot was lying face down on the duvet. She wasn't doing performative crying, making a big loud fuss about everything so people would hear. Instead, she was sobbing gently, like a real child, rather than the changeling she sometimes resembled.

'Hey,' said Flora. 'What's gone so wrong?'

'Miss Lorna said,' sniffed the child. 'Miss Lorna said if we were

310

good and wrote to Santa Claus we would get the thing that we wanted. And I was SO VERY GOOD.'

'Were you?' said Flora doubtfully.

'I did not shout in class! And I did not do CHATTING CHATTING CHATTING and when Miss Lorna said "Agot, no chatting" I DID NOT DO CHATTING. And I took hands with Hamish when it was time to take hands and I did not say "Yuck yuck yuck". I was very, very good; ask Miss Lorna!'

'I will do that,' said Flora.

'Everyone says "AGOT IS VERY NAUGHTY",' said Agot, looking heartbroken.

'They don't say that,' said Flora, stroking the girl's long pale hair.

'Yes,' said Agot with a resigned look. '"AGOT, SHE IS VERY NAUGHTY AND SPOILED".'

'Oh sweetie.' Flora took the small body in her arms. 'Well. You're still one of the very favourite people I've ever met.'

'You love Bugliss now. Everyone loves Bugliss now.'

'There is room,' said Flora. 'There is room to love everyone.'

'My mummy and daddy didn't have room. Then they did.'

Flora hugged the little girl harder.

'Grown-ups are complicated,' she said. 'And they are very sorry about that. But everything is all right now, isn't it?'

'But! I did try,' wept Agot. 'I did try to be good for Santa. So I could go ice skating. But he brought me . . .'

And her voice wobbled on the brink of total collapse.

'. . . stuuuupppiidddd Shopppppppkinnnnnnssss.'

Flora stayed with her until, to her surprise, Agot actually dozed off on the bed, having been up at regular intervals to midnight, and from two a.m. onwards. Flora rather fancied joining her, but it was a very busy day. She tucked the child in and went back to the sitting room, where the pleasant smell of scrambled eggs from the yard and locally smoked salmon was filling the room. Eilidh had given in to temptation and poured everyone a buck's fizz, which Flora reluctantly refused.

'There's nowhere for her to skate!' Eilidh was trying to explain. 'If I'd given her the stupid skates, there would just be a big tantrum after that!'

'Well, she's having a sleep,' said Flora. 'I'm sure she'll feel better after she's woken up.'

'Ready for the big day?' said Innes. Flora grimaced. It had seemed such a good idea at the time.

'You're asking the wrong person,' she said.

Chapter Sixty-seven

Fintan woke up curled in the strong arms of Gaspard, who was snoring gently beside him. It took him a moment to remember, just as he was waking, that they were sleeping in the house Colton had paid for, which he had built and funded. And that he was betraying the man he loved.

Who was dead.

Suddenly Gaspard's tattooed arms felt like a trap, too heavy on him. He stared at the handsome, scruffy, dissolute Frenchman, whose face, unfurled from its customary snarl, looked younger and softer in the clear white light. Fintan looked at it for a moment . . . then thought of his day ahead, and his heart sank.

No. He did not want to walk the halls of Colton's great dream. Did not want to oversee the kitchens that had been Colton's pride and joy; look around the ridiculously over-tartaned dining room, remember Colton's absurd tartan outfits – he had liked nothing better than dressing up as monarch of the glen, stag feather in his cap and all.

He hated the Rock, and everything about it. It was a millstone, nothing else. He jumped out of bed crossly to get ready to head to the farmhouse first and see his family before pulling himself up to play the jolly host at their grand opening lunch. He assumed everything was ready; Flora had been sticking her nose in all over the place. And Gaspard had told him not to worry, although that was also when Gaspard was trying to get him into bed, so he may or may not be able to take that as gospel. There were almost certainly issues involved in guiltily sleeping with your chef, but Fintan pushed those onto the huge pile of problems he had that couldn't get any higher and slunk off to the shower, the weight of the world on his shoulders.

Gaspard sat up.

'YOU ARE SAD,' he shouted, but it wasn't really a question. Fintan turned back.

'I don't know what's going to happen,' he said.

'Nobody knows what's going to 'appen.'

'I hate the hotel.'

'So walk away. Whenever I am sad, I walk away.'

'Are you sad now?'

Gaspard eyed him up seriously.

'*Non.*'

* ❋

Joel watched Flora carefully when Fintan came in, trying to smile as he handed over another huge gift for Douglas. 'You'd better try and dress him,' she said. 'I'm crap at it.'

Joel went over to her.

'You're not,' he said, surprised. 'Of course you aren't.'

Douglas was already waking up from his morning nap and preparing to make a wail. Joel looked at Flora's face – she was almost flinching, and suddenly something dawned on him.

'Darling,' he said. 'Can I take you next door for a second?'

⋆ * ❊

In Flora's old bedroom, beside a snoring Agot, Joel took Flora's hands in his.

'All this time,' he said quietly. 'All this time. I didn't realise.'

'What?' said Flora, anxious to get on to the Rock.

'Darling,' said Joel. 'Have you had trouble staying at home with the baby?'

'No!' whispered Flora loudly. 'I love him!'

'I know you love him,' said Joel with infinite patience. 'I mean. Have you found it difficult?'

Flora froze. He knew. He had seen it. She had tried so hard to make it look like she could do everything. When it was obvious that she couldn't. That she was failing Douglas. Jan was right. She barely saw him. It was awful.

She burst into tears.

'He doesn't love me!' she whispered. 'He prefers you! I'm shit at it! I get bored and frustrated and distracted and he cries *all the time* with me! *All the time!* He loves you and I'm shit at it!'

Joel wanted to laugh, although he sensed, correctly, that this perhaps wasn't the time.

'He cries all the time with me too,' he said soothingly. 'He's a baby.'

'But you're so patient with him.'

Joel looked at her.

'But this is all new to me,' he said, astonished it wasn't as clear to her as it was to him. 'I've never had a family before. You've been surrounded by brothers and children and relations and so many people your whole life you don't even realise it! I've had nobody. Nobody ever. And then I had you and now I have Douglas, and oh my God, Flora. Oh my God.'

They were both crying now.

'But ... you don't think I'm a terrible mother? For doing other things?'

'God, no,' said Joel. 'You're great. And wanting to run the Rock ... It's okay. I'm not sure but between you and me, and I'm sure absolutely nobody else has noticed ... I'm not sure Fintan is quite cut out for it.'

Flora swallowed a half-gulping half laugh.

'You mean that?'

'I take absolutely no responsibility for interfering in MacKenzie business,' said Joel. 'But I am happy, Douglas is happy and everything is well. Fintan is miserable and as for you ... you'll be fine, my darling.'

He hadn't been planning to do it *quite* at that moment, but suddenly it seemed fitting.

'I'm not sure if this is the time, because you are very, very tear-stained but ... I bought you something to go with that diamond necklace ...'

And he took a small box out of his coat pocket.

'If you can get enough time off between shifts ...'

Now he was going down on one knee. Flora was just staring at him, astounded.

Then she wiped her face furiously.

'Oh my God, this is *so* unfair,' she said.

'I know,' said Joel.

'Oh my God.'

'In your own time.'

He smiled up at her widely and she returned his grin.

'Oh my God.'

'I know, Mark and Marsha are going to kill us for not doing it when they were there.'

She flung her arms around him.

'YES PLEASE! YES PLEASE! YES PLEASE!'

'Ssh,' said Joel. 'You'll wake them.'

But it was too late. She heard the familiar wail from the sitting room. But somehow, somehow, it wasn't as hard as it usually was. Just knowing that Joel understood . . . and OMG she was engaged!

She danced into the sitting room.

'Where are you, my darling little man?' she crooned.

Joel stayed behind in the bedroom for a moment, slightly stunned with himself.

'I KNEW THAT WAS A BAD BABY BUGLISS,' came an unrepentant voice from under Flora's old duvet.

Chapter Sixty-eight

It had been a hard night's work, but a hard night's work was exactly what Konstantin didn't mind anything like as much as he'd always thought he might, and he couldn't sleep anyway so it had made sense.

Now he was hovering, waiting for sun-up. He couldn't help it: he wanted to see her face. However alone he felt, there was someone who might be happy to see him.

He had been dreading going back to the kitchen during the day. Having to face Isla. Knowing she felt he'd let her down, that she hated him, thought him some sleazy, lying player. It had taken so long to break down her defences, to feel that she trusted him, like a little bird in a funny way. And then just as he'd thought they had reached an understanding, and as he was getting to know someone better than he ever had before – certainly better than any of the girls he'd been with – well.

He could see it from her point of view. And he had wanted to get away, desperately at first.

Now though, Christmas Day dawned bright and frosty, the ice crackling over the fields with the short shaggy cows and their big horns mooing enthusiastically, the beautiful, endlessly long beach with the clear blue sea to the horizon, the little painted houses huddled round the harbour, the abundant fresh air, the scent of warm baking. He could see why people loved it too. He didn't mind it at all any more, in fact, as he strode through it, warm in his darned jacket.

As he reached the MacKenzies' farmyard, he saw that the family were up as smoke billowed from the chimney, and he could see figures moving inside the low windows.

Taking a quick breath, he knocked at the door.

'It's the prince,' said Fintan uninterestedly when he opened it up.

'I am not a prince,' said Konstantin awkwardly.

'Is everything okay at the hotel?' said Flora immediately, taking two seconds off from looking at her beautiful new ring from every angle and waking Mark and Marsha at four a.m. in New York, as was traditional.

'What should he care? He's only passing through,' said Fintan.

'I wish you cared as much as he does,' shot back Flora, then remembered what Joel had said, and held her fire.

'Actually . . .' said Konstantin politely.

'Come in, come in, it's freezing,' said Innes, who knew exactly what was up, beckoning him in and handing him a cup of tea, which left both Flora and Fintan feeling rather ashamed of their lack of goodwill.

'Happy Christmas,' said Flora. 'Sorry.'

'She was just shouting at me,' said Fintan.

'Well, I like your local Scottish traditions,' said Konstantin, taking a sip of the tea, which was disgusting to him, and wincing. He had never got used to it.

'I have coffee too,' said Flora hastily.

'I was actually looking for Miss Agot,' said Konstantin gravely. She had in fact emerged when the knock at the door had come and stood rubbing her eyes at the hall entrance. 'I owe her something.'

'Are you really a prince?' she said.

Konstantin shrugged.

'Oh well, for you, why not?'

Agot took a look at Douglas's pile of presents by the wall, all wrapped in blue animal paper.

'And who are they for?' she said suspiciously.

'I have brought you something,' said Konstantin quickly.

Agot blinked.

'Did you bring anything for Bugliss?'

'I brought nothing for Bugliss.'

'Okay.'

Konstantin winked at Innes, who vanished obediently.

'What's going on?' said Eilidh suspiciously.

Presently, Innes returned, bearing a white box.

'But!' said Eilidh, but Innes hushed her and handed it over to Agot.

Eyes wide, she opened it.

Inside was the most perfectly beautiful little pair of skates, white and trimmed with white fake fur, with pink laces.

Agot gasped.

'NOOOOO!'

She lifted them out of the tissue paper wrapping as if they were the most stunningly lovely things she'd ever seen. The silver blades caught the light, flashing and glinting in the early winter sun.

'But where is she—' started Eilidh.

'Ssh,' said Innes.

'And you see here,' said Konstantin, pulling out a pair of skates. 'I too have my skates.'

'You brought your skates from your palace in Norway?' said Flora.

'Of course,' said Konstantin, looking confused.

He lent the little girl his arm.

'Would you like to come skating with me?'

And he led her out into the farmyard to a sight that provoked a gasp from all of the others too.

Konstantin and Innes had had one more conversation before he had left the Harbour's Rest, and met later that night. Then they had used old tarpaulin as a liner, filled it half full of water, waited overnight – and now, Konstantin was using a kettle and a broom to carefully smooth it flat. On a flat piece of grassy ground, out by the cowshed, Konstantin had done something very simple. With Innes's help, he had built a small wooden fence in a rectangle, about fifteen centimetres high.

It was a perfect little rink.

Agot's eyes were wide as saucers.

'Now,' Konstantin said. 'You have to be careful not to trip over the ends. That is why you have to hold my arm.'

'I would like to hold the arm of a prince going on an ice rink,' said Agot gravely, and she sat up in the tractor seat while he tied her laces carefully and then bundled her up in her warm clothes. He took one hand and Innes took another and slowly and steadily they led the little girl round and round the rink.

Chapter Sixty-nine

Everybody laughed and cheered as Agot went round and round until she finally found the courage to go off by herself, her low centre of gravity helping, her tiny knees knocking together.

'I have to get ALL MY FRIENDS! FOR SKATING!' she shouted, her cheeks pink in the cold and her eyes bright with happiness and desperation to share it.

The others gradually retreated inside as Eilidh filmed endless hours of footage, and Flora took Fintan's arm. He was resistant at first, but she dragged him back over to the dairy, quiet today, normally busy turning out the island's sensational butter, and the milk suppliers turning up to take the milk.

Fintan spent no time in here these days. It was now run by a lad from the village, but he missed the happy days he had spent in here, experimenting with cheese – fabulous, some of it – tinkering and working and simply being his own man.

'What are you showing me this for?'

'I was wondering,' said Flora shyly, 'if … if you would like it as a gift?'

Fintan frowned.

'What are you talking about?'

'Look. Joel and I have discussed it. I'm useless on maternity leave. It's not that I don't love Douglas,' she added fiercely.

'Uh, nobody said that,' said Fintan.

'But I love the Rock too, Fintan. I loved what Colton was trying to do right from the start. It's where I met Joel. Where I fell in love. Where everyone fell in love. It's where I've had more fun than I can remember. I want his legacy to be right. I want to do it, Fintan. I can do it. If you like … I could take over the Rock. As a real job. And you could go back to making cheese.'

He looked at her suspiciously.

'What's the catch?'

'There's no catch,' said Flora. 'The only catch would be if you desperately wanted to keep doing the Rock and didn't want me to do it.'

'Oh *God*,' said Fintan, his face brightening suddenly. 'I'd *love* you to do it! Then I wouldn't feel like I was letting down Colton by selling it or giving it away.'

'You'll need to pay me,' said Flora.

'No, I realise that. But I don't … I mean, this is … this is …'

He looked at her, eyes red.

'Thank you!' he said. 'I thought you were just interfering to be a putz.'

'And I thought you were being lazy because you too are a putz,' said Flora.

They grinned at one another, and hugged in the freezing dairy.

'I miss him,' said Fintan, starting to cry. 'I can't believe I still miss him so damn much.'

'Because you're not an idiot,' said Flora. 'Of course you do. Make the best cheese you can in his memory. That's what made him fall for you in the first place.'

'Actually, I think it was my fabulous butt,' said Fintan.

'Yeah, yeah, whatevs,' said Flora. And properly arm in arm this time, both beaming, they made their way back to the house.

Chapter Seventy

On Christmas morning, Iona had scampered back to her mother's place, looking forward to a full day of the pair of them drinking Prosecco, eating sausage sandwiches and chocolates and watching TV in their pyjamas. Isla in contrast had come down to a silent kitchen and her wounded-looking mother being passive-aggressive, hoarding the teapot at her end of the table and making her disgruntlement very clear.

'Happy Christmas,' Isla had tried and her mother had harrumphed.

'For you maybe,' she'd said inaccurately. There were presents under the tree, but for once, neither of them was interested in looking at them. It was heartbreaking.

'Well,' said Isla finally. 'I'll see you at lunchtime? I think Flora's put you next to Mrs Laird and that nice Dr Saif.'

'Will he eat the food? They eat weird stuff.'

'Um, he's fine, Mum.'

Vera sniffed. Although the doctor might enjoy hearing about her rare symptoms. That might be something. Other people had common-or-garden complaints, but she was a medical mystery.

'Mum,' said Isla. 'I need to talk to you. I think I'm going to move out after the New Year. In with Iona.'

Her mother's hand went to her throat.

'You're moving?'

'I don't think ... I don't think we're making each other very happy.'

'You're getting a flat! You're growing up! That's *wonderful*!'

Isla was completely and utterly taken aback.

'I don't need you here fussing round me!' said Vera. 'That's just ... I'm so pleased for you, my darling. Your life needs to move on.'

Iona was slightly astounded as they hugged.

Gaspard came down to the kitchen looking uncharacteristically happy for once and, even more surprisingly, kissed them all and handed out large tins of mystery duck, which made no sense to anyone, and announced:

'Today will be *'uge* success. And those who 'ope it will be *poor success* will be so wrong they shall cry into their steam 'orse pudding thing you like.'

Gaspard had never got the point of mincemeat, and he wasn't about to start now.

'Where is the young prince?'

'He's not a prince,' said Isla automatically, then wondered why she was defending him. 'I don't know. He might be gone.'

''E is not gone. There are no planes, no boats, nothing. He is lazy. Go wake him up.'

Isla flushed.

'I don't think—'

'*Allez! Allez!* Now! We have much to do! Go!'

Isla slunk out of the kitchen despondently and mounted the beautiful stairs. Everything looked even more spotless than usual. Gala on the desk was already busy, checking in the very first customers with a broad smile. It was actually happening! After three years, the doors of the Rock were finally open! Bertie the boatman was bringing people round from the village. There was a mix of people who were genuinely interested, people who were there for an ironic break after all the fuss in the papers, some Norwegian star-spotters, locals and even – which would have surprised Joel – some of his old party friends who were tiring of the London lifestyle and wanted to see what the big draw was up here. The ferry had come in – a special service – but, to Candice's pure annoyance, wasn't going back again. The captain was staying for his Christmas lunch too.

There were a small group of old friends of Colton's, greying, fit-looking men who smiled ruefully at one another and traded sad anecdotes. And there was Candice, standing crossly in the middle of the foyer, her plans in ruins. The fact that she had had an unbelievably comfortable bed last night was just irritating.

The waiting staff were already fetching coffee and shortbread into the drawing room as people waited to get checked into the brand-new rooms. There was a palpable air of excitement.

All the way up in the eaves, everything was quiet, the rooms empty. Isla remembered the very first morning she had come here, how shocking she had found him. Well, now it all made sense, she supposed. She hadn't liked him then. She shouldn't like him now.

But even so. She remembered his face as the statue went up; the boyish enthusiasm he'd allowed to run riot. Even how nifty he'd got with a kitchen knife. The look of concentration when his too-long hair flopped over his face. The way his hand had felt in hers . . .

She almost let out a groan. The room was empty. Of course it was. He had gone.

And she was alone, but it was worse than before. Because before, she hadn't known what she was missing, hadn't realised there was something bigger out there, hadn't ever – she hated to admit it to herself – hadn't ever fallen in love, even if it was with a cad.

Almost out of habit, she glanced at her social media, even though she was terrified of seeing anything about herself on it. Konstantin was in loads of papers but she ignored it all.

Then she saw one thing. On Eilidh's Facebook account, of all people. It looked impossible, but it was true. A picture of two blonds: Konstantin, holding Agot's hand as they ... were they *skating*? The clear winter light was hitting their hair; it was beautiful.

Underneath, Eilidh had written, 'The prince built us an ice rink!'

Isla stared at it for a long time. He had really gone and dug an ice rink. He had really gone and done something for someone else, no thought to himself, just so that Agot would be happy on Christmas Day. This wasn't something she would ever have thought him capable of before. She stared at the photograph for a long time.

When she finally turned away from his door, she suddenly heard boots. It couldn't be. She steeled herself. He was coming back to pick up his stuff, that was all.

He walked slowly. After the excitement of seeing Agot, all his miseries were back. His face was sad, and his back stooped as he got to the top of the stairs. Even Bjärk looked disconsolate next to him. Then he glanced up and saw her, and his face changed completely.

'Were you . . . looking for me?' he asked.

There was a long pause.

'Gaspard was wondering where you are,' stuttered Isla.

'But not you?'

Isla shrugged.

'I thought you'd be heading back.'

'Where?' said Konstantin instantly. 'Where? You know the truth about me. I got thrown out of my own country. Thrown out. And I have heard nothing. Not from my dad, not from anyone. They were more than happy to see the back of me. And now everybody here thinks the same. You'll all be happy to see the back of me too. So it hardly matters where I go, does it?'

He walked straight past her.

'But you have loads of friends! Everyone knows you,' Isla found herself saying.

'Everyone knows me,' came the voice heading into the room, 'and nobody gives a damn.'

And he pushed the door shut behind him.

'I do,' said Isla in a very small voice. 'I give a damn.'

There was a squeak as the door pulled open again.

'What?' said Konstantin. 'What did you just say?'

Isla was flushed.

'Tell me!'

'I said, I give a damn,' she said very quietly.

'You didn't when you stormed off.'

'I didn't say I don't think you're a jerk.'

He looked deep into her eyes.

'But you make me not want to be a jerk,' he said.

'Well, I'm not sure it's working.'

In response, he took her face in his hands.

'I need to ask you,' he said gently as the mood instantly changed. 'I need to check and I need to tell you that my intentions with you . . . are not exactly pure. But – can I say good? Or at least better – but you make me want to be—'

Before he got to the end of the sentence, she grabbed him and kissed him hard.

Chapter Seventy-one

Of course Gaspard was yelling for them before thirty seconds were up, and no, it couldn't possibly be but was that a smile? A tiny hint of a smile on his face as they catapulted down the back stairs. Surely not.

Isla pulled Konstantin back just as they were preparing to enter the kitchen, flushed.

'I . . . I just wanted to say I don't care. If you're here for ever or if you're just passing through or . . . well. I've decided. I don't care.'

He turned to her, hands outstretched.

'Darling, I have nowhere else to go. I'm here.'

She looked back at him.

'That's not very flattering.'

He leaned over and kissed her.

'And there's nowhere else I'd rather be. Happy Christmas.'

She watched him go into the kitchen, put on the freshly

laundered whites naturally, pick up his knife and swish it round, cheerfully and full of confidence, and her heart blossomed suddenly, full of excitement and thought and plans. Maybe ... could this happen? She scuttled after him into the kitchen.

Flora arrived in her best red dress, the diamond bracelet, the brand-new ring and a smile the size of the Endless Beach, because after all it wasn't every day you got engaged *and* became the manager of the loveliest hotel for miles around, *and* stood in the foyer smiling and welcoming everyone in.

She'd tell the kitchen later. And also have some quite strong words with them about how they spoke on the record about the business.

There was an empty table which had been vacated by the councillors, led by Malcy, with Jan and Charlie out in solidarity, but she'd managed to fill it, so the boycott was hardly going to cause them too much trouble.

Otherwise it was such an interesting group of people: hipsters, possibly looking for a giggle; proper, serious-looking foodies with guidebooks, including one or two who followed Gaspard wherever he went; locals, of course, plus some older people from the mainland who had seen past the daftness of the videos and into the loveliness of the remote surroundings; she even noticed some old flames of Joel's, looking around for the 'prince'.

She smiled. He may not be a prince, and he may have done some pretty questionable things, but she couldn't help smiling, thinking about how happy Agot had been that morning.

At one p.m., all the MacKenzies turned up, Douglas resplendent in a ridiculous baby-shaped full tartan outfit, also courtesy of Marsha and Mark, of course, but gurgling happily in his increasingly heavy car seat. Fintan had changed back into a paisley shirt and soft jumper and his face looked a decade younger. He shot straight off into the kitchen for possibly the first time ever. Joel and Flora looked after him, confused.

'Okay, what's going on?'

Joel laughed.

'What?' said Flora.

He shrugged. 'It's just . . . we always thought I was the Type A in this relationship, Mrs Binder.'

'People change,' she said, kissing him and closing her eyes with happiness of just being near him, as she always did, because she always was.

* ❄

'No falling down,' Gaspard was saying severely. Bjårk Bjårkensson was imprisoned upstairs just in case, which he was dealing with by steadily ripping apart every single one of Konstantin's socks, which was going to make it slightly ironic that Konstantin wouldn't be able to complain about getting socks for Christmas this year because he wasn't getting anything that year. Everyone was lined up, ready to go. Kerry was looking more furious than ever as Fintan came into the kitchen.

'Hello, stranger,' said Konstantin, but Fintan didn't look the same at all. He looked exuberant if anything.

'Happy Christmas, everyone,' he said jovially. 'I know you'll be wonderful today.'

They glanced at one another.

'But also ... I wanted to announce that Flora is taking over as the proprietor of the Rock!'

They looked at one another again.

'What, she wasn't?' said Konstantin.

'She recruited me,' said Isla. 'I thought she was.'

'Who are you?' said Kerry.

In response, Fintan went up and kissed Gaspard in front of everyone.

'I'm just some guy,' he said. 'I might have some cheese to sell you.'

Gaspard beamed. Only Isla saw Kerry's face fall even further and realised, finally, why the silent stolid girl had followed the mercurial chef when all around him had tired of it, and her heart went out to her.

'Okay, *allez allez allez*,' said Gaspard, glancing at the clock. 'Starters, please.'

*   ❅

At two p.m. precisely, everyone was seated in the dining room, drinks in hand, canapés circulated, and finally the blessed lutefisk (or smoked salmon if you'd rather) starter was plated up and there was a moment, just before service, when Gaspard got them all together and held their hands.

'Well,' he said finally. Isla was acutely conscious of Konstantin's hand in hers. She waited for some inspirational words.

'You've all been completely, my God, so very, very *not useful* for so long. But now! Please let us say this will not be another terreeble deesaster. Bless you all!'

And no one said anything until Konstantin said:

334

'Uh ... amen?'

And they laughed, and Gaspard rang the bell, and service began.

* *

Everywhere, thought Flora, looking around, there were happy faces as the courses came out, seamlessly and delicious. There were, miraculously, vegan options for the fussy people from London, but good hearty dishes for the older people too: a splendid local beef; goose, of course, delicious; an absolutely stunning lutefisk made in Konstantin's honour; and a chestnut soup of glorious lightness.

The cellar was cheerfully emptied, the new young waiting staff always immaculate, cheerful and sweet. Flora kept looking fairly ferociously at Candice, who rolled her eyes at her. Yes, it was amazing. Yes, she was being chatted up by two frankly incredibly hot men either side of her, Ewan the polis and Fionn the fisherman, neither of whom she could understand a word of but really did it matter when there was this much good food and laughter and quiet music and jollity? And they showed Dan up, who had sent a couple of very strangulated passive-aggressive text messages that had very much made her wonder if someone so uptight was quite right for her and for God's sake, she had barely meant to upset his mother. What, she thought, about all the times when she would deliberately want to irritate her in the future? That would be awful. And yes, okay, so she was going to have to file something; that irritating flea Iona was already taking pictures of her. And she didn't normally eat carbs of any sort, of course, but was that why the roast potatoes were so good. And 'World's Worst Hotel Comes Up Trumps' wasn't a bad headline anyway.

By the time the Christmas pudding had been served, and they were onto coffee and liqueurs and the band were setting up for a ceilidh, Flora couldn't have been happier. The Rock was alive, brimming with happy, well-fed people. The cheerful buzz of noise and laughter hummed, with the children running around the huge tree, brandishing their best new toys, and the women giggling in the lovely bathrooms, reapplying lipstick and glancing at their hair. For the first time ever, the place felt fully lived in, properly doing what it was supposed to do. She wished so very much Colton were here to see it. She looked over at Fintan and realised that of course he felt exactly the same. She got up and squeezed his shoulders.

'He'd love it.'

'He'd wish I'd done it.'

'He wouldn't give a rat's ass,' she said, using one of Colton's favourite expressions, which made him smile.

'I think he liked quite a lot of MacKenzies.'

She passed on, thanking the waiting staff, and heading into the kitchen.

'I think people want to see you,' she said to Gaspard, who had disappeared out for a cigarette.

'*Vraiment?*' said Gaspard, but he wasn't unused to this. He'd always known he could cook. He just hadn't thought there'd be a kitchen that could hold him.

He dragged them all out in front of the room, in fact, which erupted into a loud round of applause (more drink had been taken at this point).

Konstantin, to his surprise, found himself a little overcome.

336

Service had been fast and intense and he'd amazed himself by how hard he could work, and how much he could do when he tried, when he really tried. He found himself turning a little pink as he faced the clapping even though it was silly, it was only lunch.

Then someone at one table stood up, and he froze.

Chapter Seventy-two

It couldn't be. He dropped Isla's hand immediately and she turned to look at him, puzzled. Then he stepped forward.

The short man at the table stepped forward also, beaming.

'*Pappa?*' said Konstantin in a very small voice.

He looked at the rest of the table. It wasn't just his father: his aunts, his friends, even Anders, his dreaded nemesis. He stepped towards him like he was sleepwalking. Isla's face suddenly dropped as she realised who was there.

'We thought we'd surprise you,' said his father in Norwegian. 'But you have surprised us. And I am so proud of you.'

'But . . . in the papers . . . I looked such an idiot . . .'

'That is when we decided to come!' said his father. 'When we saw you with the dog! We did not think "idiot". We thought . . . look at my boy. He is *working*! And we are so proud of you. Your chef said you were doing so well.'

'I deed not – you are eediot!' came a voice from far off, but Gaspard couldn't possibly understand Norwegian so they both ignored it.

And, completely in opposition to everything he had once thought he would do when he saw his father again – the harsh truths he would unveil; the cold disdainful words he would give to the family who had banished him – Konstantin found himself burying himself in his father's arms like a child again.

'AND HE MAKES ICE RINKS,' announced a small voice loudly. 'Are you the king? When I am bigger, I am going to marry him. Maybe NEXT YEAR.'

The older Konstantin looked faintly perplexed. 'Well, thank you for the advance warning, miss,' he answered formally, as the younger Konstantin buried his head further in his father's shoulder in order to hide his tears.

＊ ❋
＊

Gaspard led the rest of them back to the kitchen and the waiting staff poured back in with crockery as there was still much to be done to clear the tables for dancing.

Isla, stony-faced, stood by the sink alone. It was ridiculous: two hours before she had been building castles in the air, fantasising about the two of them – just the two of them – going out properly, making a life together, working in the hotel, celebrating Hogmanay and Burns Night, then enjoying the spring that lay ahead and the long summer months.

And now it was all over. His rich family – she had seen the way they were all dressed – was back and of course he was going to want to go with them, off to where all his bloody trees were and all his great fun and sleigh bells and skiing and parties and all those skinny rich blondes.

And she'd be left behind as she'd always been.

She scrubbed a pot particularly hard. Kerry came over.

'They're not worth it,' she said dully. Isla looked up at her, wondering if there was more wisdom coming.

'Men,' said Kerry slowly, 'are all minky, manky, spinky, spanking copper-bottomed bollock-wobbling FUCKING DICKHEADS.'

Then she shut her mouth, turned round and went back to tidying up her station and helping with the mountain of plates coming through.

Isla put her ugly hat back on, and got her elbows soaking wet in the suds. She should be wearing her gloves, but who even cared now if her hands got red and chapped working in the water and with knives all day? What did it matter if she grew careworn and old back here, hidden away – well, yes, just like a scullery maid – while the young dukes and princes lorded it around outside, just as it had always been, just as it was always ordered to be.

'*Only at Christmas time,*' came on the radio, which was just what she didn't need right now, and she was very close to tears by the time the kitchen swing door banged open once more.

One of the waiters yelped.

'A dog in the kitchen!' he howled, as Bjårk immediately turned round, stupid doggie eyes shining brightly as he smelled the many delicious scents of the forbidden area, and he jumped up with two paws on the kitchen unit and started licking down the dirty plates.

'Oh, *Bjårk,*' said Isla, then she looked at him. 'Well, I suppose you're being helpful for once,' she conceded, caressing the stupid animal's big pointy ears as he panted appreciatively.

'Bjårk!' came another voice, rushing in. 'I brought you down to say hello to your *family*, not *eat the kitchen.*'

He stopped short at Isla.

'And you too,' he said. 'Aren't you coming to say hello?'

Isla looked at him.

'Not like this,' she pleaded. Her apron was dirty; her hands were filthy and soaking wet.

Konstantin came over, unpinned her cap, then carefully pulled the pins out of her hair, which came tumbling down. She looked up at him, scared.

'Let me kiss your mouth rosy,' he said, then proceeded to do so.

'Okay,' he said. 'Now you're perfect. Come on.'

And he tossed the cap to the side and led her out through the swinging doors.

Bjårk stayed behind and dealt very efficiently with the gravy.

341

Chapter Seventy-three

The dancing was in full swing through in the dining room, with an energetic Strip the Willow going on. The usual lines of four or eight couples appeared to have morphed into all sorts of numbers, and Agot and Ash were racing hand in hand through every archway whether it was their turn or not, so it was pretty much business as usual.

Isla could never have known how delighted Konstantin Senior was to meet – for the first ever time – a friend of Konstantin's, properly introduced, who didn't look like an overindulged party girl or behaved like a spoilt brat. Someone sweet, pretty, normal and kind. She was still very conscious of her apron though, and her damp hands.

'It's lovely to meet you,' said the old man genuinely, and, feeling slightly ridiculous to be meeting a strange white-bearded man with rosy cheeks and a Scandinavian accent on

Christmas Day, Isla smiled back and managed not to accidentally curtsy.

'Ahem.'

There was a clearing of throat behind them, and Isla turned round. There sat her mother, refusing to get up, clutching her handbag.

'Ah,' said Isla. 'And this is my mother.'

'Enchanted,' said Konstantin Senior with all the charm he could muster. Please don't be rude to them, thought Isla with all her might. Please don't be off with them.

Vera rose and stood up to her full height, extending a hand as if she herself were royalty.

'I see your son has had the very good fortune to meet my daughter,' she said calmly.

Chapter Seventy-four

Boxing Day dawned clear and bright. Breakfast was tasty and done quickly; there would be no further meal services that day. Konstantin looked nervous, Isla realised. He had stayed up late, speaking Norwegian to everyone, and she had taken her mother home, the pair of them getting in and opening their presents. One of Isla's was a new, cool, Cath Kidston teapot.

'I thought you might like it,' said her mother shyly. 'For the new place.'

'I do,' said Isla. 'Very much. But not as much as yours.'

* ❄

They still had the emergency council meeting that morning.

'What's the worst they can do?' Isla said.

'Just the idea that people hate it makes me sad. They could tear it down,' said Konstantin, frowning.

'I know.'

'I just wanted to do something nice. I thought it would be nice.'

'You don't know who hates it.'

'All the powerful people who run everything,' said Konstantin, gloomily munching a sausage.

Isla plucked up the courage to ask:

'And then ... are you going back? With your dad?'

'Yes,' said Konstantin, and Isla's heart dropped. 'For a visit. Can you come? There's no more meals till Hogmanay.'

'What?'

'I mean, we could go for a few days? I could show you around.'

'And then come back?'

'Well, for now, yes. I've got a job. I like it. I'm trying to get a girlfriend, although I will tell you up until now it is going very, *very* slowly.'

Isla smiled in delight.

'And then what?'

Konstantin screwed up his face. 'Come on. I've barely got my first job started; don't ask me my five-year plan. Also, I'm in some danger of getting banished from here too. Two countries in one year would be quite good going, I think.'

'Even for a playboy.'

'Even for a playboy.'

In fact, the papers, desperate for copy, were already running Candice's glowing review of the beautiful Christmas lunch. Candice herself was staying on a couple of extra days; Fionn had promised to take her out on his boat and catch her a lobster, and she was absolutely feeling rather up for it.

Fifteen minutes before the emergency council meeting was

due to start, they looked round the empty kitchen, then nervously headed towards the town hall. The Angel towered above them, glinting in the sun. It was as beautiful as ever. But today the glow gave it a sinister cast, as if it knew it might have to come down.

Hand in hand, they walked to the doorway. Where they saw the most amazing thing. They'd noticed a lot of people around the village, but assumed everyone was heading for the Loony Dook later that morning. Many were carrying blankets and flasks and Mrs Brodie was rattling the tin for the school fund as usual.

But as they reached the door, they heard a great swell of people and a noise. 'NOW!' came a voice, and everyone took hands.

'What's going on?' said Konstantin. Malcy, arriving at the same time, looked around crossly.

'What the hell is this?'

Right up the street from the town hall, leading to the statue, was a human chain of people – Billy and Effie from the airport, all the children, more or less, from the school with Lorna, and a pilot, who had flown in to speak for all the pilots who loved it for navigation, with a message from ships likewise.

The council man harrumphed, following the other members into the town hall, including poor slightly terrorised Marsali.

Then everyone from the chain trooped behind Konstantin and Isla, and took up every single space in the hall.

'We are here to vote upon the removal of a non-planning per-mission object on the island,' said Malcy. But every time he tried to get people to be quiet, they started up again, chanting, 'KEEP THE ANGEL! KEEP THE ANGEL!'

Malcy spoke at some length about how it was an eyesore and completely illegal, and there was some harrumphing. Then Konstantin looked at Isla and winked. He stood up.

'May I speak? I wish to name the angel the Malcolm Marsali

Aoghas Fraser William Effie Angel,' he announced grandly. 'And I personally will pay for a plaque to commemorate the full name to be placed at the base,' he added.

There was some silence over this. People started cheering and shouting, 'Vote! Vote! Vote!'

Obviously, Malcy did not want a vote as he did not know how he could win. There was some private conferring.

Eventually he returned.

'The provision is this: the statue will stay as long as Konstantin undertakes to keep it in good order and to return and tend to it. And make the plaque with all our names on it.'

Everybody cheered.

'Thank you,' said Konstantin gravely. 'I realise you are an important man in this town.'

He turned to Isla delightedly.

'I'm not sure you can get rid of me that easily. It's the law now.'

Chapter Seventy-five

The visiting Norwegians were well used to getting into extremely cold water and only had to be reminded once more that here it was done with swimming trunks on, so they were all up for the Loony Dook.

The children were doing it because it was fun and naughty and it meant their parents had to do it to not look like wusses.

Candice decided to do it because she had a fabulous figure in a bikini so any excuse. Also, the light and the colours of the water and the pale white sand on the Endless Beach made it look like she was actually in the Bahamas, if the temperature hadn't been three degrees Celsius, so she could take lots of excellent pictures for her Instagram. She was getting quite the following. She noticed Iona taking selfies in a particularly fetching spot and copied them exactly, to Iona's stone-cold fury.

Fintan and Gaspard were very much staying at home and doing something else.

Just before eleven a.m., there was a piper burling up and down the beach and much laughing and bantering and remarks and swearing about how cold it was just to take your jumper off, but there was nobody not ready to jump in apart from the older members of the community, who stood with warm towels and blankets and coats and flasks full of hot coffee laced with whisky, and bacon sandwiches wrapped in silver foil. Just to the side, Flora noticed Jan trying to placate Christabel who was having a tantrum of extraordinary, gut-busting proportions in front of the entire town. She made a mental note to have a kind word later. They surely had plenty to talk about.

At eleven sharp, the entire island lined up along the sand. There was a great horn blown – by Agot, naturally – and, hand in hand, the entire long line ran down the Endless Beach and into the freezing churning water, screaming their heads off.

Several words were heard that truly would not have passed muster in front of the children, but it was only once a year. There was much shrieking and most of the children ran in only up to their waists, figured that was enough and immediately turned and charged back the other way to be scooped up by adoring grannies and rubbed fresh pink.

The others, bolder, swam.

Konstantin loved the cold water, and took Isla with him, deeper and deeper, and when he thought no one was looking, finally kissed her flushed face full on and laughed at her shock and joy as she wrapped herself around him.

Flora and Joel held hands and Flora jumped up and down screaming while he endured the freezing water with complete and utter calmness and she burst out laughing and said, 'I am sure this is a metaphor for something about the two of us!' and he laughed too and grabbed her close and they ran back out together, heading for Douglas, who was laughing and giggling in the blanketed lap of his doting grandfather, to swing him up between them.

Saif and Lorna swam out further and further and moved just close enough so their toes could entwine in the water, for it is not deep, and the sand that joins the world flowed over their numb toes. They could not feel one another but they were still together, because sometimes even when we cannot feel one another we are still together.

And the town laughed as one, and ran back in, glowing and jolly, feeling refreshed and cleansed and freshly alive under the watching eye of the great Mure Angel, bright in the winter sun, lighting the way, keeping them safe.

لذلك سوف أميل دائما قلبي
أقرب إلى روحك
كما استطيع.

So I will always lean my heart
As close to your soul
As I can.

Khwāja Shams-ud-Dīn Muḥammad Ḥāfeẓ-e Shīrāzī

Eg stansa vel uviss, utan svar,
som framfor eit ukjend land,
om ikkje min kjærleik til deg var
for meg som ei lykt i mi hand

I paused uncertainly without answer
Finding myself set against an unknown land
To see whether or not my love for you
Was a lantern in my hand

Halldis Moren Vesaas

Tha caoin-shlios mo leannain mar eal' air a' chuan,
Nas gile nan fhaoileann air aodann nan stuadh,
Mar shneachd air na beannaibh, mar chanach nam bruach,
'S i furasta, suairc na giùlan

My love is a swan on the ocean
Brighter than gulls on the waves
Like snow on the mountains, like wild cotton
It is easy, and I shout aloud with joy

Dugald MacPhail

Acknowledgements

Thanks: Kjersti Herland Jonson, my Norwegian publisher, who answered all my Norwegian questions so helpfully and kindly; Layla Al Ammar, Tom Holland and M. Lynx Qualey for their help with Nizar Qabbani. Nicole Moore at Lynne Reinner Publishers. Also Nicole Moore . . . and Guri Vesaas.

Huge thanks to: Jo Unwin, Lucy Malagoni, Milly Reilly, Donna Greaves, Joanna Kramer, Charlie King , David Shelley, Stephanie Melrose, Gemma Shelley, and all at Little, Brown; Deborah Schneider and Rachel Kahan at William Morrow; Alexander Cochran, Jake Smith-Bosanquet, and Kate Burton.

Did you enjoy *An Island Christmas*?
Then you'll love escaping with
Jenny's festive new novel ...

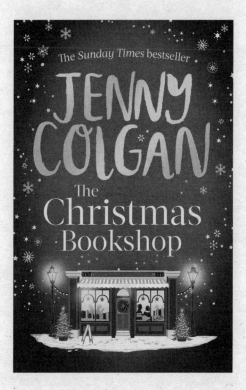

Can't wait to find out what happens
next to the residents of Mure? Read on for
a sneak peek at the next in the series . . .

The *Sunday Times* bestseller

JENNY COLGAN

An Island
Wedding

Coming May 2022.
Available to pre-order now.

Chapter One

It was the tail-end of March, and the Rock hotel on Mure was booked absolutely solid. The visitors had got lucky too: the end of the Atlantic storms had brought snow and ice well into the third month of the year, but for the last week the sun had shone bright every day.

As long as you had a decent coat and some stout shoes (the hotel would of course lend you some wellingtons), the island looked glorious: the sand on the Endless Beach was so pale it was practically white, the water lapping turquoise and clear, the sky huge and blue as a child's painting. The little brightly painted houses lopsidedly leaning against each other in the harbour were jolly and gay, and the fishing boats were freshly painted and eager to take to the waves.

'It is absolutely. Sodding. Freezing,' said Flora, stepping out into the bright sunshine, going round to check the gardens around the back of the house, where the daffodils were in full bloom.

Her fiancé Joel, on the other end of the phone, let out a barking laugh.

'It's because you heat that hotel so much you've got soft.'

Flora sighed. This was almost certainly true. In the McKenzie farmhouse, where she'd grown up, the windows were single-paned and draughty and you had to hurtle to the damped-down peat kitchen fire every morning, your feet freezing on the icy stone, to stir it up again, then heat your chilled fingers around a warm, strong cup of tea.

The Rock, on the other hand, a huge old grey stone building, had been converted into a hotel by a rich Texan who couldn't bear discomfort of any kind. The traditional-style windows were triple-glazed; a heat pump had been installed, giving out vast amounts of cheap energy; and every bathroom had underfloor heating. There were thick rugs and cosy blankets everywhere, as well as deep carpets in the library and sitting rooms. Colton, Flora's brother Fintan's late husband, had basically compared living at the very northern tip of the British Isles to living in a ski resort, and built accordingly. Except, as a newcomer to Scotland, he had gone for what he thought would be a design to blend in with the locals, and as a result there was tartan carpet of deep greens and blues and stags' heads everywhere. At first, Flora had thought it was naff and ridiculous. Now, she rather loved it. It reminded her of Colton every time she strolled the long corridors or opened the door to the restaurant (then quickly shut them again, if Gaspard the temperamental chef, was shouting at someone in the kitchen).

She found her way round to the side of the hotel which faced the water; there was a little dock there, and many people arrived by boat. The gardens by the wall hosted a suntrap a wind could not reach, and they had benches for people to sit and watch the big boats go by in the distance, on their long journeys up and over the fjords. In the direct sun, it was incredibly pleasant. She sat down for two seconds' break from the endless demands of running a hotel and a café. Nobody could see her from here, but it wasn't hiding exactly – and she continued her conversation with Joel.

'How's it going?'

Joel sighed in a way that indicated he didn't think he'd be back soon. He administered Colton's trust fund, which had contributed to the development of a global vaccination programme. It had made him busier than they had ever thought possible, particularly after he'd moved to Mure for a quiet life.

'That well?' said Flora, glancing at her watch. It was 6 a.m. where he was in Mexico City.

'It is going well,' said Joel. 'This is a problem. They think it might be down to me.'

'Because it is,' said Flora. Joel was the best and smartest man she'd ever met, in her opinion. The rest of the world catching up to this fact didn't surprise her in the slightest.

Joel harrumphed. 'I think several thousands of actual scientists might have something to say about that. Anyway. I am desperate to get home.'

Flora looked out at the sea. It was habit, scanning the horizon for whales. There was a pod due, she felt it in her bones, though the horizon was choppy but clear. Everyone on the island knew the Mackenzie women were descended from selkies, the seal people. It was clear as day in their pale hair and translucent eyes; creatures who came from the sea, who might one day return. Of course it was absolute nonsense, Flora would harrumph. Nonetheless, there was no denying she did have a connection with the wild creatures around the shores of the island. She did feel a kinship, particularly with the whales. But surely every islander felt that way, she told herself.

'Come back before the whales come,' she said. 'Then the whole of summer will be ahead of us.'

'Okay, my selkie girl,' said Joel, smiling to himself. He liked thinking of Flora as a sea spirit sometimes. Even though Joel himself hated the water, which was one of the many surprising things about him ending up on a very small island in the middle of the Atlantic Ocean. 'I'd better get back to it.'

'Be careful,' said Flora frowning. 'Is it dangerous where you are?'

She could hear the smile in Joel's voice.

'Everywhere is dangerous compared to Mure,' he said. 'It's not rational, what you think is dangerous.'

That was true. Ewan Clark, the local policeman worked pretty much full time on his farm, was only occasionally called to an altercation outside the Harbour's Rest hotel late on market day, or to sort out some optimistic parking by tourists who didn't quite understand that the strong discouragement to bring cars over on the ferry also applied to them. Children roamed free most of the year, and everyone knew everyone else, more or less.

'How's Douglas? Walking yet?'

'Stop pressuring Douglas!'

All the MacKenzies had been apparently, 'nine-month walkers' and, now that Douglas was almost one, the pressure was on.

'No, I don't want him to walk! I want to be there!'

'Oh well. In that case, he's pretty much still all drool and snot.'

'Good, good,' said Joel, who as someone who had never known much parenting himself had nonetheless turned into the most devoted father imaginable.

'Also, we need to talk about . . . Oh, it can wait.'

'What?' said Flora, sitting up straighter. Nothing good ever came from the phrase 'we need to talk' in her experience. 'What do we have to talk about? What?'

'Oh, nothing, honestly; wait till I'm back.'

'That's not for days! And now I will panic and think it's something bad.'

'It's nothing bad,' said Joel. 'At least I don't think so'

'What? Oh my God oh my God oh my God *what*?'

'Nothing! Honestly!'

'TELL ME!'

'When I'm home ... Can we talk about the wedding?'

'*Our* wedding?'

'No,' said Joel, 'all those other weddings I take a deep and abiding interest in. Probably a Kardashian one.'

Flora headed into her office after the phone call, wondering what he meant exactly – presumably he didn't mean "cancel' the wedding if he was making jokes about the Kardashians, but even so. He'd proposed at Christmas, and it had just been wonderful and gorgeous and there seemed no reason to delay having it this summer – but he had been rather cagey about discussing actual wedding details and the like. Flora would have been perfectly happy if he had said 'do what you like' given she had a hotel, a chef and a lot of good pastry at her disposal, but he hadn't said that either. And if they did want to do it this summer, they had better get moving ...

She looked out at the north end of the Endless Beach. Tourists had taken up residence in wildly optimistic swimsuits and more realistic windbreakers. Every so often someone would dare go up and touch the water, pale blue as a Caribbean shore, lapping gently up to the perfect white sands – then jump back in absolute horror as they felt the temperature. Flora smiled. It didn't really matter how hot the sun shone: it was still the north sea. They had lots of so-called wild swimmers who turned up all winter with lots of expensive kit and huge dry robes talking about how wild swimming was amazing and had completely changed their lives and how fantastic it was, before running in and out for five minutes. On Mure, they just called it swimming.

The phone rang in the office the second she opened the door, and Flora looked out of the window as she picked it up. Oh, there they were – she thought she'd run into them on her way to the garden. Eck, her dad, and Hamish, one of her three brothers, were trying to persuade Douglas into a standing position. Agot, the daughter of Flora's brother Innes, who had followed her in, looked out and sniffed dismissively.

'That baby is RUBBISH at walking. *Tha e gòrach.*' Agot was learning Gaelic at school and liked to mutter in it, particularly remarks too cheeky to say aloud.

Flora's funny, serious-looking baby, the spit of his dad, was sitting in the grass, toggled up in the nine layers of knitted wool considered essential by Mure knitters, ie, most of the population, was eyeing them suspiciously. It was a look Flora knew well from his father, and it said 'whatever you think you're talking about, I'm going to do exactly what I think is right in my own good time'. It was what made Joel an excellent lawyer and an occasionally frustrating partner.

Still, they made a pretty sight, three generations of McKenzie boys, plus Bramble of course, looking for the muddiest patch of the flower beds to roll in, and avoiding the enthusiastic attentions of Bjårk Bjårkensson, the huge and rambunctious kitchen dog. They really shouldn't have a kitchen dog, Flora thought, for the nine thousandth time, as she answered the phone.

'Hello? The Rock hotel.'

'Yah, hello?'

The voice was calm and flat. It was, from the first syllable, a voice that sounded used to getting its own way.

'Am I speaking to the proprietor of the Rock hotel?'

Flora's heart sank. Whatever they were selling, she didn't want to buy it and couldn't afford it anyway.

'Yes, hello, this is Flora, but we're not really in the . . .'

'Jan MacArthur gave me your number'.

Ah. Jan was a local woman who ran a camping and survival courses and had an entirely explicable dislike of Flora, who had got off with her husband years ago. Way before they were dating, in fact, but somehow this didn't seem to let Flora off the hook.

'Oh, great!' Flora said brightly.

'Actually, she tried to discourage me, but I'd seen your article . . .'

A journalist had come to the hotel last Christmas to sneer, but had ended up thoroughly enjoying herself and had written a massive rave.

'Anyway. I want to talk you about weddings.'

Flora was ready for this.

'I'm sorry, we don't do weddings,' she said apologetically.

The plan was that soon they absolutely would do weddings; they got called all the time about them, and a more photogenic spot could barely be imagined . Once Flora was confident that the hotel, which had only been open for six months, could handle it, that Gaspard wouldn't have a meltdown, that guests wouldn't throw up in the flowerbeds, that they could serve a hundred people at the same time, then she was definitely going to start running it as a wedding venue. She and Joel were going to get married first – well, at least, that was the plan – as a test run, and after that they'd go for it.

But there was a little more to it than that: she couldn't forget Colton and Fintan's wedding. It had been the most glorious day, the most perfectly planned occasion, wonderful in every way – weather, food, guests, toasts, speeches, everything a dream under a bright blue sky – and it hadn't saved him from the cancer that had spent the following year eating him from the inside out, breaking Fintan's heart in the procress. It had made everyone a little superstitious.

The voice was nasal and sounded like it was used to getting its own way.

'Jan said you would make an exception for us? My name is Jacinth; I'm calling on behalf of her sister?'

Flora's eyes went wide.

'*Olivia?*'

'Yah!'

Escape with
JENNY COLGAN

Escape to a remote little Scottish island and meet the
charmingly eccentric residents of Mure...

**'Charming, made me long to
escape to Mure. Total joy'**
SOPHIE KINSELLA

Escape with
JENNY COLGAN

In a quaint seaside resort, where the air is rich with the smell of fresh buns and bread, a charming bakery holds the key to another world…

'Deliciously warm and sweet'
SOPHIE KINSELLA